D1475234

To my best friend, and my biggest supporter who only ever read 1½ of my books – my husband. Love ya!

Air

By Terra Harmony

Copyright 2011 by Terra Harmony

A Patchwork Press Title

www.patchwork-press.com

Editing Team: Jessica Dall, Cathy Wathen, and Extra Set of Eyes Proofing
www.readitreviewit.wordpress.com

Cover design by Keary Taylor
www.indiecoverdesigns.com

Forward

Air is the second book in the Akasha Series, a set of contemporary eco-fantasy novels. This book is for mature readers only. It contains sexual content, some of it non-consensual. Comments and criticism are always welcome and can be sent to terra.harmony11@gmail.com.

If you enjoy the book, please consider leaving a review online at Amazon, Goodreads, Smashwords, or Barnes and Noble. Happy reading!

Terra Harmony

Terra Harmony

Chapter 1

Breath of Life

"I can see my breath."

There was no response from the small, handheld radio nestled in my thick glove.

I clicked on the talk button again. "Did you hear me, Micah? I said I can see my breath. Time to go."

Finally, a voice answered, though not through the radio. *Do you not understand the concept of silent ops?*

He was using our telepathic connection. I immediately shut it down. There were things in my head he need not know – not yet anyway. I couldn't take the chance he would find them while tooling around in there. I clicked the radio again. "Then why did you bring the radios?"

I could almost hear his frustrated huff through the vast expanse of the Pennsylvania pine forest that lay between us. He had explained it to me before we separated; the handhelds were there in case we suspected someone intruding on our telepathic connection.

He came back, over the radio this time, and said, "I am almost to the cabin. Let me just check it out and then we can go. I am going silent – for real this time."

"Don't you dare turn off the—" my best warning voice was cut off by the hum of the radio, letting me know I was no longer connected to my counterpart. It was tit for tat with us.

I huffed, the same way I imagined him doing it. My breath formed a cloud of fog that lingered lazily in front of my face. I played with it, sucking it back in, then blowing out to form bigger clouds, and swishing it away with my hands. Anything to keep my mind off the cold. The wind picked up as clouds moved into the valley, darkening the midnight sky further.

I squinted, trying to pinpoint the cabin in the dark. The moon, fully hidden behind thick clouds, was no help. We had tracked Shawn this far, despite my protests. In my opinion, it had been far too easy – like following bread crumbs. But Micah's need for vengeance surpassed my own.

Giving up on the cabin, I exhaled again. A gust of cold wind met the fog. I narrowed my eyes. This gust had come in against the oncoming storm. I watched as my breath cloud was sucked into an invisible black hole and disappeared, sizzling as it went. The wind followed its trail, straight into my lungs.

I turned, flailing my arms out to ward off whatever was attacking me. But how can you ward off air? The sucking persisted, panic and fear taking hold of me more thoroughly than the cold that had bit its way into my bones. Had it not been so dark out already, I'm sure I would've already seen the forest go black.

Falling to my knees, I reached out for the only element of which I had a strong grasp; water. Particles were drawn from the clouds, the soil, and the trees. They rushed to meet me, then wavered in front of my face, hesitating. I wasn't sure what to do with them. But there was more than just me at stake. In a desperate, final act, I sent them down my throat, into my lungs and into the very thing that sucked the life out of me. I flooded it with far more water, volume-wise, than the amount of air it took. Shortly, it proved to be too much, and the mysterious void of nothingness expelled everything. Water and air both flooded my system. I sputtered, choking up the water I had so desperately called to my aid.

As soon as I lifted myself from the ground, thoroughly soaked, I thought of Micah. Whatever, or whoever it was might be going after him too. The trail leading up to the cliff was steep and full of loose rock, causing me to slide most of the way down. Once my feet hit solid earth, I took off running. The forest was dense, but I avoided the protruding roots and clawing branches easily enough. There was only one thing on my mind. Without thinking, I opened up the telepathic connection and screamed his name, *Micah!*

There was no answer. I ran faster. The forest opened up into a small, circular clearing. As I entered it, I spotted Micah clearing the trees on the opposite side in a dead run toward me. We met in the middle, coming to a stop a few feet apart, both hunched over with our hands on our knees. A cursory scan of each other while still gasping for air was enough until words came to us. He was out of breath, but he was unscathed and handsome and dry – and I hated him for it.

Before he could say anything, I went first, in between breaths, "Well – was there anything in the cabin?" I didn't bother keeping the bite out of my voice.

He held up a piece of paper in his hand, at least having the mind to look sheepish. "I found a letter." He folded it up and put it in his pocket. "What happened to you?"

I fixed him with a stare as cold as the wind, "I found trouble." Then, because I couldn't help it, I shivered.

He sighed, taking off his jacket and wrapped it around me, "I guess I shouldn't expect anything less from you, Kaitlyn."

Chapter 2

Dark Moods

I had barely left my bed in the two days since we had returned from Pennsylvania to Simeulue Island, and the Chakra compound. Three thick blankets were almost enough to keep away the bone numbing chill that seemed to creep in and take residence during our half hour stint in the pine forest. Blankets also provided good cover for the swell of my belly – an inevitable consequence of pregnancy.

I was starting to outgrow my clothes. I was just frumpy enough to look silly in my usual garb, but not quite big enough to warrant an entire wardrobe change. It was a wonder they didn't take me to the nearest stream and drown me in a burlap sack like a litter of unwanted kittens.

"I have bad news." Micah entered the room, face drawn. His consistently gloomy mood mirrored mine as of late.

"No burlap sack?"

His eyebrows furrowed. "What?"

"Nothing." I waved it away, annoyed.

He looked at me for another moment before continuing, "The letter I found at the cabin is coded – it'll take some time to work though it and figure out the next step in finding Shawn."

"Oh, darn." I rolled my eyes.

The Seven had ceased all operations in order to thwart Shawn's efforts of creating his own, parallel organization. *More than likely, they are playing into Shawn's plan perfectly*, I thought.

"There were too many P's in that sentence," I mumbled.

"What?" Micah looked at me, more hopeless than confused this time.

I flinched, realizing I had spoken aloud. I was starting to lose it, and was going to lose Micah as well, if I hadn't already.

"We need to talk." I put aside all sarcasm, attempting to sound serious.

Micah sat down on the bed next to me, rubbing his eyes then scratching the stubble at his chin. Lately, he constantly had that five o'clock shadow, like his chin's hair growth was suspended in time. "I've been trying to *talk* ever since we left the hospital in San Diego. I know you've been to Hell and back—"

"Am I back? Can't be sure."

He ignored me. "But we can't go on like this forever."

At 'forever' I closed up again. Beyond telling him I was pregnant, and didn't know if the child was his, there was the issue of what happened to Gaias, a role I currently played with the Seven.

"There is no forever with us," I spat. He didn't know Shawn had shared the fact that once another, stronger Gaia came along, it was Micah's job to send me to greener pastures.

It was Micah's turn to flinch. "Kaitlyn, stop. Can't we just—"

"No." I cut him off. "I don't think we can. Not yet, anyway."

Micah's face fell. He backed up, turned, and attempted to leave the room. In the process of stomping out, he almost bumped into his sister, Susan, who was bringing me a tray of food.

"Watch it!" she exclaimed, frantically juggling the tray, food sliding dangerously.

"You watch it!" He barely glanced at her, disappearing to wherever he spent most of his time these days.

Susan watched him go, sighed heavily, then entered the room and set the tray down next to the bed. "You're certainly doing a number on him. I've never seen him like this."

My jaw dropped. Of anyone here, she should be siding with me. She was fully aware of my condition. I couldn't very well hide the balloon of water growing inside me from the Nerina. Her powers were to sense, manipulate, and interact with the element of water.

Seeing the look on my face, she added, "You need to tell him."

I rolled my eyes and looked away from her. "If he hasn't figured it out by now, he will soon enough."

Susan pulled down the blanket, flipped up my oversized t-shirt, and laid her hand on the slight swell. "How could he know? You walk around in baggy clothes and you two probably haven't spent more than ten consecutive minutes together since we found you." She removed her hand, giving me a glass of water and my daily prenatal vitamin she kept discreetly hidden in her own belongings.

Following my brief stint in the hospital after a rescue from Shawn's camp on the Galapagos Islands, the whole crew returned to the Chakra, headquarters of the Seven. Cato, the leader of our rag tag bunch, gave Susan a room so she could stay while we regrouped. It may have been smarter to let us go our own separate ways. Forced to stay together, even in a place as large as the Chakra, darkened everyone's moods as well as the weather. There were steady, gray clouds covering the island that hadn't broken up in weeks. They threatened rain, but it never came. As if to emphasize my point, a low rumbling of thunder erupted in the distance.

Susan looked out the window, but before she could comment, I interjected, "Can't you do something about that? Draw the rain out or something and send the clouds on their way?"

She shook her head. "That has more to do with the air and wind. Besides, it wouldn't help. Once gone, more clouds would form in a matter of hours. The weather is reflecting the mood of everyone here. It's sort of fitting. Now, take that." She gestured to the small vitamin still in my hand.

I downed it just before Cato entered the room. Susan and I exchanged a glance that said, 'that was close'.

"Ah, my two favorite women."

"Cato, we're the only two women you know," Susan said. She briefly blocked his view of me while I pulled my shirt down over my belly and covered back up with the thick blankets.

"That's beside the point." He waved her off, moving to stand next to the bed, and grabbed one of each of our hands. "You two have been spending a lot of time together."

I looked sideways at Susan, hoping she would come up with an explanation. She didn't disappoint.

"We have a lot to learn from each other. Kaitlyn has a different perspective on the element of water, and has shown me things I've never encountered before."

Cato peered at me. His eyes had gone a dull, almost translucent blue with age, but I could almost hear wheels turning behind those eyes.

I looked down, purposefully avoiding his gaze.

That may not have been the best idea.

"I believe there's something else you're not telling me; something that involves all of us, or at least more than just you two." He said.

I chanced looking at him. Cato stared me down, one eyebrow raised.

I glanced at Susan again and she nodded in encouragement. No way was I going to tell *him* before Micah. "Perhaps there is something, Cato, but now is not the time. When we're ready, we'll let you know."

They both looked disappointed, but Cato nodded, reluctantly. "Well, let's just hope the truth is revealed soon. I am going rather pale from the lack of sun."

Susan and I murmured in agreement while scrutinizing the color of skin on our arms.

Cato let go of our hands and sat next to Susan on the bed. "You've heard of our recent failure?"

"Hmmm," Susan acknowledged. She liked their targeting of Shawn even less than I did.

Cato went on, "He must have found out we were coming. The cabin was cleared out before Micah got there."

"Maybe you need to forget about Shawn and concentrate on more important things, Cato," I interjected.

"We need to discover his intentions. He could interfere with all of our successes in maintaining a balance." Cato said.

I exploded. "He already has! You've put everything else aside in order to find him. You've halted all operations, all of your studies, all training – everything! If and when a final showdown occurs, we'll be completely unprepared."

More thunder rumbled in the distance as Cato disagreed, "We'll find him before that's necessary. It won't be long now; we get closer every time."

My shoulders sagged. "It's just an illusion, Cato. Don't underestimate him. He lets you get closer so you are enticed to keep trying."

I could have been mistaken, but I thought a flicker of pride crossed Cato's face. It was covered up quickly with that warm, fatherly smile he was so good at giving. "If that's the case, maybe we can fight back with our own illusion." Cato pat my hand as he stood up. "Let me know if you come up with any ideas."

He walked toward the door, paused, then turned in the doorway and announced, "Almost forgot why I came. I wanted to let you two know we have a visitor arriving tomorrow."

"Who?" Susan beat me to the question.

"Our Shu, Vayu."

I waited until Cato left, and then looked at Susan. "Who is Arshuvayu?"

She laughed. "No, Cato meant our Shu. S-H-U," she spelled out for me. "One who can manipulate the element of air. His name is Vayu."

"Vayu isn't much better," I defended my mistake.

"Self-named after the Indian God of wind and air," Susan explained. "He thought it was more fitting than John. He is a very…interesting character," Susan said delicately. "A bit of a diva. But, who knows? Maybe he's exactly what we need to lighten things up around here." She glanced out the window. "Literally."

Chapter 3

Diva

Having spent the entire previous day in bed, I woke to see the clouds turn lighter as the sun reached its apex. A twinge of expectation had dragged me from sleep. I had to think hard to remember why. *Oh yes, our guest, Vayu.* Feeling a sense of purpose for the first time in a long while, I dragged myself out of bed and through a shower. I picked out clothes that made me feel like a functioning human, while still concealing my slightly bulging belly. After drying and combing my wild hair, I brushed my teeth and broke into my makeup drawer. I could've sworn there was dust on a few items. I even plucked my eyebrows. Satisfied with my appearance, I emerged from the room.

The halls felt foreign to me; different somehow. As I approached the kitchen, it dawned on me. They felt different because I felt different. The usual sickness that accompanied me was gone. I smiled and took a deep breath in. This was going to be a good day.

The smell of coffee drew me into the kitchen but once there, my growling stomach usurped my need for caffeine. I prowled the cupboards, came across a bag of bagels and popped one into the toaster. I turned back to the coffee pot.

Should I drink coffee? Was it bad for the baby? This is where a doctor would have come in handy. The smell of coffee beans kept me hovering around the pot. *Maybe just a deep whiff would appease my craving.* I took the coffee pot from its warmer, removed the lid, and inhaled deeply. I sighed. *Nope, craving still there. Maybe one more time would do the trick.* I inhaled even deeper and longer with my eyes closed, concentrating hard – willing the smell to appease me. The bagels popped out of the toaster with unexpected vigor, causing me to jump. Coffee sloshed over my hands, and down my front.

I swore, bending over, inspecting the stain on my clothes with one bright red hand and balancing the now half empty coffee pot in my other bright red hand.

"What are you doing?" The voice startled me even more.

I jumped to the side, away from the intruder behind me, bumping into the cupboards and the rest of the coffee, and pot, crashed to the floor. I grimaced, rubbing my hands, sending a dirty look toward the most convenient person to blame. Micah.

"What are *you* doing, sneaking up on me like that?"

"Me? I'm not the one snorting an open pot of coffee like some coke fiend." He said, brushing past me to look at the mess.

"Well, I, ummm…" I started pushing some of the shattered glass into a pile with my shoes while I thought up an excuse, "I was just trying to figure out the brand before I poured myself a cup."

Micah took a step closer to reach around me, pulling out the bag from behind the coffee maker. He turned it toward me. "Local brand – Sumatra coffee, same as always."

"Oh," I took the bag. "Thanks." I looked down, trying to avoid his green eyes boring into me, and frowned. My wet shirt was clinging to my belly, revealing too much.

"You look good today, Kaitlyn." Micah's comment was unexpected, as was my responding smile. I looked up and was hooked. It was all I could do to keep from closing the rest of the distance between us.

"Thanks, I feel good today." I looked down again, reminded of the shirt situation. I peeled it away from my skin. "I need to go change. That coffee was hot."

"You want me to come?" Micah asked, and then hesitated, confused by his own question.

"No, I got it. I'll be right back," I said. I jogged back to the room to search the closet. *How can I be sexy but covered at the same time?* I settled on a low-cut baby doll blouse that billowed out at the waist. A quick look in the mirror – I needed more makeup. Another look – I ran a brush through my hair. Yet another look convinced me to pick up my blush but I put it back down again. *Can't be too obvious.* I sighed. Life was so much easier when I chose to mope.

I made my way back to the kitchen, hoping the second try would be more graceful than the first. By the time I got there, Micah was plating eggs and diced fruit. It was much more tempting than my bagel that had turned cold in my absence. The coffee mess was cleaned up and a newer, albeit smaller pot of coffee, was brewing. The smells had drawn several others out of the woodwork. Susan and Cato were chatting while waiting for the coffee to brew and a few maintenance workers stood in line clamoring for eggs.

Micah handed the first serving to me. "Sorry guys, beauty before brains."

Before I could retort, the plate was snatched out of my hands.

"Well if that is the case..." Alex piled more grapes and kiwi on the plate. I couldn't help but smile. Alex, my weapons trainer and the sole person responsible for logistics on our missions, always knew how to make me smile, even on my darkest days.

Out of the corner of my eye, I caught Micah frowning.

Predictably, Cato stepped in to make peace. "Alex - perhaps you didn't hear, but Vayu will be making an appearance in a few minutes."

Alex froze with his first forkful halfway to his mouth. "Vayu? Here? Now?"

"Yes, and I thought we could all meet him out front."

Alex handed the plate back to me, spouting excuses, "You know, I just remembered. I am behind on inventory. We don't want any pistols going missing. And flights for the next trip need to be arranged. And ground transportation and our hotel..." Alex was nearly out of the room. "But give Vayu my best. I'll catch up with him…later."

I looked at Cato for an explanation but all I got was a friendly wink. Next I turned to Micah, who seemed satisfied with the situation.

"Don't think you are off the hook, mister." I pointed my finger at him.

"What?" He widened his eyes innocently.

"If I'm beauty then I suppose you're what? The brains of this operation?"

Smirking, he held up his arms. "Was it ever a question?"

I took a fork from the pile on the counter and poked him in the arm. "Bastard."

He recoiled, "Brute!"

Cato interrupted, pretending not to notice our quickly escalating fight. "I think I hear the truck rolling up. Come on; let's give Vayu the greeting he always insists on having."

Everyone shoved their last bits of food in their mouth, dumping their plates in the sink for some unlucky soul who would eventually get stuck with dishwashing duty, and shuffled for the door.

The rusty farm truck rolled up just as we emerged. The old brakes squealed as they did very little to slow the truck down. The security guard driving cut the engine and metallic rattling died out. The truck was the only form of motorized transportation on the island, and it looked to be about as old as the island itself. I had the very unpleasant experience of riding in it a couple times, and from the looks of the passenger climbing out the side door, he hadn't found the experience any more pleasant.

The man's face was white. His shoulder length, bleach-blonde hair clung to his cheeks. He paused at the truck's side-view mirror, primping himself, and smoothing out the wrinkles in his shirt before acknowledging us.

Cato was the first to reach him, "Vayu – welcome back! I trust your travel was adequate?"

The newcomer snorted. "If by adequate you mean it got me here, then yes, I suppose it was adequate. But Cato – that truck is on its last leg. The brakes don't exactly do their job, and its constant stalling on the way here is the only reason we didn't run off the road into a tree." He squared his shoulders with Cato, smiling. "Give us a hug, old man."

Cato hesitated. "Oh, well…"

Vayu didn't give him a chance to back out. He swept Cato up into a bear hug, holding on much longer than necessary. Cato broke free, "Ah, yes. Good to see you too. Sorry about the ride, but as you know – our money is better spent elsewhere. Now if you'll excuse me, I'll just see to the truck." He side-stepped around Vayu to speak to the driver about the maintenance of the truck.

Micah stepped up. "Long time no see, Vayu. Your usual room is ready." Micah stuck his hand out, well out of hugging range.

Vayu smiled at Micah and shook his hand, but touched him on the shoulder with his other hand all the same. "Always a pleasure, Micah. I'll be sure to come see you after I've settled." Still holding onto Micah's hand, Vayu peered around him narrowing his eyes, "Where is Alex?"

"Alex couldn't get away," Micah said a little too quickly. "We can hunt him down later." He looked at the old truck, frowned, moved toward it. "I'd better go help Cato out. Hey…don't touch that, Cato, it's probably still hot!"

Fresh out of men to accost, Vayu finally turned to Susan and me. "Dears, you are looking quite lovely this morning." He kissed each of our hands.

"Thank you, Vayu." Susan cleared her throat. "This is Kaitlyn, our newest Gaia."

Vayu turned to study me, lips pursed, his right hand stroking his clean-shaven chin.

Suddenly, it dawned on me. "Oh, you're—" I clamped my hand over my mouth, cutting the rest of my sentence off as my brain had a chance to catch up with my mouth.

"Oh come off it. Say it with me. Gaaaaay." Vayu prompted.

I laughed nervously, the only sound that would come out of my mouth. I cleared my throat, "Sorry, I didn't mean to offend. You just sort of took me by surprise."

"As did you, dear," he said. "After all, you are the first pregnant Gaia I've seen."

I nearly stumbled back in surprise.

"Don't look so shocked, honey. I know my shapes."

I shook my head, looking around to make sure no one had overheard. Thankfully everyone else seemed to be preoccupied.

Vayu stepped closer without warning, and laid his hand on my belly. "How far along are you?"

I gruffly pushed his hand away, glancing at the group by the van before glaring at Vayu. "It's a secret!" I hissed.

"Oh, right." He shut his lips tight and gestured as if he were locking them. "Have you seen a doctor yet?"

I rolled my eyes; figured I might as well answer before he kept asking in front of the others. "I think I am about five months along and no, I haven't seen a doctor yet. Not an easy thing to ask for if you don't want anyone to know."

"Well, that won't do." Vayu put his hands on hips and scrutinized me from top to bottom. "I had a relationship with a midwife once who was all too eager to share the more gruesome parts of pregnancy and childbirth. I suppose I could examine you myself."

"I don't think so," I scoffed, lowering my voice as Cato and Micah approached. "Besides, I can't keep it secret much longer."

"Already sharing secrets?" Cato asked. I swallowed a grimace. His hearing was deceptively good for such an old man.

"Secrets of the spoken word." Vayu lied, waving away the premise with one hand, and putting the other around me. "It can be more powerful than magic itself." Vayu steered me away from the other men toward the building.

After we were out of earshot, he spoke under his breath, "What I said was true, you know – about the spoken word."

I raised an eyebrow. "What?"

"The spoken word can be more powerful than magic."

I studied him for a moment as we walked, and finally gave in. "Care to demonstrate?"

He smiled. "I thought you'd never ask."

Vayu stopped walking, closed his eyes and took a deep breath. When he let it out, words escaped with it. The words were a mix of two languages; Latin and the English translation as far as I could tell, but somehow spoken simultaneously.

"*Sol iustitiae nos illustra* - Sun of righteousness shine upon us."

The words rode on the wind of Vayu's breath, becoming fainter as they flew further away and then louder as the wind raced back toward my ears. The wind and words played with my hair a moment then floated up to the sky, straight to a darker part of the clouds looming over the Chakra. Moments later the clouds parted just enough to let a sliver of sunlight through. The sun's warmth invigorated me. I closed my eyes, soaking up its brilliance. It didn't last long, the clouds quickly closed up again, but the sun had saturated my whole body – right down to the bones.

I looked at him in awe. "I will pay you a thousand dollars each time you do that. Once a day would do wonders for my mood."

He laughed. "I'm thinking there won't be a need soon enough. See? The clouds are already weaker."

I followed his gaze upward and thought he might have a point, but I couldn't be sure.

"Things will get better for you," he said, "and so will the weather."

Chapter 4

Code Breakers

She was familiar enough with her dreams to realize this one was different. It didn't seem to be driven by her subconscious. The dream had a mind of its own. She was trapped, subjected to the dream's whims, if there were such a thing. It wasn't pleasant. The atmosphere was tainted and cold. She shivered, wrapping her arms around her body.

The dream answered her need. The skies opened up and a crash of lightning in front of her sparked a small fire. She floated toward it and settled herself, stretching her hands out to soak in the heat. The fire crackled and sizzled and spoke to her, 'lightning man'. When the dream felt she was sufficiently warmed, the fire died down, but did not disappear.

As her eyes adjusted to the dimming light, Shawn appeared across the fire. She sat completely still, a strange calm forcing its way inside her. Still, the tainted air kept her alert.

'They call me mellow yellow…' the words to the 1960's song vibrated through her head.

Shawn smiled, his expression friendly, but his eyes cold. When she shivered again, the fire flared up. It grew and grew, fueled by an intruding wind until everything was consumed.

* * *

I spent the majority of the next day evading Vayu's attempts to examine me. I was bribed with more bouts of sunshine, food, and massages but didn't care to have

Vayu's amateur hands probing me God knows where. I only got rid of him once I sold out Alex's hiding place. As Vayu walked off with a spring in his step, I sent a silent apology to Alex, knowing it wouldn't be received. He didn't have the same abilities as the rest of us.

Searching for something to do, I found myself in Cato's library. I scanned the walls of books for something to read, and was disappointed to find no fiction; just rows and rows of boring textbooks, some dating back to the 1800s.

How accurate can those be?

Distracted by the books' uselessness, I turned, knocking over one of the stacks. They scattered, mixing in with notepads and loose papers on the floor.

"Crap," I muttered at the room. I was going to have to get used to my changing body.

"Is that you Kaitlyn?" Cato called from deeper within the library.

"Yes, yes," I responded, trying to put the pile back in some order, not that it had had much of one before. "I'm coming."

Making my way to the sound of Cato's voice was a trial. His office was ten times more packed than it was the last time I'd seen it, something that should not have even been possible. I worked my way around an especially large pile of junk and found Cato sitting at a desk under the giant tree growing in the middle of the room. The tree looked diseased. Its leaves drooped, some turning brown. The lack of sun was affecting more than just us humans.

Cato cleared his throat, averting my attention from the tree. Micah sat across the desk from Cato, settled on a torn, ratty couch.

"This is the letter Micah brought home from your trip to the States." Cato motioned to a letter. "We have been studying it for the last few hours. On the surface it doesn't make much sense, but we believe it is coded. Do you want to look?"

I stepped closer to the desk after a sideways glance at Micah and leaned over the letter.

Prepare Your Fire And Rock my Worthiest opponent, in Mass quantities.

The subject line sat written in clear print across the top.

Cato continued, "The first line serves as a key to the rest of the letter. We pulled out several words and phrases. Depending which it is, we can decipher the rest of the letter. Does anything jump out at you?"

Cato pushed his notebook toward me and I scanned over the list of words.

ruin kim
warm
wary
eye norm
pour a worm
ray of arts
aye dot
princess

I didn't need to review the entire list; I knew it when I saw it. They should have guessed by the simple clarity of the word.

"Princess - it's what Shawn calls me," I said it quietly, hesitantly. I looked at Micah but couldn't read his expression. Cato took back the notebook and began to decipher the rest of the letter. Taking a seat on the dusty couch next to Micah, I could feel his eyes boring into me from the side. I turned to face him. "What?"

He looked a second more, face stony. Finally, his eyes softened. I didn't even want to know what was going through his head. He covered my hand with his own and put his other arm around me. I moved closer, welcoming his warmth. It was the closest we'd been in a long time. We sat in silence until Cato finished his puzzle. It didn't take long.

"Take a look." He motioned us closer. Micah stood quickly, me a little more awkwardly, the sagging couch fighting against the growing weight of my stomach. Luckily, the men didn't seem to notice. I joined them; all three of us leaned over Cato's scribbling.

Princess – Come find me where our dreams meet.

"Does that mean anything to you?" Cato asked, studying me intently.

"Maybe, I...I had a dream about him last night." Micah tensed beside me. "It doesn't happen often."

"Well," Cato interrupted, "where were you in the dream?"

His question gave me pause. I tried to think back to my dream but nothing came to mind beyond the fire. "I don't know. We were ... nowhere. I mean, there was nothing around us. "Is there anything in there about a lightning man?"

"No," Cato said, studying the letter again. "Why?"

"Never mind. Just a thought."

"Fire?" Micah spoke up. I didn't know if I had spoken my thoughts aloud or if he was reverting to an old, unwelcome habit of reading my mind.

Cato didn't give me time to address the issue, "That is most unhelpful, Kaitlyn."

I shrugged my shoulders and he grudgingly bent back over the letter, looking for more clues. Micah motioned toward the door and we started off, leaving Cato in peace.

We hadn't gotten far from the library when the quiet hallways erupted with Vayu's excited voice, "A fire!"

His words were chilling, and the wind that swirled around Vayu made me shiver. I immediately grabbed for Micah's hand.

Micah moved to stand in front of me, and asked Vayu, "What fire? Where?"

I peeked around Micah's shoulder and saw Vayu eyeing our posture. I detected a hint of jealousy in the look he sent my way. The wind picked up. Micah spoke up again, "Vayu – calm yourself! Get your element under control!"

Vayu made a visible effort to relax and the wind died down abruptly. "Australia, in the Northern Territory. One of the largest brush fires they've ever seen – it's being spread too rapidly by the winds to get it under control. I could help…we could help. We could be there by tonight." Vayu had barely taken a breath while rushing to get everything out, and was now breathing hard, his lungs working to catch up.

I squeezed Micah's hand, moving to his side to look up at his face. "Do you think—?"

"Yes," he interrupted. "It's too much of a coincidence not to be him. We'd better tell Cato."

The three of us turned back toward the office. Vayu, in all his excitement, reached the door first. Just as he began to pull it open it Micah slammed it shut again. "Make sure you're under control." Micah gave him a pointed look. His eyes slid to me. "We're still reorganizing in there after the last windstorm."

Vayu smiled. "I appreciate the concern, sweetheart. But I'm okay now."

Vayu attempted to open the door again. Micah pushed it closed. "Don't call me sweetheart."

I could see a spark in Vayu's eyes; the altercation was exciting him even more. I stepped in between the two. "Ok, guys. Break it up. Business first, quarrels later." I pushed both of them back and opened the doors myself.

Vayu was relaying the information to Cato before we could even reach him. By the time we got to him, Shawn's letter sat discarded to the side, and he had produced a detailed map of Australia. "Where did you say the fire was?"

Vayu answered, "In the Northern Territory. It's covering some 2,000 square miles."

They all leaned over the map, and Vayu asked, "If this is Shawn's doing, how does he expect us to pinpoint the meeting place in all of that?"

Slowly, all heads turned toward me.

I huffed at the thought of helping them find the only man I wished to never see again, but studied the map anyway. Vayu pointed out where he remembered most of the fire being shown on the news and I squinted at the names of cities and other places. Finally, I zeroed in on the most obvious possibility. "There, in Kakudu National Park. Yellow Waters."

The three men followed my finger.

"Are you sure?" Cato asked, reaching into his shirt pocket for glasses.

I'd never seen him wear glasses before. "Pretty sure. Yellow was part of the dream, too."

Micah opened his mouth, forming a question.

I interrupted before he could even start, "Don't ask."

"Well then." Cato took his glasses off and rubbed the bridge of his nose. "We have a destination."

Vayu jumped up and down, clapping his hands.

Cato frowned. "Vayu, find Alex and brief him on everything. He'll need to arrange transportation for all of us, including Susan and Kaitlyn."

I straightened, preparing for an argument and racking my brain for all the reasons I shouldn't go. Cato and Micah's stares convinced me otherwise and without a word spoken, I had lost the fight.

"Lightning man makes sense now, was that part of your dream, too?" Cato asked.

"Kind of."

He pulled a dusty book down off of one of the higher shelves. "Namarrgon is an aboriginal legend meaning lightning man."

"What does that have to do with me?"

"Nothing," Cato said. "It is Shawn letting us know this fire isn't natural. He most likely started it. This is his way of ensuring we go to battle it instead of letting nature take its course."

Cato gave me a chance to respond but I couldn't come up with an argument so he continued, "He wants you there, Kaitlyn. We are going to oblige because we need this lead."

I felt Micah's hand on the back of my neck, giving me what support he could, but his warmth did nothing for the chill growing in my body.

Chapter 5

A Fish out of Water

"Now *that* is a warm welcome."

No one laughed at Vayu's joke as we made our way down the steep flight of stairs from the plane onto the open tarmac. We all eyed the ominous orange glow visible in the distance.

As we passed a baggage handler his radio crackled to life and a thick Australian accent came over the airways, "Ok guys, that is the last plane in. We are going to start the evacuation process. Make sure…" the man with the radio walked out of earshot.

I felt my heart beat faster. I glanced up at Micah, sticking close by my side. He met my look, but kept all emotion hidden behind the stone wall of his face.

Having packed carry-ons only, we were able to leave the airport quickly. Stuffing ourselves into a rental van, we were pressed up against one another, two seatbelts short of accommodating everyone.

Cato sat in the front passenger seat, studying a large map of the Northern Territory. He looked at Alex, "We are supposed to meet my associate here. He is with a local fire brigade and can direct us to where we will be most effective without being detected."

Micah leaned forward to consult how to get there while making our best guess on avoiding fire-ravaged roads. I looked behind me to the back row where Vayu and a haggard Susan sat.

I furrowed my eyebrows at Susan's pale face. "What's the matter? Are you all right?"

She took a sip from her water bottle and nodded her head. "Yes, I'm…well, no." She leaned forward and lowered her voice sending a furtive look at Micah. "It's the air – there's no water in it. The fire's dried out the entire area. I feel like…well, a little like a fish out of water." She managed a smile. I reached back and took hold of her hand, squeezing tightly. Maybe being closer to me and the extra water my body carried would give her some comfort. She leaned back in the seat and closed her eyes. Pink returned to her cheeks.

White ash began to fall on the windshield of the van. I swallowed hard, forcing my attention to Vayu. He ignored us and looked anxiously out the window, closing and opening his eyes, concentrating on something no one else could see.

Ten minutes later we pulled up to a large gathering of firemen, fire trucks, and emergency personnel. Cato looked at us, speaking quietly before we left the van, "I don't want to draw any attention to us, which is what will happen if we all go. Alex and I will stay here with the fireman and will let you know where to go."

Alex began shuffling around in a large duffel bag by his side. "I brought handhelds. Here." He handed a radio to Micah and kept the other to himself. "Channel Two."

"That's my boy." Cato winked at Alex. They got out and disappeared into the sea of yellow coats. Micah crawled forward into the driver's seat and took us back out onto the roads, checking in with Alex over the radio every 15 minutes. I stayed where I was, holding Susan's hand. Alex began spewing directions over the radio, leading us onto unmarked dirt roads. We passed a small neighborhood of a dozen houses, all of which should have been evacuated, but residents still stood outside watering down their roofs and lawns. The orange glow and the roar of the fire grew louder as we continued.

"These idiots are going to be trapped soon..." Micah mumbled under his breath.

A few minutes past the houses, Alex's voice began to fade in and out, leaving static for longer and longer stretches.

Micah stopped the van, "This is as far as we should go. I don't want to lose radio contact." He turned to Vayu, who was still lost in his own world. "Vayu...Vayu!"

Vayu snapped his attention to Micah.

"Can you work from here?"

Vayu nodded, taking a long moment before answering. "Yes, I think so. We need to walk a little further in but this will be good."

We opened the doors and immediately began to choke on the tainted air.

"Come on, let's make this fast." Micah coughed, handing us backpacks, each stuffed with random items Alex thought might be useful.

We began to see the flames not far from the van. The roar seemed to shake the forest, punctuated by loud bursts when dry trees went up in flames. I glanced at Micah – his hair was as white as his sister's skin. I frowned. All of us were turning white as ash stuck to us.

A cry made us spin. Susan fell to the ground. Micah and I rushed to her side, each taking one of her hands.

"I don't think I can go anymore, I need water now."

Micah rifled through his bag for a water bottle and handed it to her.

"No, not that. I need more." She coughed.

"Am I not enough?" I asked.

Micah looked confused, but didn't question me.

"No, not anymore." She closed her eyes in concentration and Micah and I waited, helpless. Finally she spoke, "There is water that way, not too far. You could carry me there Micah."

"Yes, of course." Micah began to pick his sister up.

"I need to go this way to be most effective," Vayu said, pointing east, right into the heart of the flames.

Micah shook his head. "No – no one goes alone." Realizing the situation he had just put himself in, he laid his sister back down gently and looked from me to her. We all waited impatiently. Vayu had crossed his arms, making it apparent which way he was going regardless of Micah's verdict. Micah finally reached into his backpack and pulled out the only fire blanket Alex had. He turned me around and stuffed it into my own backpack. He grabbed Vayu's arm. "If—"

"No if's. We'll be all right." Vayu interrupted. He followed Micah's gaze toward me and rephrased his statement, "*She* will be all right."

Micah nodded, picked up his sister, and walked away without glancing back.

Vayu pulled me in the other direction. I hesitated. His direction meant higher temperatures, more smoke, and significantly more risk. Up until now, I had taken Micah's comforting presence for granted. I sighed, then coughed. I tried to keep my arm over my mouth, breathing in the cotton fibers of my sleeve instead of the poisoned air.

Only a few minutes later, something on all fours came lumbering out of the smoke.

"A koala bear!" I exclaimed. It was the first wild koala bear I had ever seen, and it was also limping. I angled toward it.

Vayu stopped me. "We don't want to scare it back into the fire."

As it came closer, I noticed a small baby clinging to the koala bear's back. My stomach turned over. Both baby and mother had singed hairs on their backsides. I forced myself to stand still while they passed, wanting to help. The mother walked awkwardly on her paws. It soon became apparent the bottoms of her feet were burnt. Suddenly my trials as a mother-to-be seemed rather insignificant.

Vayu shook his head, face wrinkled with pity. "Slow moving creatures. They fall prey to wildfires too easily."

"We have to help it." I spoke, just short of yelling to be heard over the roar of the fire.

"No. There isn't much we can do. Besides, if we can stop this fire from moving forward, we'll save the town back there and the koala bear."

I agreed and followed Vayu deeper into the bush, encountering no more animals.

Only the stupid ones would still be here, I thought. *Humans notwithstanding.*

A thick wall of fire came into view. Vayu stopped. "Here. This is the front of the fire."

He turned to me and I realized how wildly unprepared I actually was. Wind was the most unpredictable of elements, the most difficult to control. I hadn't had much practice with it.

Vayu said, "I don't have time to teach you, but we can do this one of two ways. You can either feed me energy or you can try to copy what I do as best as you can."

It didn't take me long to choose, remembering what happened to Micah last time he willingly gave me his energy. "I'll try it on my own."

Vayu scrutinized me for a moment, trying to judge my abilities as if he could by just looking at my face.

I frowned. He hadn't seen any of what I could do. "Vayu – Micah wouldn't have left me if he didn't think I could handle it."

Vayu accepted my reasoning, which in turn gave me more confidence. Amazing how Micah could change things without even being there.

Vayu took a deep breath in, and flows of energy left his body as he exhaled. There weren't streams as I saw or felt with Susan or Cato, but more of an all-encompassing net that went out from his body. The net expanded, retracted, and grew thicker or thinner at Vayu's will. I felt it allow air through in some places and block it in others. The net quickly grew to the left and right of us, expanding beyond my sight. Somehow, Vayu knew what to do even in the places he couldn't see.

Following his lead, I took a deep breath in and immediately sputtered on the smoke. Vayu spared a sideways glance, but kept most of his focus on the job at hand.

I remembered Cato's words. *Everyone has a different way of doing it. Knowing how one person does it won't help you figure out how to do it on your own.* I thought back to all the other times I had used my powers. I had either drawn energy from within myself, drawn energy from another element, or used raw emotion to conjure weather. Thinking briefly of the koala bears, I decided I couldn't draw energy from within and risk the baby; it was the least I could do as a mother. I also lacked any significant emotion, barring the fear building up in the pit of my stomach. I had never really operated on fear before. It was anyone's guess how the elements would react.

I closed my eyes and concentrated on elements around me. Water was obviously in short supply, the air was tainted and I didn't want to interfere with Vayu's element. That left fire and earth. Could I possibly draw energy from the very element I was trying to defeat?

I shrugged my shoulders, "Why the hell not?" The fire was far too loud for Vayu to hear me. Good – the less crazy he thought I was, the better.

Drawing energy toward me from the fire, I shifted its direction before reaching Vayu's net and converted it into wind. I directed the wind over the fire, quelling what flame I could and cooling the entire area.

"Good," Vayu called over the noise. "That is helping – very good."

He looked surprised, and I smiled. I liked surprising people, as long as it was with my skill and not the lack thereof. I continued to concentrate on my wind, cooling down the fire and occasionally letting a gust blow over the top of Vayu's net to cool us down.

Blackened landscape came into view as we pushed the fire back. We moved constantly, to the sides and forward, following the fire as it retreated. Several loud bursts to our left shocked us from our concentration. A small grove of trees had succumbed to the fire and were exploding into flames, one right after another.

"Move your wind to only that area," Vayu yelled.

I refocused my efforts as Vayu's net grew more intense. I worked for what seemed like hours, no longer sparing wind to cool us down. I was drained.

A strong wind on our right caught me off guard and blew over me with malicious force.

"What are you doing?" I yelled at Vayu.

"Not me – when a fire gets too hot it creates weather of its own."

Despite the heat, chills crawled up my back. We were no longer fighting just a fire. It was a living, breathing monster, and a crafty one, at that. The fire's weather pushed quickly through Vayu's net on our right and we angled our bodies to combat it. We had to move backwards into the burnt terrain to avoid being singed ourselves. Now we were on the losing side of the battle.

Something caught us from behind and we both ended up on the ground.

Vayu recovered faster. "Damn log." He got up quickly and rebuilt his net.

"Vayu." I swallowed hard, not moving. "It's not a log."

"What?" He shouted down at me without looking.

"It's a person." I sat, frozen for a moment, then finally shuffled around the charred body and looked for signs of life. The hair was mostly burned off, leaving only sporadic patches of fuzz, but judging by the size of the body and width of the shoulders, it was a man. He was lying on his stomach, his head turned toward me. His back rose in a shallow, irregular breathing pattern.

"Is it Shawn?" Vayu asked, not able to spare a glance down at the body.

I looked at his face, and shook my head. "No."

The man's eyes, probably the only unscathed part of his body, were a light brown, not Shawn's icy blue stare. I couldn't look away; there was too much white in his eyes. His lids were almost completely burned off. Bile rose in my throat.

He began to gurgle in an effort to say something.

I whispered back, "Shhh.....don't say anything. I'll get you help." I touched his shoulder and bits of something flaked off. I couldn't tell if it was skin or clothing. The entire body was either black or red; he wasn't going to make it no matter what I did. I didn't feel the same sense of pity as I did with the koala bears; I felt physically ill. I looked at him again and mouthed the words 'I'm sorry'.

Recognition flashed in his eyes. I believe I had just been so kind as to help him realize his own death was close at hand. I lay down next to him, oblivious of the fire around us. The least I could do was stay with him until the end. Vayu was yelling something, but my priorities were clear. I wasn't a Gaia right then, nor was I Kaitlyn. I was simply the last connection this man would have in his life.

Vayu, still yelling, rustled around in the pack on my back for something. My body jerked as his search became more frantic.

The man resumed his attempts to speak, despite my insistence that he lay still. I leaned in closer, trying to interpret a phrase he said over and over. Only two words in the garbling were comprehensible, and they were enough to freeze me in place. "One less, one less."

He began shifting his body and grunting; I couldn't subdue him with my hands for fear of causing more damage. Finally he leaned away from me, pulling out a bag from underneath the blanket. It was shiny; possibly fireproof. Inside the bag was a thick, neatly bound document. He must have been protecting the document while sacrificing his own body. The white pages were a stark contrast to the blackened earth below and his charred hand. He pushed the document feebly toward me, leaving streaks of ash behind on the pristine paper as he pulled his hand away. On the cover was one simple symbol, the same symbol worn on my shoulder as a permanent scar of Shawn's doing.

Suspicions confirmed, my body went numb.

"I was chosen to be one less." His smile, no matter how much it anguished him to do so, was the last thing I saw.

Vayu threw himself over me holding the fire blanket around both of us. It was only big enough for two. He pinned down as many sides of the blanket as he could. The temperature inside spiked, the fire a deafening roar around us. Despite being smothered by Vayu's weight, the air inside the blanket was breathable. No smoke seeped in under the blankets edges. Vayu had to have been using a trick to put oxygen in the air under the blanket. We could do nothing but lay there and wait for the fire to pass. The image of the symbol, clear and foreboding underneath streaks of ashes, was seared into my brain. Half hoping the document was now burning in the fire, I reached out gingerly to search for it. My fingers made contact and I quickly retracted my hand. Vayu had to have shuffled it closer while trying to get the blanket down, probably not even realizing what it was.

I tried to force my mind to more pleasant images and immediately thought of Micah. *Oh, God – Micah!* He was out there, left to face this quick-moving monster with a sick sister to slow him down. I thought about reaching out to him, mentally, but no, distracting him for my own selfish knowledge wouldn't help him. Agitated, I could no longer lay still under Vayu's weight. I heaved him off to the side. He struggled to keep the blanket pinned down under my sudden movement. I took control of one side to help him. It was surprisingly difficult as the fiery wind constantly tried to work its way underneath, ripping and pulling at the blanket.

"Don't fight it," Vayu yelled at me. "Work with it."

By applying pressure in different places, I figured out what he meant. The blanket went lax and I was no longer struggling to hold on. The fire seemed to roar in agitation at our endurance. I held my focus on the gray blanket, watching it waver almost leisurely now. Finally, the fire gave up. Once the roaring died down to a dull rumble in the distance, Vayu peeked out, then lifted the blanket off of us.

My jaw dropped, looking at the landscape. Everything was either black or still smoldering in bright orange embers. Trees were twisted or bent over in agony and thin plumes of smoke rose like spires into the sky. I turned to Vayu then followed his gaze from the skies down to our feet. The man now lay in a charred heap. I turned away quickly.

"Nature's way of renewing the earth," Vayu whispered.

I shook my head, "It could have been contained – we failed. I failed."

He didn't answer me.

We stood in shock for a few minutes longer. I snapped out of it, trying to focus on getting us back to safety. I stuffed the blanket back into my backpack and picked up the document. "Which way to the neighborhood we passed?"

Vayu, bringing himself out of his own trance, started to look around. "I'm not sure. Everything looks different." Panic hit his face. "We don't even have the radio – Micah took it."

"I can find Micah…maybe." I put a calming hand on Vayu's arm. *If he isn't dead.* I closed my eyes and took a deep breath, preparing myself for what I might find. I pictured myself, standing in the blackened landscape alone and lost. I solidified the image then sent it out, hoping Micah would receive it. He did. I felt it being absorbed and returned with an image of him helping his sister out of a large pond. I smiled in relief. They'd managed to find enough water to submerge themselves in until the fire passed. "This way!" I yelled to Vayu, barely waiting for him to follow me. The thought of Micah's arms around me, strong and sturdy, urged me on.

It wasn't long before he came into view, pulling his sister behind him. I broke into a sprint, oblivious to the charred shrubbery and sticks that scratched at my ankles. I tripped and landed hard on the ground.

Leave it to me to ruin a Hollywood moment, I groaned inwardly. The document floated away, landing just out of my reach, at Micah's feet. He stopped dead in his tracks, staring at the symbol; a painful reminder to us both of his failure to protect me. He bent down to pick it up, completely ignoring the fact that I was sprawled out beside it.

"That tells me where I stand," I said getting up and dusting myself off. "Or lay, for that matter." I looked around but no one got the joke. Micah, and now Susan, who had approached from behind, were staring at the symbol. And Vayu was staring at them, trying to interpret their faces.

"Where did you get this?" Micah finally looked at me.

I thought of the man and had to fight back the bile that rose in my throat. "I think it was left for me. By Shawn."

Micah's eyes flashed. "You saw him?"

"No." I snatched the document out of his hands and stuffed it into my backpack. "Let's just get out of here – we can talk about it later."

Micah stared at me, questions coursing through his expression and his eyes willing me to explain.

"You can just stop with your eye tricks," I said, harsher than I intended. "If I talk about it now I'm going to be sick all over the place – then you'll really have something to stare at."

He looked away. "Fine. Later, then." He pulled out his handheld, calling Alex. Just static. Micah sighed, "The van is this way. Hopefully it didn't catch fire. Careful where you step. The hotspots will burn right through your shoes."

Micah set off and Vayu followed. Susan and I looked at each other, exchanged sympathetic expressions, then held hands for support as we followed the men back to civilization.

Chapter 6

Cleaning Up

Our walk back to the van was silent. We avoided looking at the charred houses that only hours ago stood secure and strong. I hoped the owners made it out unscathed, but I had no desire to go looking for more burnt bodies. I'd seen one too many already. Even the world seemed silent, the air eerily void of the sounds of bugs, birds, or whatever other animals might be out and about in Australia on a warm spring day. Besides our footsteps, only the occasional cracking branch giving in to its injuries filled the dead space.

Alex and Cato didn't ask any questions as we reached them, we all just shuffled to allow room for them in the van and headed for a hotel. There were few other guests, most having voluntarily evacuated, leaving enough space for us each to have our own room at their discounted disaster rate. I went straight for the shower. I scrubbed my body from head to toe, over and over again until my skin felt raw. I only stopped once the water running off my body and down the drain was clear – not the sinister black of charred forest. I released a breath. Better raw than seeing one smudge of ash to remind me of earlier. I dried off, turned the television on max volume, not caring what channel blared through the room. Cocooning myself in the thick covers of the bed, an Australian fishing competition was just loud enough to drown out my own thoughts.

* * *

The next morning, with the smell of fire and ash still thick in the air; I emerged from my cocoon only when my bladder gave me no choice. Washing my hands, I caught a glimpse of myself in the mirror and almost gasped out loud. The dark circles under my eyes were nothing compared to the mess of brown and gold strands hanging from my head, knotted and crinkled from the roots to the tips.

Trying to occupy my mind with nothing last night was so effective I didn't even remember one of the most important beauty tips my mother gave me – never go to bed with wet hair. It was crinkled in some placed, and sticking straight up in other places. I tried pulling at my hair in vain. The only solution was another shower.

Two showers in eight hours. I had never been so clean in my life. My physical cleanliness did not mirror my emotional state. I began to chase away visions forming in my head. Burning trees that reach out for me, and bodies lumped on the ground, making it impossible to get away. I definitely needed a distraction and soon; something more powerful than TV.

As I was stepping out of the shower, I couldn't hear the TV. Thinking further, I realized it wasn't even on when I woke up.

Distraction achieved.

Had someone come into the room without me even knowing? Were they still there? I looked around the bathroom for something to cover myself just in case. Two towels did the trick; they were the only option next to the clothes I wore yesterday now piled in a black heap next to the toilet.

I poked my head out of the bathroom, "Hello?"

The intruder spoke, "I put clothes in front of the door there for you."

I craned my neck out further and saw him sitting on the corner of the bed with his back to me. "Cato?!"

He didn't respond; keeping his head respectfully turned away.

I looked at the clothes he had left for me, complete with undergarments. I made a face. "Well, that is kind of disturbing."

"Not as disturbing as this." He held up the document given to me yesterday. I growled at the thought of having to discuss it with anyone but scooped up the pile of clothes and changed nonetheless. I ran a comb through my hair, vowing to take a blow dryer to it before I went to bed again.

Cato spoke before I could. "Have you read any of it yet?"

I shook my head, joining him on the bed. "I can't look at the thing without feeling sick."

He eyed me critically, as if wondering what could have been that bad. "I see. Micah let me know about it, and I've read through some of it while you were still under your blankets. Sorry for the intrusion, but this isn't something that can wait."

"What is it, exactly?" I asked, trying to avoid glancing at the white paper still marked with streaks of ash from the deliverer's hand.

"It appears to be a business plan."

"What?" I now leaned over to see.

Cato opened the document to the table of contents; *Mission Statement, Description of Corporation, Feasibility Studies, Location, Personnel, Financial Data...*

Cato explained, "He is starting his own organization, with a mission similar to ours but carried out with extremely different principals."

"We knew that much, but why share such detailed information with us? It's like he is giving us a roadmap to bring him down." I flipped over to the page number that supposedly held the organization's location information. It was blank. "Oh."

"He conveniently omitted a few parts." Cato pushed himself up from the bed stiffly. Yesterday must have been hard on him, too. "Susan, Alex, and I are leaving today. There isn't much more we can do here. We will be counting on you, Vayu, and Micah to continue to help contain the fire until it is manageable enough for the local authorities to control it on their own." He closed the document still in his hand. "Here."

I put up my hands in protest. "I'd rather not."

"I am insisting, Kaitlyn. This was given to you, and although we may not understand exactly why, I think it best that you read through it."

I stood up angrily. "Shawn put me through hell and back. I went through things you could never even begin to understand. I don't want anything more to do with him!"

Cato kept his cool as always, meeting my fiery stare. "I know. But it seems as though Shawn wants everything to do with you. And I think we both know him well enough to know that you don't have a choice in the matter." Cato tossed the document next to me on the bed. "Read it. Analyze it. Understand it. Know it from front to back. Witnessing the lengths that Shawn will go to, such as with this wildfire, I admit I was wrong. I now believe there is a large, drawn out battle approaching, and this may very well be the key to saving your own ass one day."

That was the first time I heard Cato curse. It sounded ten times more atrocious coming out of his mouth than from anyone else. He took his exit before I could recover from shock.

I sat in silence for a few minutes, occasionally glancing at the document with wary looks. It felt as though it were Shawn himself sitting next to me. Finally, I decided it could wait a little longer, and I went out into the hall to look for Susan, or Micah, or anyone else that could keep me occupied. I soon realized I had no idea where any of their rooms were. Well, we were the only current tenants of the hotel as far as I knew. Finding them couldn't be hard.

I walked down the hall, pausing at each door to listen for signs of life. After hearing nothing the entire length of the hallway, I turned around and yelled, with my outdoor voice, "Hello?!"

The word echoed down the hallway. My pulse raced, as the terrifying feeling of abandonment hit me. Finally, a door opened and Micah poked his head out, "We're in here."

Sighing in relief, I walked a little too quickly into his room. He didn't seem to notice. Three backpacks and a spread of supplies covered his bed, everything in triplicate. Fire blankets, first aid supplies, water bottles, walkie-talkies, and dehydrated food. Vayu began packing everything in the backpacks. "Ready for another round?"

I sighed, but a job which prevented me from going back to my room, and back to what awaited me there, was better than nothing.

* * *

The next three days were filled with on-the-job training on how to fight fire with wind. My nights were spent holed up in my room reading the paperwork given to me. My days were significantly better than my nights. The document words resonated through my mind as if Shawn were reading them to me in his pompous voice. I read each night until I could bear no more of him in my head.

By the end of the third day, Micah announced we had done our part. We'd leave the next morning. Vayu and I merely nodded in acknowledgment. It was a struggle to expend even that much energy. Perhaps Micah was the only reason I could still stay on my feet. The entire time we were out, Micah strayed no further than a few yards from me. His closeness was comforting, and the few brief moments of physical contact sent chills through my body, even in the blinding heat. A brush of the hands or accidental bump of the shoulders seemed enough to keep me moving to the end of the day.

That night, Micah stopped me before I could put my key card in the door to my room. "I want to take you to dinner tonight."

I looked up at him with tired eyes. As much as I wanted to crawl into bed, I also wasn't ready to leave him. Despite our long day, his eyes were bright and his skin looked smooth, amazingly hydrated. He must have been a stark contrast to my chapped lips and smudges of black across my forehead and cheeks. Were we not just in the same fire fight?

"I have to warn you," he continued, "I want to talk to you about the document."

Ah, so there's the rub.

I weighed my options, but in the end couldn't resist his green eyes boring down at me. "Fine. Let me get cleaned up – give me 15 minutes." I realized I could smell my own body odor, even over the smoke that seemed irreversibly soaked into my pores. "I mean half an hour, give me half an hour."

He smiled. "Deal."

* * *

Some of the restaurants had reopened. Micah chose a small diner, requesting a seat in the corner for privacy. Privacy from what, I don't know; we were the only customers. As it was, the waitress had plenty of time to hover over us, attending to our every need, which gave us very little opportunity to talk. She seemed a little too entranced with Micah. I bristled. Once our food came, I asked for the check and dismissed her, saying we'd call her over if we needed anything else. She huffed and turned away; probably disappointed she wouldn't have more excuses to flaunt herself in front of Micah. He smiled at the look I gave her. My jealousy surprised even me after not having any intimate contact with Micah for months. Maybe that would change…

"So what did you find out about the document?" Micah interrupted my thoughts.

So much for intimate contact tonight. I frowned, mood officially ruined.

I put down my fork, wiped my mouth and came right out with it. "His organization is much stronger than we thought. He's been busy."

"How so?"

"Mostly seeking financing for his projects, setting up corporate partners and such. He's also delving into high-tech gadgets to assist in his missions. His missions are pretty much the same as ours, but on a much bigger scale, and set up to bring him as much publicity as possible." I paused to let Micah interject but he stayed silent. "Oh, and he's been recruiting…heavily. There is a list of Elementals he has already recruited." I leaned over to get the document out of my small bag. I opened it to the personnel page and handed it to Micah.

He scanned the list. "All of the strongest."

"Then why don't *we* use them?" I asked. I honestly wasn't sure who worked for us, but I knew there was usually just one person for each element. Shawn listed several for each.

"There's such a thing as being dangerously strong." Micah raised an eyebrow. "But besides that, there are those who don't agree with what we do or the way we do it, or whose personalities don't mesh with the rest of ours. Others are just downright uncontrollable. Anyway." He flicked his finger at the paper. "You can't put more than one of the same type of Elemental on a mission– the results are too unpredictable."

"Doesn't he know that?"

"Yes!" Micah shifted in his seat, "He knows it all. From first-hand experience, in some cases."

I shrugged my shoulders. "Maybe he's found a way around that."

"Why are you…?" Micah nearly lifted himself out of his chair with the force of the words. He caught himself and lowered his voice. "Why are you defending him?"

I fixed my eyes on Micah and stared him down until he averted his. It was quite the coup for me – he had a major advantage when it came to the power of the eyes.

"I'm sorry. I didn't mean to imply you sympathized with him. I'm just upset," Micah continued to stutter excuses.

I looked down and rubbed my temples, trying to fight off the massive headache I could feel coming on.

Finally Micah fell silent so I spoke, "I hope you understand how difficult it has been for me to even read this thing." I grabbed the paper out of his hands and stuffed it back into my bag. "I'm only doing it as a favor to Cato. If I had my choice it would have burned in this God-awful fire." I paused briefly to take a deep breath and began to rub my temples again, avoiding Micah's eyes. "Shawn has, for some reason, given us this information. What we choose to do with it has to be smart. It can't be what he expects us to do with it, and it can't be more wild goose chases. He has us running around all over the place chasing after him while he can put his plan into action."

I looked up to see Micah smiling at me. "What?" I snapped.

"This is the most I've heard you say in a long time. You must be feeling better."

"On the contrary, I feel like crap." A sudden gust of wind blew open the restaurant doors. The otherwise bored waitresses chased down the paper menus that scattered across the room. "Unless you want this fire to flare up again, I suggest you take me back to the hotel."

Micah didn't hesitate. He fumbled around in his pockets and left a few Australian polymer notes on the table. I fiddled with the plastic currency. The wind died down slightly as I realized the difference in lifestyle that I had not had a chance to witness. *I should get something touristy before we leave. A shot glass, or t-shirt or something.*

Micah interrupted my thoughts, placed his hand around my upper arm and led me out of the restaurant.

"Let's go," he whispered. I barely noticed the jealous stares of our waitress. I was too tired to care.

Chapter 7

Cold Weaves

The next morning I awoke to Micah moving around my room, packing my carry-on. I swallowed a growl. Second time in a week someone had entered my room without me knowing. Besides, my headache had, if anything, gotten worse through the night. I sat up in bed and cleared my throat.

Micah turned toward me. "Sorry, I wanted to let you sleep as long as possible."

"Yes," I mumbled with a raspy morning voice. "You seem to be doing a lot of apologizing lately."

"Sorry," he said again, then smiled.

Despite my best efforts, his smile lifted my mood. I shook my head, swinging my legs out of bed. "Let me just run through a shower. Give me ten minutes."

"Ok. Meet us downstairs when you're ready. Our plane leaves in two hours."

I padded across the room, careful to face away from him lest he get a whiff of my morning breath. By the time I left the bathroom, Micah had emptied the room of everything save one small bag for whatever items were left over. I met them downstairs and Micah greeted me with a small peck on the cheek.

Vayu interrupted our moment, "Taxi's waiting."

Throughout the trip home, Vayu continued to interject when Micah and I might have had a moment to talk, or even simply to hold hands. When we arrived at the Chakra, Susan greeted us with an entire medical team on standby to give me a checkup. Personally, some alone time with Micah seemed a little more important than finding out I was dehydrated, but the recent lack of personnel with which to perform medical intervention had them too eager to assist me. In all the craziness, Cato captured Micah, no doubt so they could debrief each other.

I sighed. *Maybe next time.*

Susan stayed by my side, pestering me for information about our trip. Blissfully, she didn't ask about the document.

She finally paused for a moment, gesturing to the medics. "Just so you know, they know."

I narrowed my eyes. "Know what?"

"You know…"

I didn't want to say it out loud, in case we weren't talking in code about the same thing. "You mean," I looked down at my belly, "that thing?"

She nodded.

"Why?!" I half squeaked, half yelled.

She rolled her eyes. "Puh-lease. Don't you think it isn't obvious to them – or to anyone else for that matter?"

"Well, it isn't obvious to Micah." I attempted to keep from pouting like a child. "And I'd prefer to keep it that way until I am ready to tell him – on my own terms." I fixed her with the same stare that had triumphed over Micah.

She didn't notice. "You don't have much time left. The wrong position, or just the wrong angle would reveal everything. You're showing."

"I know, I know." I would almost have rather talked about Shawn's document at that point.

"All I'm saying is you need to start thinking seriously about what you're going to say." She brushed back a stubborn lock of hair that kept falling over her eye. I had to remind myself of her fierce loyalty to her brother.

I changed the subject, "Let's go find out if Cato and Micah have come up with a plan for Shawn yet."

Susan got the hint. "*I'll* go see what they have in mind. You can join us when you are a little less tied down."

I looked at the myriad of needles going into me and huffed, "Fine."

Several hours and two IV bags later, I found everyone in the living room. I walked in, greeted by papers being shuffled away and several open books closing at once. Then all eyes were on me.

I frowned, "What was that all about?"

"Sorry, dear. We think it best you don't know the details of what we're planning." Cato explained, folding his hands in front of him.

"Why not?"

"He comes to you in your dreams, does he not?"

I glanced at Micah but he was avoiding eye contact. "He has once, yes..."

"Then he has some connection to you. If he were to get any bit of information from your subconscious it could put us all at jeopardy."

"I see." I walked over to an empty chair included in the circle of people and sat down. "What *can* you tell me?"

A collective sigh of relief rang out as if they had all been on edge waiting for me to overreact.

Vayu took initiative. "You and I are going to send a message to Shawn. We need to meet with him in person."

Cato walked forward and held out a slip of folded paper. "Here is the meeting place. It will be three days from now. Why don't you and Vayu go start on that now?"

I looked at the paper, but didn't take it. "I'm not going." I looked at Micah again for some sign of support but got nothing. He was avoiding me.

"I'm sorry?" Cato asked.

"I'm. Not. Going." I stood, annunciating my words and crossing my arms.

Now Cato looked to Micah for support. Micah was staring resolutely at his shoes.

Hah.

Vayu stood, took the paper from Cato and my arm, turning me away from the group, "Well the least you can do is help send the message."

I let Vayu escort me out of the room. I was too tired for a fight, anyway.

Once outside, Susan caught up to us, "I think I can help, too."

Vayu put one arm around her and one arm around me. "Just us girls, then. Let's go somewhere private."

"How about the rock?" I suggested.

They turned without my direction toward the infamous landmark.

The cherry blossoms weren't in bloom. I had a flashback of falling white and pink petals surrounding Micah and me on the small bench in a warm wind. One of the many talks we had had there. I felt a sharp pang in my heart, longing for that kind of relationship once again. Shawn had come between us in more ways than even he knew.

"Kaitlyn," Susan said. "I know this is hard for you, but we really could use your help here. If you come this time, I promise this will be the last trip you have to make for Shawn before the baby is born."

I sighed, she didn't quite get it, either. But the deal may be worth keeping everyone off my back so I could concentrate on growing a baby. Eat raisins and yogurt, or whatever it was pregnant women did. "If I goes this time, it will be the last trip I make *ever* for Shawn."

Susan smiled, "Deal. I'll hold off the hounds, I promise."

I nodded as Susan, Vayu, and I walked further into the garden behind the bench, pushing our way through trees and shrubbery. This part of the grounds had not been tended to for some time. We stepped into an area that was now cluttered with fallen branches, overgrown weeds and other bits of nature's debris. In the middle of it all was a large boulder. The center of the Chakra, as Micah once described it, where a large part of the energy contained within the Chakra resided. Micah had given me a handmade necklace made from a piece of the rock. My hand went to my neck, eager to feel the smooth rock in its butterfly frame, but it wasn't there. Another unfortunate casualty of my time as Shawn's prisoner.

We stopped in front of the rock and looked at each other, each waiting for the other to say something.

Susan finally spoke. "Kaitlyn, do you remember sending messages out to Micah and me while you were on Galapagos?"

"Yes," I said softly.

"How did you do that?"

I closed my eyes, trying to recall my spell while blocking out the unpleasant memories. "It was an impromptu prayer to water. I held my hands over a bowl of water and said a chant. Then I used heat to evaporate the water hoping the wind would catch it. Sometimes I also blessed water then spilled it onto the ground whenever I could manage. I'm not sure which way worked."

I looked at Susan, prompting her for her side.

She responded, "We were still in Spain. We didn't want to leave since we weren't sure if Shawn was keeping you there. I can't explain how I received your message. It was more like a feeling. That's the way Micah described it too. I can say that I tend to be more sensitive to water in the air than in the ground – as you might have guessed from my reaction in Australia." She smirked at her own comment, but her eyes said it was still too fresh in her mind for jokes.

Vayu interjected, "The elements of air and water balance each other. They're good partners." He nudged Susan with his shoulder. "Air expands your consciousness and represents truth. It's also associated with thought and language, the breath of life. I very much believe your messages were delivered by the wind."

"Wind it is then – besides, I've had plenty of practice with it as of late," I mumbled.

"Ok," Vayu smiled. "Let's do it a little differently this time. Susan – we are going to need some water."

"I'm on it." Susan nodded, and began to weave a water-tight bowl with stems and leaves laying on the ground. As she wove, she chanted a spell of intent into the forming bowl.

Vayu, just as interested in the basket it seemed, forced his attention away from Susan to me, "We are going to bless the water but send it out a little differently. After you evaporate it, you are going to have to intertwine the evaporation strands with my wind. We'll send it out together."

"How are you going to know which direction to send it?"

He shrugged his shoulders. "I won't, but we will know once it has been absorbed."

"How?"

"You'll see." He winked at me. We looked back at Susan. She had successfully completed a small bowl and moved on to collecting water from some of the plant life. A made a mental note to have her around if I was ever stranded in the desert.

"Here you go," she said, balancing the bowl in the middle of the large boulder.

"Well done," Vayu congratulated her. "Your turn Kaitlyn."

"Ok, here goes nothing." I directed a small amount of energy into the bowl. It didn't take much, especially since all my powers were heightened at the Chakra instead of depleted like on the Galapagos. Moisture in the air just above the bowl increased. The strands of evaporation almost slipped away before I could get a hold of them.

Susan coached me, "Careful, if you squeeze too much they'll disintegrate."

I loosened my grasp on the drops and wrapped weaves of air around the strands.

"Good, good," Vayu said. "Now I'm going to slip in there; don't let them waiver."

His weaves of air crept forward and slowly intertwined with my own. Combining powers with him instantly turned my stomach. My own weaves faltered. Everything turned cold and slimy. Vayu's magic slithered forward insistently, enveloping the extensions of my body. It took everything I had not to retract my energy.

"Oh come on, honey – it can't be that bad."

I quickly wiped the look of disdain off my face, "Sorry, it just feels…weird."

"Ok, we'll try going northwest first, to cover Europe – then we'll try east as far as the States. Air always flows easier going east."

I let Vayu lead. His weaves stretched my strands to the point I thought they would snap back.

After a few minutes, Vayu spoke again, "I can't find him there. Let's go another direction."

Instead of reeling in our strands then casting again, Vayu shot them straight over in the opposite direction. I almost fell over with the sudden shift in momentum. Susan grabbed my shoulders, physically steadying me. I ignored her, too deep in concentration. It didn't take much longer before I felt the weaves vibrate with a sudden tension. An even deeper cold crept down our energy streams and into my skin. I shivered, resisting the urge to retreat.

"Don't!" Vayu yelled, startling me with his intensity. "That's him. Keep the connection. Send the message."

"Oh crap." I suddenly realized my mistake. "I forgot to bless the water before I evaporated it. That is how I did it last time."

"Better think of something fast," Vayu pressured me.

"Ok, ok. Just let me think." I pulled out the piece of paper Vayu handed me, doing my best to read it while the chill grew, threatening to snap the connection. *Wyoming*. I blinked, trying to comprehend the one word scribbled in the middle of the paper. "That isn't very helpful. Where, exactly in Wyoming?"

"Your choice," Susan said. "Don't ask…"

I closed my eyes to think, concentration shattering a little bit every time Vayu tapped his foot impatiently. I've only been to one place in Wyoming on a photography assignment, Yellowstone National Park. Kind of ironic, the similar names of meeting places. It would be easier to send the message though.

"Got it," I announced. Blessing the piece of paper in an impromptu prayer, I placed it on the rock. After a few seconds of deep concentration, manipulating two elements at once, a tiny spark flared at the corner. The entire paper went up in flames within seconds. I urged the smoke from the fire toward the weaves Vayu and I created, letting all the elements mix themselves together. "I pray to Water, Air, and Fire, and the God and Goddess Spirits that governs them. Send this to Shawn, wielder of power over Gaia; that he may find me."

I would have never admitted his power to Shawn's face, but a pleasing message might be that much easier to absorb. As my energy neared its breaking point, I'd take all the help I could get. I looked to Vayu. "Do you know that Mellow Yellow song?"

"Yeah, why?"

"Sing it."

He raised an eyebrow.

"Just do it," I snapped. "It is part of the plan."

He broke into a hesitant, non-melodic song.

I opened my mouth to chastise him when Susan interrupted with her own version, which was slightly better. Encouraged by each other, the song grew confident. Their feet tapped out the beat

"Good, that's good," I said. "Now let the song move your weaves."

Their voices got louder and I found myself joining in. Rhythm vibrated through my body and back down the cold strings of power. The water vibrated, and smoke in the air fluttered in time to the music. After we ran out of words to the song, we slowly let the weaves slip from our grasp. I shivered and hugged my arms around myself for warmth. No one spoke.

Vayu finally forced a smile. "A little unorthodox, but I think he got the message."

"Um, Kaitlyn?" Susan asked. "What was the message?"

"Yellowstone National Park – near Yellowstone Lake. I think he'll be able to figure it out. There are only two backcountry trailheads near there. They are accessible by road but completely private."

"Good choice - Yellowstone Lake is the second largest freshwater lake in the world above 7,000 feet. I've always wanted to go!" Excitement bubbled out of Susan.

"Hmmm," Vayu and I said in unison, failing to share her same enthusiasm.

"Come on, let's go brief everyone else," Vayu said.

"You go ahead, I need to talk to Kaitlyn a minute," Susan said.

As soon as he was out of earshot, I looked at Susan. "What about?"

She glared at me sideways. "About you, your powers, and your baby."

Here we go again.

"I'm sorry to have to say this, Kaitlyn, but if you don't tell Micah soon – I am going to tell him for you."

I stopped. "Don't you dare. That would turn out worse than you think."

"Perhaps." She motioned for me to keep walking. "But each day that they don't know makes the entire situation worse. They will continue to do things like put you in the middle of one of the largest wildfires Australia has ever had."

I grumbled something incoherent even to my own ears and changed the subject. "What about my powers?"

She looked at me, as if making up her mind if she was going to let the last issue slide. She sighed. "I've never seen someone tied so emotionally and physically to their powers as you. Maybe that's a part of what makes you so strong, but I worry about you. I think that you also take more damage than normal because of it. Coming back from Australia, you were much worse off than Micah and Vayu – and knowing Micah, he probably took care of you better than himself out there."

She gave me a chance to interject but I kept silent. "Would you consider, only temporarily, not using your powers until we have a doctor check you out?"

I pressed my lips together tightly, and fixed her with a stare. "Fine, on one condition. *You* refrain from telling Micah anything until I do."

Apparently my health, and perhaps the baby's health, were priority. "Deal."

"Pinky swear?" I held out my right pinky finger.

We walked into the house shaking our pinky fingers in a truce worthy of any two childhood girlfriends.

Chapter 8

Better Plans

I was the outcast…again. Several times in the days before our trip and once on the way to Wyoming, I walked into the middle of a discussion and the speaker was quickly hushed. They were planning for our meeting with Shawn, anticipating his moves, working in weapons, spells and when and where to use elemental magic. Although I understood the precautions, I didn't like them.

After three days of travel, Micah drove Susan, Vayu and me down a dirt road toward one of the Yellowstone Lake hiking trailheads. Micah gritted his teeth, trying to focus on the curvy road over the music Vayu insisted on blaring. Susan ignored both men, leaning in to coach me. "No powers this time. Not until we can figure out how to deal with it in your current…state."

Like I have a disease.

She continued, "If Shawn deciphered our message, it'll be you he wants to talk to, but don't worry, we won't let anything happen to you."

Like last time, when you didn't let anything happen to me and Shawn had me for months?

I bit down the retort. It wasn't worth the effort of arguing over Vayu's music.

The car pulled into a dusty, deserted lot meant as a starting point for hikers on the thick forest trail. Micah put the car in park and turned off the music, to Vayu's annoyance, but he didn't kill the engine. They all turned to look at me.

"What?" I frowned, looking between each of them in turn.

"This is your stop, honey," Vayu smiled.

I continued to look between them. "By myself?"

Vayu nodded. "Oh, you know it."

Susan and Micah looked away from me. It suddenly sunk in. "I am the bait?!"

"We need Shawn to think you're alone." Micah stared at the steering wheel. "He may reveal more that way. Hopefully we'll catch him off guard. But we'll be right there the whole time. You won't be alone. I promise." He twisted around in his seat, his deep green eyes boring into to me, willing me to accept the plan.

Disgusted with them all, I got out of the car without another word, slamming the door behind me.

"Oh no she didn't," Vayu's muffled voice followed me, and Micah hesitated before he drove off. But he did, leaving me behind to wait for Shawn, alone.

Minutes crept by. I made symbols in the dirt with the edge of my shoe to occupy myself while I stewed in my anger. *If I'm the bait, where the hell is the catch?* I began to mimic a chirping cricket. It didn't work. Shawn was bigger than a fish. Maybe imitating a lamb would work.

A vehicle coming down the road shook me from my thoughts. I craned my neck, hoping it was Micah coming back to me to apologize and instead go home and make sweet, sweet love.

No such luck.

A mud-covered blue jeep rolled into the parking lot and stopped on the end opposite me. A car door on the far side opened then closed, and the Jeep rolled away, back up the road.

Through the dirt cloud kicked up by the jeep's tires, I could make out a silhouette standing in the parking lot. I didn't have to wait for the dirt to settle back down to know who was there. Shawn. A chill blew in from his direction. I tucked my arms in closer to my body, drawing as much warmth to my center as I could.

Where is Micah? I reached out for him telepathically. He was too far away, directly through the thick forest.

Shawn sauntered toward me, his lip curled up in a half smile. I stood my ground, but said a silent thanks when he stopped several feet away.

He looked me over, "You read our doctrine?"

I studied his expression, careful not to give anything away with mine. His hair had grown out to where it almost rested at his shoulders. Rough, patchy facial hair and thick eyebrows along with new tattoos down his arms darkened his appearance. His shadowy facade only accented his bright blue eyes.

"I scanned it," I commented, pulling my arms in even tighter. Still no Micah, and our surroundings were strangely quiet, even with a lush forest surrounding the barren parking lot on three sides.

"Good. I left it specifically for you."

"Why?" My question was dry, as if I didn't care about the answer.

"I want you to join us." Shawn never beat around the bush.

I smiled, remembering his resolve to replace me as soon as possible when he held me captive on the Galapagos Islands. "What's the matter Shawn, can't do any better than me? Maybe you're not trying hard enough."

His smile disappeared and he furrowed his eyebrows, but before he could respond, I continued, "Thanks but no thanks. I have better plans for myself."

I slowly turned toward the forest, in Micah's direction. Shawn didn't speak. I moved, finally sending a cautious look back, wondering if Shawn's offer was just that, or something he wasn't prepared to negotiate. He stood his ground, even as I began walking.

Just as I picked up my pace toward the trees, he shouted after me, "How is the shoulder?"

I stopped in my tracks, frozen for a long moment before I turned to see he had lifted his shirt. His sheathed athame was visible, hanging from his belt. He didn't need to show me the blade for me to know it was the same knife he had used to carve that damned symbol into my shoulder. The wound still stung; a constant reminder it would never fully heal. I looked toward the tree line; it was fifty feet away.

Skids on the loose gravel snapped my attention back to Shawn. He came toward me at a dead sprint, closing the distance between us fast.

Shit was my first thought and *run* was my second.

I took off for the safety of the tree line, awkward from weeks of inactivity. Thirty feet…twenty feet. My breath came hard and fast but I fell into my stride. I had a chance. Ten feet to the tree line. He was closing the distance. I could hear his footsteps behind me, the crunching gravel getting louder, uncomfortably close. Half turning my head I saw the glint of metal directly behind me. At the tree line, I stopped and crouched. He didn't have time to dodge me and stumbled, falling more gracefully than not, like he had meant to go down. He rolled right back onto his feet, knife still in his hand.

I attacked, hoping to catch him off guard. I grabbed the nearest, thickest fallen branch I could find, swinging it at his head. His forearm blocked it. Using the momentum of his block, I swung my body in the opposite direction, and my foot connected with the other side of his head. Off balance, he caught himself before hitting the ground on a tree trunk, bracing himself with both hands. I swung the branch again, connecting with the back of his neck. The crack echoed through the forest. Half the branch flew off, shattered from the half I held. I ran. After what seemed like a good ten minutes, my lungs felt on fire. Convincing myself I had lost him, I stopped, one hand clutching my protruding belly, the other went to the painful cramp in my side.

Slowly, I caught my breath, and was able to straighten again. I looked around, trying to regain my bearings. There was no one in sight, and no landmarks. Just endless trees. My stomach twisted. I knew Shawn. Shawn didn't give up easily. The longer I looked for Micah and the others, the longer I gave Shawn time to look for me. I closed my eyes, concentrating on the sounds around me. Besides my labored breathing, I heard nothing. Not even birds chirping. No twigs cracking under the weight of a human body. No wisp of leaves brushed by an arm. I tensed, sensing a body. Not ten or twenty feet away, but right in front of me.

I should've known he was able to do that. Even I had underestimated Shawn – I should have kept running. Sighing at another inevitable fight, I lashed out, hitting him in the nose before even opening my eyes. A small trickle of blood ran down his face. My other fist, even with open eyes, wasn't so successful; he caught it in mid-punch, and twisted. I was forced to face away from him. He kept a tight grip on my wrist, locking my arm behind my back. I kicked my leg back, aiming for his stomach, a futile move so close to him.

Knocking my leg down, he pulled me close, wrapping his free arm around my body and holding the knife up to my face. The chill crept out of his body into mine. My marked shoulder stung, stronger now, as if it had been freshly cut. The only thing that kept me from shivering was his familiar body against mine. As much as I detested him, at least I knew him. I survived our last encounter. I could survive this. I closed my eyes and began to reach out for the energy of the forest. Shawn would be able to block it, but I might have a chance if I did it quickly.

"Let her go, Shawn."

The booming voice interrupted my concentration. My eyes flew open.

Micah appeared from nowhere, just as Shawn did, several yards in front of us.

Shawn ignored Micah and put his lips to my ear. "Come with me." The whisper was as much a demand as a plea. I winced. He gripped me tighter.

I closed my eyes tight and forced a quiet, "No."

His breath was hot.

I felt a sharp pain below my left eye where the knife rest.

He tried again, more forceful this time, "Come with me. I don't have to give you a choice."

Warm blood trickled down my cheek.

Micah saw it too and took a few steps forward, body tense.

Shawn only held me tighter, forcing my back to arch. It was in that precarious moment, with my slightly bulging belly forced out even more, that the wind blew. It circled our bodies and tousled our clothes. After playing for a few seconds, mixing the scents of the forest together with our own, it dipped towards my feet then up again. My loose shirt was forced up, exposing a truth kept hidden until now.

Micah's eyes traveled down. They went blank, staring for a moment, and then his mouth dropped open. I swallowed. Not necessarily a reaction you hoped for from a father. Then again, I wasn't positive he was the father. Shawn curiously followed Micah's gaze down my torso with his hand. He couldn't see my rounded belly from his angle behind me, but he felt it. His hand was too cold on my exposed skin, and I had an immediate need to protect the life inside me. Keeping my movements slow and controlled, I placed my hand gently over Shawn's and pried it loose. I stepped away from his grip and turned to face the both of them.

It didn't take long for them to find their voices.

"You're pregnant?!" they exclaimed in unison.

I didn't answer. I'd have thought that fact was fairly obvious by now. Instead, I looked from one to the other, trying to read their faces. No joy from either, but then again, no despair. No fear, no panic. Just shock.

Let them stew in their shock.

I waved them off and turned away, whispering, "Better plans."

I didn't get very far before I felt Micah's hand on my shoulder. "Wait. Is it..." He swallowed hard. "Is it mine?"

I turned to face him again. Shawn still hadn't moved. I looked from one to another, trying to hold back tears that threatened to flood my eyes. "I don't know."

My lip quivered. I turned and walked as quickly as I could toward what I thought was the parking lot. My vision was blurred by tears. I clawed at overgrown branches, walking blind. With an occasional sob managing to squeak past my lips and the hiccups that developed, I wasn't evading anyone. Those sounds gave away my location better than a tracking device would have.

Soon enough a pair of footsteps caught up, and I felt sturdy, strong arms wrap themselves around me. I didn't know whose they were, and for a moment I didn't even venture to guess. I was just grateful for the close contact that had been missing from my life as of late. I leaned back into the embrace and took a hesitant, deep breath. I breathed in Micah. Relief flooded through my body as rampant as the tears were now. I shook, shivered, and sobbed, relying on him to keep me upright. He didn't say anything, and neither did I.

He led me to the road, where the car, Susan, and Vayu were waiting. Micah and I sat in the back seat, still holding each other tight, until I managed to gain control over myself. "Why didn't you just finish it – finish him? What happened to your plan?"

Micah looked down at me, "Killing him wasn't part of the plan. I'll explain later."

Exhausted, I placed my head back into the dip of his shoulder. Staring at the back of Vayu's head as he drove, I realized he could have created had created the wind that revealed my secret, and Susan probably convinced him to do it. Too emotionally drained for any more drama, I let it go. Besides, it had effectively deterred Shawn, and Susan had kept her promise by not necessarily telling Micah. I suppose I should have been more specific.

Chapter 9

Tonight

"Tonight." Although it was just a whisper, Micah's demand was loud and forceful in my ear. Dropping me off at my room at the Chakra, he left me gawking after him like an idiot as he walked down the hall and turned a corner, out of sight. During the two days we spent returning from Wyoming; hardly a word was spoken between us. Now that he did speak, it was the first and last thing I wanted to hear.

The rest of the afternoon dragged by, half of it spent cleaning myself up and the other half was spent debating when 'night' officially fell. I dared not leave the room. With my luck he'd choose those few moments to come by and get all the wrong signals. What did he consider 'night' anyway? Sunset? Twilight? Complete darkness? Could evening hours qualify as night? Would he really force me to wait until dark?

As the sun slowly disappeared from view, streaking the sky in pink and orange hues, I sat on the edge of my bed, sufficiently worn out from pacing. The doorknob turned and Micah entered the room, shutting the door behind him. I jumped up off the bed, startled.

Damn, I rebuked myself. *I look too anxious. I should've thought this through better.* As if I hadn't been thinking it through for the last five hours.

He didn't look unsure of himself. No, he was quite sure of himself. Full of himself, almost.

Crap, I thought again. *He wants answers. He wants dates, and he's going to try to figure this whole thing out himself.*

I tried a preemptive, "I don't really feel like talking."

"I'm not here to talk." He took a few steps toward me.

Good and bad. My heart fluttered and I felt the need to go check myself in the mirror. I looked toward the bathroom.

Darn. Too obvious again.

I put my hands over my ears to drown out all my craziness. "You are driving me insane!" I blurted out.

He laughed, "Kaitlyn, I have been there and back several times since I've met you. Welcome to the club." A few more steps and he closed the distance between us.

Suddenly, the moment I'd been wanting for months had come too soon. I placed a hand on his chest to stop him. "Wait."

He shook his head, "I can't."

I tried again, "You don't have my permission."

"I don't need it."

"But you *want* it." With those four words I reminded Micah of everything that separated him from Shawn.

He didn't step back, but neither did he move forward. With the sun gone, the room had fallen into shadows. It was a good thing too. If I had been able to clearly see his eyes I wouldn't have had a chance against him. It was difficult enough just seeing the dark outline of his silhouette and breathing in his musky scent. He'd spent a good part of the afternoon cleaning up too, if I had my guess.

Oh, what the hell. Can't let his efforts go to waste.

I removed my hand from his chest and that was all the permission he needed. In an instant his lips found mine. A moment of stiff resistance passed, melting away into acceptance. My feet came off the ground. I don't know if I was floating from pure pleasure, or if he was lifting me up that effortlessly, extra baby weight and all. The outfit I had so carefully picked out was practically ripped to shreds. It dotted the room in bits of pink and white material. His clothes were off too, although I couldn't remember exactly how it happened. We both floated back down onto the bed, his frame pressing into mine. I squeaked out a small 'umphh' and he immediately lifted himself off of me, "Does that hurt?"

"No," I lied.

He didn't buy it. "Come here."

He pulled me so we both lay on our side, facing each other. He suppressed his urgency and instead took the time to caress me from head to toe. His strokes sent both shivers and bolts of electricity through my skin. When I tried to return the favor he stopped me. "I want to do this for you. I want to please you, protect you, have you always. No matter what." His hands stopped and rested on my belly. "You should have known that."

Tears started to form in my eyes. "It is more complicated than that, and you know it."

"We'll figure it out. From now on, only truth between us. I want you to tell me everything."

"Now?"

"Later." He rolled on top of me, this time more gently, giving me the space needed on certain parts of my body. My other parts melted into his so that I couldn't tell where I ended and he began. Distracted by his mouth on mine, sucking the very breath from me, I barely noticed his knee snaking up between my legs to give him access. When he entered me, it was sharp;

painful almost. He was on the verge of ripping old wounds open.

I took a loud and abrupt breath in and froze with my back arched underneath him as far as it would go.

He held my hips in place with his hands. "I'm sorry, I cannot stop now." He started whispering in other languages in my ear. More apologies, perhaps. His words rippled through my mind and body, soothing both. I was on fire on the outside but inside I was cool liquid. It was that part of me that willed him to continue. I slowly relaxed into him and he pushed deeper into me. The entire time he whispered, sometimes in English, sometimes in Irish or French and sometimes in languages I couldn't recognize. His words sent me into a trance, heightening the experience. I didn't last long. He pushed harder and faster as he felt me coming to my peak, not stopping until we climaxed together. Finally we lay still in each other's arms until the aftershocks subsided.

After a while he looked down at me. "Are you ok?"

I smiled back. "I might be a little sore tomorrow, but I think I'll survive." He could honestly have done that ten times again before morning and I wouldn't have stopped him.

"I'm sorry," he whispered again, resting his forehead just above my ear.

"Promise me something." I propped myself up on one elbow and looked at him.

"Anything," he said.

"Promise me you will stop apologizing."

"Oh." He didn't look happy with the thought. "In English or…."

"In *any* language. We aren't going to get through this if you keep apologizing for the past."

He paused, and finally agreed, "Deal. But I think now is a good time to share with me what happened on Galapagos. I want to know everything. Every detail."

"Why now?" I looked for a reason to stall. "We have all day tomorrow."

"Yes, but sometimes it's easier to expose the truth while naked. Besides, we always seem to do better when we are touching."

I glanced at my shredded clothes on the floor. "Speaking of – you owe me some new clothes."

"What about me?" He reached down the side of the bed and produced his shirt turning it so I could see it had been ripped partly down the back.

"How did that happen?" I frowned, inspecting the shirt.

"That was all you, babe."

"Nooooo," I denied it with a slight hesitation in my voice.

"Yeeeessss," he mocked me.

"Ok," I conceded. "We'll call it even."

"Ok."

Another deal made.

We sat in silence for a long moment.

"So about what happened…."

He wasn't going to let me off the hook, and there was no way I could possibly tell him what happened.

What to do, what to do.

After a short time of playing with the pillow's edges, I came up with an idea. I sat up in bed, bunching the blankets up around me so at least from the waist down I wasn't exposed. "Sit up. I know how we are going to do this."

He obeyed without question and sat across from me on the bed.

I explained, "So basically, I want you to read my memories."

"What?"

"I've done this before, trust me. It'll work. I'm just going to open up my memories to you, and you just, well...receive them." I was trying to recall exactly how it worked with Shawn, but this time I was on the giving end instead of the receiving end. "It is going to feel weird, because they are my memories. You will feel all the emotions and physical senses I experienced, or at least how I remember them. Don't try to control anything. Just let it happen."

He looked hopeful. "You are full of surprises. Just when I think you are way too inexperienced for any of this, you come up with something that is years of training beyond any Gaia I've known."

I studied him for a long moment. "You're sure you want this?"

He nodded eagerly. "If this works, it'll be everything I need to understand what happened."

"Yeah, we'll see how you feel about it after the fact," I mumbled. We joined hands and closed our eyes. I took a few moments of deep breathing to clear my head and relax my body. I needed to be completely focused. Once I was ready, I thought back to the night Susan and I attempted a mission on our own. Shawn had taken me then, and Micah needed to know everything, starting from the very beginning. Once the images were clear in my own head, I mixed my thoughts with the smallest bit of energy and sent it out to Micah. I kept the flow as steady as my own thoughts, and soon felt him absorb them. I snuck a peek at him every now and then. He looked pleased at Susan and me accomplishing the mission on our own. He tightened up when the waves came, knocking me unconscious.

I went through my experiences on Galapagos as best as I could remember, in the order they happened. I tried not to leave out any details, my penguin 'guard dog', the way the island drained me of energy, and Shawn's constant attacks – both sexual and physical. When it came to the night with the candlestick, I lingered on the off-white candle spinning in Shawn's hand. This was one image that haunted me, almost on a nightly basis. I rushed through what occurred after. Opening one eye slightly, Micah's flinched – almost constantly, like he was trying to dodge Shawn's attacks. I shared my escape plan, the episode where Shawn finished his mark on my shoulder, and the rituals and blessings that gave me hope.

I paused, gathering strength for the next part; the hardest part of all to share. I considered leaving it out altogether, but that wouldn't have been fair to Micah. If we were going to clear the air, everything had to be shared. He began to break the bond but I interrupted him, "Wait, I'm not finished yet."

He looked at me, wide-eyed, as if he couldn't imagine anything else that could have possibly happened.

I smiled sadly, and thought to myself, *you haven't seen the half of it.*

Once ready, I conjured memories of our trip to the beach and creating the storm. I showed him how Juan died. I revealed my conversation with Shawn several days later when he told me how Susan, Micah, and he had all been adopted by Cato at young ages. He also revealed Micah's role with each Gaia; including executing each one once a stronger Gaia was found.

"I would never–" Micah moved to pull away.

"Hush," I scolded. I continued forcing memories across to him, memories of how Shawn taught me to share memories, and how he shared his memory of the night of the saining – my initiation into the Seven. Micah was there to carry out the deed should I have made the wrong choice. Whether or not he would've gone through it was left unclear. I peeked at Micah again, nearly pulling back at the tears streaming down his face. I instantly felt regret, but it was too late, the damage was done. I tried ending on a positive note, my triumphant escape leading up to where Micah found me laying on the rocky shore. It didn't help, we broke the bond and Micah looked thoroughly distraught.

"I'm sorry," I started to babble. "That's hard for someone to endure all at once – maybe we should have done it in sessions."

His face was unreadable, so I continued, "Or maybe not at all; this was a stupid idea."

He held up a hand, cutting me off mid-babble. "Why are you apologizing? Those were just your memories and I think I almost lost consciousness a few times because of *that*. You actually went through it; I'm not sure anyone else would've survived."

He laid back down on the bed, deep in thought and probably in shock. I lay down next to him, giving him the silence he needed.

"You must hate me," he announced suddenly.

I had to stifle a giggle. "Yeah, because I often sleep with people I hate."

He didn't laugh.

I rolled over on my side and moved close to him so our bare skin was touching. I traced the outline of his abdominal muscles with the tip of my finger. "There are other, much worse things in the world for me to hate."

"Like penguins?" I think it was meant to be a joke, but neither of us laughed. I kept moving my hand along his stomach and down his sides. He was becoming aroused, and looked ashamed for it.

"Yes – like penguins," I whispered in his ear. "I think for now, only one thing will help us."

"What's that?" He turned, searching my face.

"More sex."

Chapter 10

The Mother

The next morning, I awoke alone. I rolled to the other side of the bed, feeling the sheets still warm from Micah's body. I stayed there, cocooned in blankets until the last remaining scent of him disappeared. Finally, I made my way out to the kitchen looking for the real thing. Micah was nowhere to be found, but his sister was. I would have to settle for her green eyes instead of his. Susan looked at me, one eyebrow raised. I blushed, wondering if she'd heard our escapades last night. She only handed me a cup of coffee.

"Thank you," I murmured, staring intently at a cracked tile on the floor. I held the cup to my lips then stopped myself. "Wait, is this safe? I mean, for the baby and all?"

"I don't think one cup will hurt the baby. Pregnant women have ingested much worse."

"Okay," I sipped. It tasted wonderful.

"Micah has already arranged for a doctor to visit," Susan said. "He should be arriving later today."

"Oh, okay. That was fast."

"Hmm," Susan commented. Of course she'd wanted it done much sooner. "I'm sorry we intervened the way we did. But it maybe worked out okay?"

"That it did," I said wistfully, remembering the more explicit events of the night before. "And it certainly stopped Shawn dead in his tracks," I quickly added, hoping she didn't see me blushing again. I pushed away from the table. "Maybe I should go find Micah."

She wasn't having it, "Maybe you should eat."

In short order she had a plate of eggs and fruit in front of me, complete with my daily dose of prenatal vitamins, no longer hidden from sight. She shook the bottle. "We forgot to bring these with us to Australia and Wyoming. Now they're staying right here in the kitchen so you don't forget to take them."

I slunk down into the chair. "Yes, mother."

Susan smiled and moved to leave the kitchen. She paused beside me, her hand on my shoulder, and bent down to whisper in my ear, "You're the mother now."

Her words resonated long after she had gone. I couldn't move as it truly sunk in. Kids had never been in my plans, much because a husband had never been in my plans – and still wasn't, for that matter.

I spent the next two hours walking the grounds of the Chakra, somewhat searching for Micah but mostly just enjoying the sunshine on my face. Pale from the months of cloud cover, I could feel my skin starting to burn. I looked around, no one, least of all Micah, was in sight. I turned toward my room. I'd wait for Micah to find me. Maybe I'd mend some of the clothes we'd torn apart last night. I smiled to myself at the memory.

"What are you so happy about?" Alex caught me off guard in the hallway.

"Nothing," I said a little too quickly.

He stepped closer and whispered, "I heard the good news."

I raised my eyebrows playfully. "What good news?"

"You know…" He glanced quickly at my protruding belly.

I continued to look at him innocently. "Know what?"

His swallowed. "Don't make me say it."

"Say what? Is it a secret?" I looked both ways down the hall, as if we could get caught at any moment.

"You know," he said. "The Buddha belly."

I laughed out loud. "Buddha belly?"

He rolled his eyes, then pressed his hands on my stomach and rubbed, "Buddha, Buddha, Buddha!"

I laughed even harder, slapping his hands away.

Someone cleared their throat.

We broke away, turning toward Micah, standing at the end of the hall. Alex cupped his hand over his mouth, speaking out of the corner of his mouth to me, "Uh-oh, he beckons." Then a little louder, looking at Micah. "It's too late, pal. I've already rubbed all the luck out of this thing." He gestured to me, or rather my belly.

I punched Alex in the arm and retreated to Micah. Micah took me by the hand and planted a kiss on my cheek before steering us down the hall. "I don't need any luck; I've got the woman," he shot back at Alex.

"Touché," Alex said quietly, turning to go his own way.

Micah led me through a door and down two flights of stairs. I hadn't been in the basement since my first couple days' induction to the Chakra and this organization. We stopped outside one of the closed doors and he turned to me. "The doctor's here. He's going to do a complete exam. He's delivered babies to women with powers like yours. He knows what he is doing."

A tingle crept up my spine. "Is he going to do an ultrasound, so I can see the baby?"

"Yes, if his equipment is working correctly."

We hesitated, neither daring to move to open the door. I spared us both the awkwardness. "I should do this alone."

I turned to enter the room quickly, hopefully leaving Micah without a choice, but he stopped me just as quickly. He grabbed me by the hand and spun me around into him. Holding me tightly, he looked at me intently. "You aren't alone anymore. I am with you always, whether you like it or not."

I smiled, feeling more relieved than I thought I would hearing those words. "Okay."

"Okay." He smiled back and leaned in to kiss me, pausing just before our lips touched. He let me close the distance, forcing me to show him I wanted it just as badly as he did. Gentle at first, the kiss grew more intense. His tongue found mine and he didn't let go. He sucked the very breath from me but then gave it back plus some. I would've been happy to stay there for the rest of time, exchanging each other's air, locking lips and holding onto each other so tightly we were sure to have bruises the next day.

The sharp metal clang of instruments hitting the ground in the next room brought us back to reality. We reluctantly pulled apart, though we left our hands intertwined.

He spoke first, "Are you ready for this?"

I took a deep breath in and let it out slowly. "Ready."

He pushed open the door for me and the sting of white hit our eyes.

Chapter 11

Promises

The doctor's visit was rough. He quizzed me relentlessly. Mostly on dates. The date of my last cycle, dates of possible consummation, dates I used my powers, and on and on. My head began to swim. There was a two week window of when I could have conceived; too close to say who the father was either way. Examining me, the doctor favored an earlier date, which meant Micah, but he followed that with a warning that it was just too close to be sure. Micah squeezed my hand.

He's with me either way, I reminded myself.

They ran blood tests, urine analysis, checked the baby's heartbeat, took measurements around my stomach, checked my pulse and blood pressure, and weighed me. Several test results wouldn't be back for a week but the doctor assured me everything he could see looked normal. He pulled a large machine on wheels next to the stretcher I was on. He smiled broadly. "Ready to see your baby?"

"Sure," I responded, not quite matching his enthusiasm. Micah's hand still grasped mine. The doctor rolled up my shirt and placed a fair amount of cold gel on my stomach. The machine whirred to life, making more noises in its old age than it probably should have. He placed a small, flat electrical device over the baby and a picture came to life on the screen facing us.

My jaw dropped. I'd expected something like a kidney bean, small and lifeless. Instead I saw a live, kicking little baby taking up the entire screen. You could count ten little fingers and toes, you saw the spine, and even the mouth opened and closed. It moved its head and all four limbs, and when it stretched out on the screen I actually felt a small push against the organs inside of me.

"You've got quite an active one, there," the doctor commented.

"That's the baby?" I said, louder than I had intended. "I thought that was just indigestion." A few of the other medical personnel in the room stifled giggles.

"In another few weeks you'll be able to feel it just by placing your hand over your stomach." The doctor smiled down at me.

I felt a small, unexpected tear roll out of the corner of my eye. I tried convincing myself it was a reaction to the old screen, but I knew better. I wiped it away quickly, feeling a little silly at being so sentimental. I glanced at Micah to make sure he hadn't seen, but he was too busy staring at the screen with the same shocked, blank face he had had in the forest.

I squeezed his hand to elicit some sort of response and he glanced at me, then back at the screen.

"Say something," I urged, trying to keep my voice as low as possible.

He looked at me again and seemed to snap out of it. "It's just, so real."

"Yeah," I agreed, realizing all he had promised me was finally dawning on him. My breath caught, and I was suddenly wondering if he was truly ready for this. I didn't necessarily have a choice; he did.

The doctor interrupted my thoughts. "Do you want to know the gender?"

"Oh, um. I don't know," I said, unprepared. "I guess so. You can tell?"

"Let's take a look here." He took a few minutes to zoom in on the baby's legs, trying different angles. Suddenly, he announced, "Here we go – you see a leg here, and a leg here, and nothing in between!" He waited for our response but all he got was blank stares in return. "It's a girl," he sighed.

Micah let out a strangled sort of laugh. I didn't say anything, letting it sink in. Suddenly, Shawn's words buzzed in my head. *The ability to do what we do runs in our blood.* The world grew cold, almost grayed out. *There can never be two Gaias that practice our ways at once.* His words kept echoing back and forth. *The ability to do what we do—*

"Kaitlyn, Kaitlyn! Wake up!" Micah's voice broke through.

I sat up; cold tiles touched my skin, "What happened?"

"You fainted and rolled off the cot." He attempted to get in between two of the other medics to help me up.

Too many hands were helping me; I felt claustrophobic.

"I have to get out of here." I grabbed for clean rags to wipe off my belly and pulled down my shirt, jetting out of the room before anyone could think to stop me.

"Wait!" Micah called after me. I caught a glimpse of him as I rounded the corner. He was caught up in the pile of medical staff, wires and the overturned cot.

I ignored him and kept running, temporarily confused by the maze of basement hallways. Anxious to get out of there before Micah caught up, I stopped and closed my eyes. I felt for my new partner, the wind element, and located the freshest air. Following it up two flights of stairs, I found my way out of the building and to the gardens.

Micah, much to my chagrin, managed to catch me, and wasn't gentle in stopping me. "What is wrong with you!"

"Me?!" I jerked my shoulder away, rubbing it where his fingers had dug in. "What is wrong with *me*?"

"Yes!" he yelled back.

"I'm having a baby girl; that is what's wrong with me!" I threw my hands up. "She is my responsibility, whether I like it or not."

"So?"

"So, what if she is blessed with the same curse we are? What if she grows to be just as strong of a Gaia as me, or stronger?"

Comprehension slowly started to dawn across his features.

"What if she's my replacement? Who will you choose to eliminate for your precious organization?" I gave him a second to think. "Well, who will it be? Mother or daughter?"

Micah was stunned into silence, searching for the right answer to my question. He didn't realize there was no right answer.

"I don't think that is something we have to worry about until we know for sure…" he finally stuttered out a response.

"Yes it is! The life of their child is something a parent should worry about from day one!" Of course he wasn't ready for such an undertaking. He was completely unfit to follow through with his promises.

On a roll now, I questioned him about something that had been bothering me since Wyoming. "What were you planning with Shawn? What changed once you found out I was pregnant?"

Now Micah rubbed at the back of his neck.

"From now on, only truth between us. I want you to tell me everything." I mimicked his hardened voice, cajoling him to come clean as I had.

He took a deep breath, "We knew Shawn wanted to recruit you. And we were going to let him."

Words stuck in my throat, "I'm sorry, what?"

"I was there only to put a tracker on you, or him – whatever I could manage. We had each direction covered, we weren't going to let you far from sight." He was speaking quickly now. "It would have been only until we found his base of operations. A quick trip – then you would be out of there while we closed him down."

"You were going to let me go back to him?" I felt like I had been punched in the gut.

"Even with Shawn gone, we had to be sure nobody would continue his work. But this was the plan *before* I knew what he did to you. Knowing what I do now, I would never have agreed to it."

"Agreed to it? Whose plan was it, then? Susan's? Vayu's?"

He shook his head, "We didn't let Susan know the whole plan. We thought you two were too close and that she might divulge some of the information. We couldn't risk Shawn finding out through you."

Shock turned to anger. I conjured a net of wind, materializing only after it passed me, catching him and throwing him back into a particularly thorny bush. I tied off the streams of energy to make the net last as long as possible before it disintegrated. I stormed off into the forest.

Before long, I came to an opening with a large pond. It was the same pond, almost the same exact spot, Cato had used for my saining ritual.

What a perfect coincidence, I thought, heading for the tree Micah and Shawn had used with their rifle sights set on my forehead during the ritual.

Instead of skirting the pond, I swam through it, fully clothed. As I emerged, shivering and soaked to the bone, Micah sent a telepathic message. *Wait*, the word came to me, *I'll take care of you. Make it all better.*

Hell if I was going to let that happen. I filled my head with static, letting it get louder and louder. Once it was as big and steady as I could manage, I sent it out. It shot straight at Micah through the forest like an arrow. I heard his scream echo over the pond and felt a guilty sense of pleasure. Good to know I hadn't lost my touch. It would go away in a moment, but it certainly sent a message. If logic prevailed, he'd leave me alone.

I made my way to the same tree with little trouble. The seasons had changed and so had the landscape, but the same tree was there. Small branches stuck out in just the right places for me to make my way to the small perch twenty feet above the ground or so. My awkward body shape made climbing difficult, but I managed with a little extra help from wind I created pushing me up. I found a seat; secure in the same place Micah and Shawn sat before. Anchoring one foot around the large trunk of the tree, I felt stable enough to stop concentrating on holding on and sat back.

I took several deep breaths in, releasing them slowly while I tried to calm down. I let my mind wander, thinking mostly of the baby girl growing inside of me. She gave me a small kick in return. I smiled. Birds began to return to the tree, landing around me, having been disturbed by my initial ascent. With my view of the calm lake I could spot fish under the surface of the water.

I almost felt relaxed enough to drift off. Sleep had a way of letting me forget for a moment all of the problems facing me. It was my preferred choice of defense as of late anyway. A commotion of flapping wings and annoyed squawks snapped me out of the blissful doze. The birds hopped and flapped, frantically trying to take flight from the tree. I didn't see the large body drop beside me from above. The branch dipped suddenly, moaning under the stress of added weight. My hold on the tree came undone and for one terrifying moment I leaned too far in one direction with nothing but flimsy air beneath me. Just as I tucked my head in, bracing for the inevitable fall, a strong hand grasped my wrist and pulled me back to safety.

Safety might not have been the right word for it. The anger in his smoldering green eyes made me shrink back into the tree. He took advantage, crowding me with his large frame and holding my wrists in a grip of steel. Partly grateful to be pinned against the stable core of the tree, the other part of me almost would rather have fallen.

"What in the hell do you think you are doing?" Micah asked, his voice dangerously low. Images of him holding the high-powered rifle aimed directly at me flashed through my mind.

I tried to swallow my fear and put on a brave face. "I am trying to avoid you." I swallowed, too aware I could not mask the tremor in my voice.

One side of his lip curled up in a snarl and I shrank back even further. "You are mine, as is the baby inside of you. By sitting up here you are putting both at risk." My fear seemed to feed his anger.

My eyes lit up; the heat in my voice matched his. "You say that now, but you can change your mind at any minute. You would have to choose between us and the rules you've served your entire life. I don't think even you are sure what you would choose." I swallowed the lump in my throat and lowered my voice. "I can't take the chance that you'll make the wrong decision."

He leaned away from me and let go of my wrists. "What are you thinking about doing?"

I took a deep breath in, drawing in the strength. "I'm thinking about leaving. For good."

"You would leave me?" His brows rose from anger to shock.

"For the life of my daughter, I think I would do just about anything," I said. Spoken like a true mother, Susan would be proud.

He sat back, withdrawing into his own mind. I rubbed the red marks he had left behind on my wrists and waited.

Finally he spoke one word, "No."

It was as casual as if he were turning down cream for his coffee, and just as definitive. It was not up for debate.

I stood on the branch, wobbling the whole way. "I'm not going to be a prisoner ever again, Micah. I've had enough of that."

He stood too, and we both performed a balancing act on the shaky branch – me trying to refuse his help and him insisting I take it. "Fine then, you can leave, but I'm going with you."

I scoffed. "It isn't the Chakra I need to get away from, it is you!"

"No," he said again, with the same resolution in his voice. "It's too much of a risk with Shawn out there, not to mention the risk of losing control of your powers."

He steadied us both, pressing me into the truck once again. I avoided his face but had to know. "Is that the only reason?"

Lifting my chin, he forced me to look into his eyes. "Kaitlyn, I need you as much as you need me. That is a cold, hard fact. Not an opinion."

Even as he said the words I understood the truth in them. Had I managed to get away I would have done nothing but think about returning to him. It would have been the worst mental torture I could've put myself through.

He leaned in to kiss me, hard and fast, shocking me into submission. His body pressed into mine and the rough bark of the tree scraped my back through my thin shirt. I attempted to squirm away, the bark only scratching more. "Micah, you're hurting me."

"I can heal you later," he responded in between kisses, reminding me the pleasure was well worth the temporary pain. Suddenly, I received images from him. His lips continued to press into mine, but a mental connection I wasn't prepared for was made. I saw him and Shawn, on the night of my saining, sitting on the exact same branch as now.

At the sight of Shawn, my whole body tensed. Micah tightened his hold on me. "Relax, I have to show you this. I have to show you my side." His kiss was persistent, and the images were crystal clear, much clearer than what Shawn showed me or what I could have possibly shown Micah.

I let the scene dance in my head, only because I did not want to stop the sensation of his lips on mine.

Shawn spoke, "Just making sure you are prepared to do what needs to be done."

"She'll do the right thing," Micah said defensively.

Shawn took Micah's rifle from him, studying it. He snorted. "The scope isn't even turned on." Shawn flipped it on, and Micah watched him aim it directly at me, across the pond. The lump I felt in my throat was Micah's. His hands began to shake as he silently retrieved a small pistol from his side pocket, kept hidden from Shawn's view. Memories of them playing together as boys ran through Micah's head, and therefore mine. His thumb felt to make sure the safety was off, but his eyes never left Shawn's trigger finger. He was prepared to use it on his own brother; the one friend he had since childhood. It was all in my defense; a woman he had barely met weeks prior.

I opened my eyes, bringing back the reality of the tree and the man who held on to me tighter than anyone ever had before. Tears streamed down my face. "I knew it. I knew you wouldn't have done it."

"Promise me you'll never leave me, Kaitlyn. Not of your own free will. I couldn't bear it," his voice was strained.

I hesitated.

"Promise me!"

"I promise," I put as much compassion in my voice as I could manage.

"As do I," he repeated the phrase a few more times but still shook his head. "It's not enough, not enough."

"What else can I give you?" It was an honest question.

His eyes suddenly brightened and a smile creased his mouth. "Marry me."

I let out a shocked squeak from the back of my throat. "Are you proposing?"

"Yes, we'll get married tomorrow – or at least perform a handfasting until we can do a legal ceremony in the States." He wasn't looking at me now, eyes moving as if he was running through the plans in his head.

"Wait, you're answering for me now?"

"Yes, I am. We are going to get married!" The excitement in his voice was contagious, and he swept me up in another kiss. The kiss mimicked his character; neither would be denied.

In the next few minutes he had us both down from the tree safely, and was rushing us into the building. He stopped at my room and opened the door for me. "I can't stay with you tonight; that would be bad luck."

I just nodded. Somehow I had gone from thoughts of leaving him to wedding plans in a matter of minutes. He certainly kept life interesting. He produced a flower from behind his back; a lily from the gardens. I hadn't seen him grab on the way in.

"I will take care of everything. Sleep well tonight. I love you, Kaitlyn." He kissed me on the forehead, pushed me back into the room, and took his leave, closing the door behind him.

"Love you, too," I whispered back, from behind closed doors.

Chapter 12

Cords of Blood

The next morning, I awoke to feet shuffling back and forth down the hallway outside of my bedroom door. Hushed voices floated by, but they were tinged with excitement so that every other syllable was spoken louder than intended. It did nothing for those still trying to sleep.

"Like me!" I yelled at them.

No one responded.

I squinted at the clock, trying to determine the time without letting too much of the green light pierce my eyes. It was already technically afternoon and I groaned, feeling I could use a few more hours of rest. I rolled back over; rubbing the sleep from my eyes trying to think what could have caused so much excitement.

"Oh, God!" I shot upright in bed, suddenly recalling Micah's proposal. I flung the sheets off of me and stepped into the hall. There were more people bustling from room to room than I even thought resided at the Chakra.

I tried getting someone's attention, "Excuse me."

The man didn't even notice.

Another man came from the opposite direction.

"Oh, can you…"

He mumbled an apology and kept going. In his defense his arms were full of raw, packaged meat.

Finally I saw Susan stepping lightly toward me. Not taking a chance of being dismissed again, I took her gruffly by the arm and pulled her into my room. "What is going on?" I asked, exasperated.

"Oh, you're awake." She poked her head out into the hallway again. "Laura – she's awake. Bring the bathing basket." Susan turned her attention back to me, quickly moving on to making my bed, as though she couldn't stand being still. "We need to get you ready for the handfasting ceremony."

"Whoa, whoa." I held up a hand. "What ceremony?"

Susan paused, looking at me over her shoulder in her efforts to make my bed. "Micah proposed to you yesterday, didn't he?"

"You can call it that, but I don't recall saying yes."

"I see," she mumbled, walking around the bed to face me. She whispered, "But you didn't say no?"

"He didn't give me a chance to—"

She squealed. "Then it's settled. By not rejecting him you ultimately accepted him."

"Do introduce me to your black and white world sometime, would you?"

"Oh, settle down Kaitlyn." She took me by the hand and pulled me to sit on the edge of the bed with her. "Handfasting is like a trial marriage. It lasts for a year and a day. It can be renewed or dissolved at that time as the couple desires. It is not legally binding, but it is a tradition that means as much to Micah as a legal wedding, if not more."

She looked at me for some kind of response. I just buried my head in my hands. "What am I getting myself into?"

She leaned into me, ready to answer my rhetorical question. "A life with one of the best men out there."

I smiled. "You're biased."

"Damn right I am. Now, which room do you think you'll be consummating the marriage in – yours or his?"

By now a handful of people had made their way into the room. It was my turn to squeal. "I don't think that is anyone's business!"

She shrugged her shoulders, "It is if you want the room to be ready. No matter," she said, waiving the thought off. "We'll prepare them both." Susan clapped her hands twice loudly to call the attention of everyone in the room. She began barking out orders as if she had been a wedding planner all her life, sending half of them off to clean Micah's room. The other half got to work cleaning mine. I was ushered into the bathroom – alone, thankfully, with a basket full of bath beads, razors, shampoos, and soaps. All things Micah had selected. I refrained from asking, with a certain amount of sarcasm, when I was to choose his bathing supplies.

I emerged from the bathroom an hour later, feeling much less stressed. The friendly mob had moved on. The room was filled with dozens of candles waiting to be lit and flower petals that littered the floor; the scent was intoxicating. Susan walked in as if she had been waiting for the bathroom door to open, a number of dresses hanging from her arms.

"This is all I could rustle up in such short notice. Take your pick." She laid them across the bed. "Most are mine, I know I'm a little taller, but I think they would work for you."

I thanked her, scanning the dresses. As much as I tried looking at the others, my eyes kept reverting back to a simple, baby-doll style dress, the high waistline perfect for my extra weight in front. The neckline plunged.

That would compensate for some of my not-so-desirable features, I thought as I lay my hand on my belly.

"That color compliments your skin tone well," Susan commented.

I picked up the dress, trying the burgundy against my skin. The deep red was lighter at the top and gradually grew darker as it reached the hem.

"Not exactly a traditional wedding dress," I said.

She placed a hand on my shoulder. "This isn't exactly a traditional wedding. You'd look beautiful in that."

By the time dusk had approached, my hair had air-dried into tight curls and, with help from Susan and company, was adorned with a band of flowers. They had even managed to weave the lily Micah had given me the night before into the band. Susan helped with my makeup, keeping it natural looking, but it definitely lent a certain glow to my face.

"Do you have shoes to match the dress?" I chewed at my lip, worried that there had to be something missing.

Susan wiggled her own bare feet at me. "We don't wear shoes for this ceremony. It keeps us closer to the earth."

I released a breath, and shrugged my shoulders. "One less thing to worry about."

"Are you ready?"

I looked at myself one last time in mirror, pleased with my appearance for the first time in months. "As ready as I'll ever be. Let's do this thing."

Susan walked me out to the gardens. I soon knew exactly where we were going; the large boulder touted as the center of the Chakra. A perfect place for the ceremony, magical prowess and all.

Micah was waiting for me at the entrance of the path that had been recently carved out leading to the boulder.

"Isn't this bad luck?" I asked.

He smiled, only adding to how handsome he looked in his black trousers and a matching jacket. He had no tie and the first two buttons of his pristine white dress shirt were casually unbuttoned. "We will enter the circle together, as one." He handed me one of two candles and lit it with a small zippo he produced from his pocket. "Now you light mine." He held the zippo out for me to take.

"Have you already forgotten whom you are marrying?" I scolded him, and lit his candle with a small amount of energy.

"Show-off."

I smiled. "Only for you."

"Come on." He took me by the arm. "Let's do this thing."

Susan rolled her eyes, "A match made in heaven."

We stopped just before the clearing. It was beautiful. Three large circles had been etched into the ground, each within another. The largest outer circle followed the edge of the clearing. A dozen or so people, mostly the workers from the Chakra, stood in one part of the circle. In the second circle were Alex and Vayu, and Susan went to stand in between them. The inner most and smallest circle went around the boulder, Cato stood with just enough room left for two more people.

Micah bent to my ear and whispered, "I'll interpret the meaning of everything to you as we go."

Rose petals, almost the same color as my dress, dotted the ground of the clearing and everyone held lit candles. That plus the moon gave enough light to see. I looked up at the sky. "It's a full moon."

"Why do you think we rushed to have the ceremony today?"

Cato spoke, amplifying his voice with a trick of energy so all could hear, "Will the couple enter the circle from the east?"

Micah stepped first and I followed his lead. "Entering from the east symbolizes the growth in our relationship," he whispered. "Communication of the heart, mind and body, and fresh beginnings with each rising of the sun."

We followed the circle around the boulder and stopped in front of Cato. We each placed our candles on the large rock. Cato began the ceremony in Irish. It sounded like a chant, though I could only catch a few words here and there. Micah didn't bother to interpret. It would have diminished the experience. Cato's words washed over us in a wave of love and support, and I felt the same coming from everyone behind us. Clouds moved in overhead and a light mist began to rain down. I felt Susan's powers at work and glanced at her, worried. She gave me a knowing wink.

Micah leaned into me. "Rain is good luck at a wedding." Just before the mist could reach us and extinguish our candles, a thick wind jetted in overhead. The wind and rain formed an orb around the outer circle, cutting us off from the rest of the world, like the reverse of a snow globe.

Cato converted to English so smoothly it took me a second to realize the change. "Micah and Kaitlyn, do you enter this union of your own free will in perfect love and perfect trust?"

In unison we answered, "We do."

"Then declare it to the Gods and Goddesses of our beloved planet."

Micah led me through the next steps, giving me verbal as well as mental clues on what to do. We faced the east and recited together, "Before the maiden of the East we declare our love for one another and ask for a blessing of the air." A small breeze blew in our direction, filling our lungs with the breath of one another. We turned to the south. "Before the mother of the afternoon we declare our love for one another and ask for warmth of hearth and home and a light to illuminate the darkest of times." The moon burst through the clouds, penetrating the orb of water and wind, reflecting the moon's rays high above us, warming us to our toes. Facing the west we chanted, "Before the crone of twilight we declare our love for one another and request the refreshing cleansing of the rain and all the encompassing passion of the sea." Some of the mist was allowed to escape the wind, lightly touching our faces. Finally, we faced the north. "Before the dark of the night we declare our love for one another and ask for a firm foundation on which to build, and the fertility of your fields in which to enrich our lives." We felt the soil beneath us bubble up in response and exude energy willingly into our bodies.

Cato smiled as we turned back to him. "The Gods and Goddesses that command the elements have blessed your union. Be understanding and patient with each other. Be free in giving your affection and warmth. Be sensuous with one another and have no fear, for you are stronger together now. The elements are with you now and always."

Cato looked over our heads to address Vayu. "Bring forth the cord."

As Vayu stepped forward with a dark red, braided cord, Cato produced a knife from the folds of his coat.

"He will make a small cut in our wrists so our blood fuses into the cord and mingles together, strengthening our bond," Micah explained, unconcerned as Cato made a small cut in his wrist. The same was done for me before I could protest. Refusal of the task would have been a bad way to start our marriage. He turned us to face each other, and began wrapping the cord around our hands. Our blood streaked parts of the cord turning it an even darker red. They reached out to each other, as if they couldn't wait to merge.

As they did, Cato commanded, "Exchange your vows."

Micah went first, "I take you, Kaitlyn, to be my wife and to be my constant friend, my partner in life, and my true love. I will love you without reservation, honor and respect you, protect you from harm, comfort you in times of distress, and grow with you in mind and spirit."

I copied him, "I take you, Micah, to be my husband and to be my constant friend, my partner in life, and my true love. I will love you without reservation, honor and respect you, protect you from harm, comfort you in times of distress, and grow with you in mind and spirit."

Together we ended the vows, "We are man and wife for a year and a day; that space gone by, each may choose another mate, or, at our pleasure, stay."

Cheers and clapping from the small crowd rang in our ears as we leaned in for a kiss. It went longer than I was comfortable with in front of a crowd, but Micah was insistent.

Cato untied the cord. "The circle is open but unbroken. May the peace of the Old Ones go in our hearts. Blessed be." He stopped with the cord only partly undone, leaving us bound together by one hand each.

I started to pull on it as we left the circle.

"Don't. We aren't supposed to untie it all the way until the marriage is consummated." Micah winked at me. He led me to his bedroom, ignoring the others, and we spent several hours joined together, bonding in ways I never thought possible. When I fell asleep out of pure exhaustion I was still tied to the headboard.

Chapter 13

Blue Eyes

The dream was lucid; clearer than a dream should have been. He was leading her by the wrist away from the bedroom, into the gardens. The dream was so real she could feel the cold grass beneath her feet and actually shivered. The night smelled of oncoming rain.

"Is this your dream or mine?" she asked him.

"Both. It is better that way," he answered without turning his head. "Faster – I want to show you something."

They continued to race through the gardens. She giggled at his excitement. They were both naked and she felt like Eve, being pulled away from her sins by Adam. "What is it? Let's go back to bed."

He stopped and turned, holding her so close his face was blurred. She looked away and realized they were at the large boulder, the ceremonial spot. He whispered, "Have you ever made love outdoors? It heightens the experience, so close to nature." He nibbled on her ear. She tensed at the unfamiliar feeling. It almost hurt.

"No, but maybe we could do it for real? Not in a dream like this." A half owl, half cat flew by as if to emphasize her point.

"Oh, no Princess, the dream also heightens the experience."

She stopped, paralyzed by his words. "What did you call me?"

He pulled back, and the haze surrounding his face cleared. Shawn's ice cold blue eyes stared back at her, twinkling under his veil of lashes. The night's stars behind him matched, twinkling in time.

She struggled to push away from him but he had a tight hold. He laughed. His laugh blew through her hair, out amongst the trees and back again. It brought with it vines from the trees that wrapped themselves around her ankles. Dozens of velvety, red rose petals followed, stopping at their feet, creating a soft, thick pad on top of the ground. The elements were working with him; she was out of her league. She resorted to a trick she learned as a child when nightmares plagued her. She closed her eyes and allowed herself to fall back, summoning a sense of panicked descent that would jolt her out of the dream and back into Micah's arms.

Shawn fell with her, refusing to release his mental hold. They struggled, back and forth between worlds. His hold was tight, and mind numbingly painful. Unable to fight any longer, she gave in and let him pull her back to the rock. A sense of dreaded déjà vu washed through her. He was on top of her, fully aroused and pressing into her. As before, there was no waiting until she was ready. He was ready and that was all that mattered. Her wrists were restrained by the very cord Cato used in the handfasting ceremony, tied to a root protruding from the ground. She jerked at it. It was planted too strongly in the earth. It wouldn't budge.

"Welcome back," he said gruffly. "We aren't finished yet."

"Finished with what?" Her thighs fought off his knees trying to snake their way in between to give him access.

"With consummating our marriage."

"I didn't marry you!" she screamed at him, exasperated.

"You didn't?" He reached up to bring an end of the marriage cord that bound her hands in front of her face. *"Look at the blood stains, how many do you see?"*

She looked closely, until the darker streaks of blood, now brown with age, revealed themselves in the red threads of the cord. Three very distinct stains intertwined together.

Temporarily distracted, he managed to open her legs wide and thrust himself inside. She threw back her head, crying out in pain.

"Why are you so tight, bitch?" he asked, grunting. *"Did Micah not officially bind the marriage tonight? With so sweet a pot, I'd of thought it would have been done several times over."*

She tried to ignore his derogatory remarks, and the pain, but he was ripping her open from the inside out. She felt warm liquid seeping out from between her legs and was sure it was blood. His teeth punctured her neck and chest, drawing out even more. He'd bleed her dry soon.

His grinding was getting faster and fiercer, and she only prayed he would be quick about it. He grunted with effort, talking in between breaths, *"I would have preferred you came to me on your own accord, but this is just as much fun. I'll have you to myself, Princess, no matter what it takes."*

His mouth slid down her chest and clamped over one of her nipples. He began to suck ferociously while squeezing her other breast, bruising the soft, white tissue. She felt an odd sensation and looked down. Her milk had come in, and he was taking it all for himself, saving nothing for the baby. He broke the suction just *long enough to mumble something about the taste of royal milk and switched to the other nipple. His pounding was harder and faster, synchronizing with the gulps of nourishing cream he stole from her body.*

Tears streaked her face, but she was more determined to fight him back now that she was fighting for two. She managed to wriggle one of her wrists free of the cord, and immediately covered her lower abdomen, protecting the baby as best she could from the thrusts of his body. Once she managed to squeeze her arm in between them, she realized her stomach was flat, void of the life that was hers to carry.

"My baby!" she cried, "Where is my baby?"

Shawn laughed again, sitting upright over her. "What this little thing?" He held the tiny, pink baby in his arms.

She reached for it but he managed to hold it far enough away while still burying himself deep inside of her. The baby cried out. Shawn reveled in it, coming quickly to his peak. He was messy about it, spilling his seed both deep inside of her and down her thigh. The sticky liquid mingled with her blood and dripped through the bed of roses beneath them.

Old wounds ripped open, leaking their poison. She lay very still while she watched him coddle her baby. Shawn looked down at her and smiled, "She has blue eyes."

* * *

"Kaitlyn, Kaitlyn! Wake up!" Micah sat over me in the same position Shawn held in my dream, minus the intimate connection.

"Get off!" I yelled.

He obliged quickly, nearly falling off the bed. "You were having a nightmare, screaming about blue eyes." He looked closer. "You're covered in bruises. I didn't do that, did I?"

My hand, shaking with fear that it wasn't just a dream, followed his gaze and up to my neck. I felt the indents of a familiar bite mark. My eyes locked with Micah's, filling with dread. My hand immediately shot down to my belly and I let out a small sigh of relief to find a large round hump. I let my hand slide down even further, until it landed in something sticky on my inner thigh. I threw back the covers and found a pool of almost-dry blood and semen.

"Oh my God."

"What? What's wrong?" Micah's voice was becoming just as panicked. "Should I call the doctor?"

"No. But something terrible has happened."

"What?" He looked as though he were about to shake the truth out of me.

"Where is the cord, the cord from our vows?"

He looked around half-heartedly. "I don't know, why?"

"Because, Micah. I fell asleep tied to it. Where is it now?!" I didn't wait for his answer. Instead, I jumped out of bed and ran out of the room, hastily throwing a robe around me, barely bothering to tie it. Micah followed, slowed down by the pants he stumbled into and was still trying to pull up and buckle while he followed my flight out to the gardens.

Our commotion attracted more attention than I would have liked, as most of the household was already awake, but only Vayu, Alex and Susan followed; some out of genuine concern and some just out for their daily dose of drama, I'm sure.

Micah caught up easily, but didn't stop me. He stayed by my side, exuding a sense of calm and confidence, letting me know he was there for me. I made my way down the path toward the rock and nearly collapsed when I entered the clearing. There, in front of the rock, was a spot where the soil was compressed and indented with a shape similar to a body. Half a dozen rose petals fluttered around the clearing with the morning breeze and drew attention to the most damning evidence of all; the red cord tied to a root protruding from the ground.

Micah knelt down beside me and untied the cord. "I don't get it – were you here last night?" As if to answer his own question, he stood and reached inside my nest of matted hair to pull out a rose petal that was buried deep within.

I nodded. "I think so. In person, or…otherwise." How could I explain it to him?

His hands felt the outline of the body in the soil, then moved down to two much deeper knee marks, "And who else?" His voice suddenly grew tight, weary of my answer.

"Shawn."

His took up a handful of soil and squeezed until I thought minerals would come out. He stood up in anger. "How? Why?"

Still bent over, with my eyes cast downward, I barely whispered, "Look at the cord, Micah. How many blood streaks do you see?" I stayed quiet for a moment, letting realization hit him.

I heard the hesitant footsteps of our three followers enter the clearing. They each looked over Micah's shoulder at the cord. Susan let out a gasp muffled by her hand over her mouth. Alex gave a very audible, "No way."

"It is done, then." Vayu said softly to Micah. "They are bound just as you and she are bound."

Everyone grew silent but I felt all eyes turn to me. I stood up with my back still to them, not bothering to brush the tainted soil from my knees.

"The hell we are. Give me that cord." I held out my hand and Micah passed it over. "Now stand back."

I heard them take a few steps back and knew it wasn't enough.

No matter, they'll scatter as soon as they see.

I drew energy that came willingly up through the ground. Almost immediately the wind picked up and clouds blew in at my insistence. The elements infused moisture into the atmosphere and charged the clouds with electrical energy. Next, I used opposite-charged energy to create a conductive path. The first lightning strike hit the cord dead-on, filling the area with a sudden light and a loud crack. My ears rang in protest. Before the effects of the first bolt wore off, I had another racing to the ground. Those behind me half-jumped, half-stumbled back. I turned my head slightly and smiled; had they not been scared shitless, they would have been proud of me.

My robe came undone. My cackle combined with hair rising from the static electricity, I was quite the insane witch in those moments. The cord disintegrated in a matter of seconds, and I set my targets to the impression of my body in the ground. Soil exploded up around me with each lighting strike, then rained down again – offering more and more energy to my cause. The lightening was coming dangerously close. It fueled my excitement.

"Do something!" Micah shouted over the noise at Vayu and Susan.

Before they could, I delved deep into their centers and retracted their energy. I had no idea I could do that until it was done. Susan actually fainted at the sudden loss of energy. Vayu fell to the ground, paralyzed. Alex moved toward me. I stopped him with a bolt of lightning at his feet. He flew back into the brush. Before Micah could try disarming me with one of his famous kisses, I did the same to him.

Clear of distractions, I concentrated on the annoying little rose petals that still had the nerve to grace the clearing with their presence. The smell of ashes floated through the air. I felt the incredible deposit of energy I had built up draining, and decided to go out with a bang. With just enough to create a very large, very powerful final strike, I focused. The lightning paused while I fueled the force-to-be.

Just as I finished carving a path of energy and released the charge from the clouds overhead, Micah took me from behind. We went tumbling across the clearing and the strike skewed off to the side in my confusion. It hit the boulder, hard. Pieces of rock shot at us through the air like shrapnel. Micah shielded me with his own body and from the corner of my eye I saw Alex do the same for Susan. Vayu was left to his own devices. When the last pieces of boulder finally rained down, bouncing several times on the ground then settling, Micah rolled off of me. Sanity took hold as I looked around, surveying the damage and my closest friends, wrought with injuries from my doing. Micah picked himself up from the ground, moving gingerly at best, careful not to press on the shards of rock buried in his skin. I heaved myself to my knees and crawled over to the others.

Alex had recovered quickly, lifting the still unconscious Susan to his shoulders. "I have to get her to medical."

I nodded my head, at a loss of what to say in my guilt. I watched him leave then crawled over to Vayu. The wind whipped all around us and rain began to pound down. Natural rain, I felt, amplified by the distress of the atmosphere. Vayu lay on the ground, his back to me. I saw his side rise and fall, a steady but slow breathing pattern. The rock pieces had torn his shirt to shreds. He had taken the brunt of the scattering debris. I ran my hand lightly over his back, surveying the damage. The wind ripped away the remaining rag of his shirt and his bare back was revealed. On his right shoulder, he bore the same scarred pattern mine did. Shawn's mark.

"What is this?" I touched the mark to ensure it was real and he winced, gaining consciousness.

He turned over, surveying his torn shirt. He ripped the rest of it off and smiled, "How do you think Shawn's blood got on the cord?"

I stared at him, eyes wide. "You...you're with him?"

He shrugged his shoulders and lifted himself off the ground, wincing as the muscles of his back moved. "What can I say? His offers are a bit more enticing than Cato's."

Vayu lifted his arms. Unnatural wind came in, growing strong enough to lift him off the ground within seconds. Vayu moved up and away from the clearing. Anyone else might've thought it was Vayu's magic, but I knew Shawn's power when I felt it. I bristled, my anger coming back. I called upon what energy was left within me and the surrounding area; there was very little. I tried anyway, copying the same wind pattern that carried Vayu away. I slowly lifted myself off the ground, eyes intent in the direction in which Vayu had disappeared. Suddenly, one of my hands was restrained, halting my upward progress. I looked down.

Micah had a tight hold on one of my wrists. "This is his element, you can't fight him with it," Micah yelled to be heard over the wind tunnel.

I started to explain Vayu had no energy of his own left, but Micah interrupted, sending his thoughts to me. *There is a better way to do this, with me by your side.* I looked into his pleading eyes; he was still holding on, unwilling to let go. I released the wind and spun back down to the earth, right into his arms. We held each other, supporting each other's weight because neither one of us could stand on our own. Finally I looked up at him. "Take me to the doctor. I need to check on the baby."

Chapter 14

A Gift

After an hour with the doctor and many assurances that the baby was fine, as well as several more assurances there was no way to determine the baby's eye color yet, he moved on to a more private exam. Micah refused to leave the room. Instead I positioned myself so Micah would be spared of some of the more gruesome sights involved.

"I've seen everything you are trying to hide from me." He held my hands and stroked my cheek.

"Not like this, you haven't."

The doctor interrupted, "Kaitlyn, you have a fair share of new wounds. Some are already scarring over, probably due to the energy of the Chakra, but they are definitely new." He looked at Micah, narrowing his eyes in accusation.

"It wasn't him," I said in defense.

The doctor raised his eyebrows, "Maybe I should leave you two alone for a minute..." he hesitated. "Is that okay with you?"

"It's fine – thank you doctor." I lifted myself to a sitting position. Micah and I sat in silence for a few minutes, looking anywhere but at each other. I turned away from him once the tears started to roll down my face. "I'm so sorry. I should have been able to get away, to prevent this. You did something so special for me, and it's all been ruined."

He quickly pulled me off the table and wrapped himself around me, letting me bury my face in his chest. "How do you think I feel? I wasn't able to protect you even while you lay in my arms."

"It's not your fault." I sobbed into his chest.

He took my face in both hands and forced me to look at him. "Nor is it yours."

I nodded my head slowly, trying to relieve myself of the guilt, and he did the same.

"Okay then," he finally said, a forced smile on his face. "Let's get you cleaned up, fed and back in bed. In that order."

I managed to smile back, grateful to let someone else take charge – this once.

He saw me to my room, ran a warm bath filled with healing salts and fragrances the doctor gave us, and left me alone to get his own wounds looked after. I felt safe enough, as long as I stayed awake. He returned with a full plate of food just as I was dressing. Prime rib, baked potatoes, fruits and vegetables, even dessert. "Where did all this come from?"

"There was a feast in our honor last night; but we had disappeared before we could partake," he shrugged his shoulders sheepishly. "I guess we were a little too anxious."

I laughed mouth already full of food. "Well, had I known…"

His face brightened. "Amazing. With all that's happened…"

"What?" I prompted

"Well, I just think you are going to be okay, is all."

"As long as I have you, honey." I gave him my best 'wife' voice. I finally motioned to the large cardboard package he brought in with my food. "What's that?"

"Oh, a gift from everyone." He walked over to it and took out a card, reading aloud, "Dearest Micah and Kaitlyn, we are so happy for the two of you. Please accept these tree seedlings and our offer to plant a forest in honor of your union. This is a gift that will grow along with your relationship and will be a constant reminder of your love for one another. As the trees grow and prosper over the years, so too will your love." Micah's eyes moved to the bottom of the card. "Signed Cato, Susan, Alex, and Vayu."

He pulled out a small bullet-shaped canister, pointed at one end and open at the other. "Aerial reforestation," Micah commented in wonder, studying the canister. "I guess Vayu was meant to help." He slowly lowered the canister and gazed off into space. "Traitorous bastard."

I almost felt guilty having been the one to reveal it; almost. I tried to change the subject. "How's Susan? Maybe I should go see her."

"That can wait. She needs her rest as do you." Micah pushed away my food tray and pulled me into bed with him. He laid me down and curled his body around me.

"Not sure I can sleep," I said hesitantly. "It's high noon outside."

"You have lost a lot of energy today, your body needs it."

I swallowed. "It's not just that, Micah. I'm, well, kind of afraid to sleep. What if he comes back again? This is like my own, personal Elm Street."

Micah's arms tightened around me in response to the prospect of it happening all over again. His breathing grew more rapid and I lay still, tucking his hands close into my chest waiting patiently while he got himself under control. His breathing returned to normal but his voice still had an edge to it, "Now that I know, I can help prevent it."

"How?"

"We can stay connected, even in our dreams."

I recalled the days when we would communicate telepathically on a regular basis, and squirmed in closer to him in excitement at the expectation to do that again. I loved hearing his voice in my head almost more so than hearing it out loud. *Sleep now, beautiful. I will maintain the connection. What would you like to dream about? Prime rib? Cake? Mountains of rolls smothered in almond butter?*

I giggled.

He kissed me on the cheek. *I love you.* I was about to respond when he stopped me. *Don't use any more energy. Relax and let me do the work. Just know that I love you and I always will. We'll get through this together, then continue to make this world a better place for our child.* His hand rested on my belly. I smiled. It was the first time he referred to the baby as 'ours'. I closed my eyes, letting his words wash through my mind. Feeling his steady heart beat against my back, I drifted off to sleep.

Chapter 15

His Everything

I awoke with Micah's arms still around me. I dreamt not of meat and buttered rolls but of our forest to be. It was beautiful. It grew strong and pure, deeply hidden from civilization and unmarred by man's presence. Micah and I spent the entire dreaming session there, exploring the hilly landscape and revering the great trees.

Are you awake? Micah sent the question cautiously.

I answered telepathically, not yet trusting my morning voice, nor my morning breath. *Yes. What time is it?*

Midnight.

Oh. I'm not tired anymore.

Do you want to go for a walk?

I turned to face him on my side and snuggled closer. *I don't want to leave your warmth.*

He sat up in bed and wrapped the comforter around me, trapping in his heat. *So take my warmth with you.*

"Come on," he said aloud. "Let's go plant our forest."

I groaned, but lifted myself out of bed.

He dressed then lugged the box onto his shoulder. "Where do you want to do this?"

I thought for a moment. The rock was out of the question. "How about the pond?"

"Okay."

I stayed in my nightgown and dragged the whole comforter outside with me, it slowed us down.

The lake was a brilliant blue, reflecting the waning moon. I spread the blanket out on the shores of the pond, just out of the water's reach. Micah set the box down in front of us and began rooting through its contents. "Cato left us some ideas of where we could place the forest – places most in need."

He leaned in so we could scan the list together.

Only about half of the forests in Honduras remain; there was a 37% decline in forest cover between 1990 and 2005. All but 10% of trees in Nigeria have been chopped down. The Philippines forests are down to 35% and Benin and Ghana retain less than 10% of their forests.

The list continued, Cato giving us more than our share of choices, but one country in particular caught my attention. Indonesia, like much of Southeast Asia, was historically entirely covered in forests. Even though 65% of those forests remain, there had been a serious decline that didn't show signs of letting up. More logs were felled in the '80s and '90s across the large country than in all of South America and Africa combined.

The Asian region only makes up one quarter of the earth's land, but holds 60% of the world's population, the letter ended.

It seemed logical to maintain large amounts of greenery where there were large amounts of people, for the sake of balance.

"I like Indonesia." I announced. Besides, its close proximity to the Chakra would make using the wind element easier; a fact I left unspoken.

"Me, too," he said. "It is rather appropriate; they came out with a new law last year that each newlywed couple has to plant ten trees and each divorced couple has to plant 50 trees."

"How many seedlings are in there?"

"I'm guessing about 1,000."

"Enough to get married 100 times over! Or divorced..." I tried doing the math in my head.

Micah interrupted my calculations by placing a canister in my hand and digging in the box for the proper map. "It doesn't matter. There is patch of land on Java that was severely damaged by a recent earthquake. Although the land is protected by the government, they gave permission for logging companies to come in and clear the area of debris. Now it's just barren land, but rich in volcanic soil. It should be easy for the seedlings to take hold. Barring any more earthquakes, the forest will remain protected."

I studied the map. "I'm not sure how I'll know I've hit the right spot from here."

Micah thought for a moment. "Well, Java was formed mostly from volcanic activity. There is a line of volcanoes running from east to west on the island."

"So?"

"So...I thought that the soil might have a similar feel to you as the soil on Galapagos."

I gave him a warning look. Searching for something similar to the energy depleting islands of Galapagos was not my idea of how best to spend our night together. "Maybe we should think this through better. Do you think this place has the same, you know, properties as Galapagos?"

"I don't think so. Not all volcanic-based places do. In fact, we know of a few that are similar to the Chakra; places that feed you energy willingly. Cato has been trying to pinpoint all of those special places around the world when he has time. He hasn't found many yet, but Asia hasn't been studied at all." He looked at me a few moments, his forehead slowly mirroring the creases of concern mine had. "Listen, why don't you try with just one? Stay connected to the plant and you'll know soon enough if it will thrive or die there."

I shrugged my shoulders. "I guess one couldn't hurt, to start off. Let me just protect it first." I recalled a spell my mother had taught me as a child when I refused to leave my teddy bear home from school. As I grew older, I always thought the spells were her silly way of getting me to do things. Come to find out there was much more to them than that. I lay the canister next to the blanket in the soil, and drew the outline of a circle within a star with my finger.

"With this pentagram, protection I lay. Guard this object both night and day. For him who should try and harm, may his body shiver and quake and warn me through charm. I now invoke the power in me. This is my will, so let it be!"

I looked at Micah. "Okay, here goes nothing." I tuned into the frequency of the wind around me. It picked up just enough to lift the canister out of my hands and up into the air. I sent it in the direction Micah pointed.

Twenty minutes after the canister left, Micah grew impatient. "Are you there yet?"

"No, I've hit a trouble spot. Something keeps drawing the seedling toward it, away from my path. I can't get past it."

"That's probably it!" he said excitedly. "If the area is full of good energy, it will attract more good energy to it – even if it resides in other elements. Just follow the pull."

I did as he directed, skeptical of his reasoning. I thought opposites attract. Within minutes I felt soil rushing up to meet my plant. I slowed the descent and concentrated on keeping the canister steady, pointy side down. Before I allowed it to bury itself in the soil, I sent out feelers for what type of land lay there. As soon as I hit the barren soil, my weaves vibrated with warmth and strength. They infused themselves with the energy of the land without me doing a thing.

"Whoa!"

"What?" Micah frowned. "What?"

I smiled in triumph. "This is a good place –a very good place. Better than the Chakra, even." Without waiting for his response, I buried the canister deep in the soil, leaving the top only a few inches from the surface. I pulled my weaves away from the soil but kept my connection to the plant. I felt life throb; like it was anxious to spread its roots somewhere.

"Will the roots be able to break through the canister?" I asked.

"It is biodegradable and will disintegrate into the soil in a matter of days. Once Susan is feeling better, she can direct rain that way which will also help."

"Okay, it is done." I leaned in for a kiss in excitement. What was meant to be a congratulatory peck turned into a long, romantic few minutes involving tongues.

Once his hands began to work their way up the lengths of my nightgown, I pulled away. "I'm sorry, I'm not fully healed yet. I need time."

"Of course, I knew that. I just got a little too enthused." Micah took a couple of deep breaths and fiddled with my hair while he worked to cool himself down. We laid on the blanket, my head resting in the crook of his arm. Clouds moved in, hiding the moon. What stars did shine through seemed extra bright. His free hand put my hair gently aside and traveled down my torso until it rested on top of my belly.

"Is she kicking much?"

"Yes, usually around here." I moved his hand to the lower part of my abdomen, the underside of the large round hump. "She's been very active tonight. She does that when I am absorbing energy; or when I'm eating."

He laughed. "A food fiend, just like her mother." Before I could retort Micah let out a gasp. "I felt it. I mean her, I felt her!"

"You did? I didn't think she was that strong yet…"

He sat back, keeping his hold on my belly, a satisfied smile on his face. "Kaitlyn?"

"Yes?"

"In your spell, what did you mean 'warn me through charm'?"

"Oh. My mom gave me several necklaces as a child that always held what she called magical charms. The charms would supposedly warn me somehow if one of my spells were being tested. I guess by heating up or vibrating or something. When I was a little older she told me I would know even without a charm if I kept my mind open to it."

"What about the necklace I gave you?"

I felt a wave of regret run through me. "The last time I had it was at the pier with Susan. Either the waves knocked it off or Shawn has it."

Micah shrugged his shoulders. "It's not like I can't make you another one. In fact, you've done all the hard work, splintering the boulder into pieces and all. I could make you a whole set of jewelry, complete with earrings, necklace, and bracelets."

"And if the Seven goes belly up, we could open a rock jewelry business together. I'll collect the merchandise – you do the beading."

We talked about everything and nothing for the next hour before remembering to send out the rest of the seedlings. It was easier the second time, now that I knew where to go. The first rays of dawn were just beginning to streak the sky by the time we finished.

"How are you feeling? Do you want to go back to bed?" Micah asked as we made our way slowly back to the building.

"No. Being connected to that place...I have more energy now than when we started." I could still feel it coursing through my body, mixing with my blood and muscles. Good to know that a boost like that was only a short distance away.

"Are you sure?" Micah persisted. "It's going to be a busy day."

"Why?" I looked at him. "What's happening?"

"Cato will order an inspection of the entire building and grounds later. He'll also have us inspect each employee for physical signs of Shawn – like you have."

I made a face. "I can't imagine that will go over too well with some people."

"It won't. But those who refuse will be escorted off the island immediately." He paused then added, "You and Susan will need to inspect the women on your own. Are you okay with that?"

"Sure." As far as I could recall, there were only three or four women on the compound.

"Great." Micah held open the door to the kitchen.

We took our time with breakfast, cooking up a feast big enough for ten. In the time Micah took to whip scrambled eggs, make banana pancakes, sausage and bacon, I had managed to butter toast and cut up a few pieces of fruit. In my defense, I had to take a hiatus to nurse the shallow cut on my finger from an unfortunate combination of clumsy hands and a very sharp knife.

Although it was only six in the morning, the smells began to lure people into the kitchen. Cato and Alex had come in. Just as my mind wandered to Susan, debating if she was angry with me for the lightning incident, she also appeared in the doorway to the kitchen. Her eyes scanned the food on the counter then rested on me. Without giving her a chance to speak first, I ran over and threw my arms around her.

"I'm so sorry," I whispered, my face muzzled into her shoulder.

She spoke back in a voice just as low. "Don't be. I would have been suspicious if your reaction was anything less. I would have done the same." She paused. "Well, not exactly the same - I would've opted for a hurricane."

I pulled back, prodding her - looking for signs of weakness. "I haven't seen you since, how are you feeling?"

She pushed away my hands. "I'm fine. I've been camping out by the pond. The water does wonders for me. Just like the soil does for you."

"Oh." I paused, processing the information. It suddenly hit me. I dropped my voice again, all too aware of the group behind us. "Oh….did you…?"

"I saw you guys sending out our gift. It was very touching." She lowered her voice even more, "I may not have completely understood your relationship with my brother, but the look in his eyes and the sound of his voice last night… It's obvious you're his everything."

"Oh." That was the only word that kept coming to mind. It was annoying. I took a deep breath and tried again, steering her toward the food. "Have some of the breakfast I made."

"You made?" Her arched eyebrow mirrored Micah's across the kitchen, who asked the same question.

"Well," I said defensively, "I helped anyway." I hid my bandaged finger and gave Micah warning glance to keep his mouth shut.

He took the hint.

As Susan piled pancakes on her plate, Cato broke the silence, "So you planted the seedlings last night? Where?"

I hid a grimace. I always forgot his ears were younger than their years.

"Indonesia." Micah puffed out his chest. "Turns out the location there is just as powerful as here, maybe even more so."

"Hmmm. Good, I thought that might have been the case. Some of the seedlings have a GPS installed. I'll send someone out in a few months to check on their progress." Cato looked at Alex, assigning him the mission silently.

"Awww. Come on, it's their stupid forest," Alex whined, but truthfully he looked forward to his trips away from the Chakra and everyone knew it.

I dismissed Alex's comment and turned to Cato. "How do you pinpoint the areas that give off that much energy?"

Cato studied me for a moment. "Perhaps that is something I can teach you. I didn't realize Gaias could recognize such a place at a distance. We'll put you to good use while you are, well – incapacitated, as you are."

I opened my mouth, ready to protest.

He put up a hand to stop me. "But that is a conversation for another time. Right now we need to discuss today's inspection."

"Yeah – where is everyone else? The smell of this sausage would wake a bear out of hibernation." Alex stuffed an entire patty in his mouth.

"I put up wards to block the smell," Cato said, "but it won't last long. We are all going to inspect each other first. I don't expect to find anything – it is just so we can disregard any biased comments from the rest of the staff. Kaitlyn, we are already aware of your mark and how it came to be, so it won't be necessary to strip."

"How kind of you," I said sarcastically.

"I am not stripping in front of my brother," Susan said.

Alex began to raise his hand, but Micah slapped it down quickly, grumbling at him.

"Of course not, no. Kaitlyn can inspect you. After each other, we will call in the security patrols first. Next will be the medical staff. Then the ground personnel, and then anyone else we might have missed. Everyone will be sequestered in the living room pre-inspection and be moved to the library post-inspection. Except for those that are suspect. They will be escorted off the island under heavy guard immediately. After the personal inspections, we can move to their rooms while they are still in the library."

I raised my hand. "Question. Don't most know about my mark? Won't it look bad to fire people while I get to stay? Also, don't you think Shawn may have thought of this? Once one was discovered, surely he anticipated we would look for the rest. Maybe he planted a few of his minions here that don't have the mark, hoping we have a false sense of confidence once some were booted."

"Very good, Kaitlyn." Cato smiled at me and I felt like I should get a gold star sticker. "We'll just have to be extra cautious even after these inspections are done. We can do them on a regular basis and perhaps get more cooperation from the staff if they are told that." Cato paused as if listening to something the rest of us couldn't hear. "The wards have worn off. We should begin."

Susan finished her breakfast and motioned for me to join her in another room. "Here goes nothing."

Micah stopped me. "Just don't go too far, and stay connected to me. Call out if you need anything at all."

I kissed him on the cheek. "Don't worry; I am a pretty capable girl."

"Yes. The phrase 'too capable' comes to mind."

"Whatever that means," I huffed, following Susan out of the kitchen.

Chapter 16

Coursing Through my Veins

Once in private, Susan stripped and I quickly glanced over her nude body, feeling more awkward than she probably did. Her exterior was free of any markings, scars or even scratches, and I couldn't help but notice its soft glow.

I coughed, looking away. "Nice skin."

"Thanks." She put her clothes back on. "Water does wonders for a body."

"Yeah, so does coffee." In all the excitement we hadn't made a pot, and being up for the last seven hours was beginning to have its effects on my caffeine-addicted brain.

"Let's get some before we see the other women."

Susan led me out, apparently just as anxious to get to the warm, sweet liquid as I was.

Ten minutes later we entered the living room, hot cups of coffee in hand. The room was packed and I realized these poor people hadn't had a chance to eat or have their own coffee yet. Half were still in their pajamas with bed head.

Micah pushed his way through the crowd toward us. "We're still waiting on a couple more, but the three women are here if you want to start with them."

"Alright, here goes nothing." Susan took charge and I was happy to let her. She called the three women, only two of whom I recognized, and led them into the kitchen. Hanging in the background with my face buried in my mug, I let her do the inspections and answer their questions. Susan handled it well.

Inspection completed, we led the women to the library, hands full of muffins and fruit to set out for everyone coming in after being inspected. One of the women also brought in mugs and a carafe of coffee. Not to would be cruel.

We stayed with the women until enough of the security guards were done being inspected and Cato gave the okay to leave the library under their watch. The men filtering in post-inspection made themselves as comfortable as possible in the dusty room. At least there wasn't a lack of reading material.

Susan and I moved on to inspecting the women's rooms. With two of the women being roommates, we moved through the two rooms quickly but thoroughly, careful to leave things as they were.

In going through a dresser, I found a small, tightly wrapped bag of white powder. "Umm, Susan?" I held up the bag with facial tissue, careful not to get my fingerprints on it. "What should we do with this?"

Susan took it from me. "Well, we can stop treating it like its evidence in a crime scene."

I threw the tissue in the trash. "It kind of is."

She rolled her eyes, stuffing the bag into her pocket. "Kaitlyn, this is Sumatra – not California. Probably cocaine. This comes in handy as justification for doing these kinds of inspections. Alex will make sure word gets around that this was found. He is good at gossip."

When we entered the living room that still had a few lingering souls waiting for inspection, Alex greeted us, "Thank God. These guys are edgy and it is only getting worse. Can you do something to lighten the mood?"

"You mean, besides our mere presence?" Susan floated by him, running the tips of her fingers across his chest. She moved to the windows and threw them open. She looked at me across the room and made a gesture with her head. I stood staring at her, befuddled. She tried again by jerking her head to the side a little less subtly. My dazed look and her epileptic motions were beginning to attract attention.

Alex cleared his throat, looking at me. "I think she wants you perform a little voodoo and, you know, bring in a breeze."

"Ooohhh." I gave Susan a thumbs up that I finally understood. She rolled her eyes. Her and I really need to work on our communication skills. Within seconds I had a cool northern breeze blowing amongst the room's inhabitants, lifting the heat off their necks. I felt my weaves waver with a touch of Susan's power. She was infusing the incoming air with tiny water particles. I looked at her while she stood by the window, absorbing some of the moisture through the skin on her face. I wondered if she and I might be able to have the same sort of mental communications as I did with Micah, or even the less desirable type of dream connections I had with Shawn.

I tried by sending out a short message. *We need to work on our communication.*

I was almost immediately answered. *What?*

Micah. The same path wasn't going to work with Susan.

I shook my head. *Never mind.*

We talked, or rather shared thoughts, back and forth for some time while he did his inspections. The room was beginning to empty rapidly and soon only two men were left besides the guards, Susan, Alex, and me. Through the open path, I felt a sudden rush of Micah's heartbeat. *What happened? Are you okay?*

He responded with grunts and curses, something I was sure he meant to say out loud. I just hoped he wasn't trying to relay the situation to those around him instead of sending it telepathically. Finally I heard a strained, *send the rest of guards in. Keep Alex with you.* I relayed the message as ordered.

I prodded Micah's mind, probably distracting him from the struggle. He finally answered my unasked questions. *One of the groundskeepers didn't want to be inspected, tried to make a run for it. Not one of Shawn's, seems to do with drugs.*

Susan and Alex relaxed as I repeated the information. Who would have thought such a rampant drug problem would have been considered good news? I looked at the last two men waiting for inspection and wondered if we would have any more problems. They certainly didn't look like drug users, though one looked considerably worse for the wear. He paced the room, emitting a nice film of sweat that covered his entire body.

"Withdrawal?" I asked Susan who had moved to stand beside me.

"No, not so soon," she said hesitantly. There was something almost certainly wrong with him. "Let's try to calm him down before sending him to Micah."

We moved toward him, trying to look as innocent as possible. It didn't help. As soon as he saw us, he met us halfway in the open area of the living room; feet shoulder width apart and arms crossed.

"Calm down, dude. It's just a standard inspection – nothing to worry about." Alex coaxed him from across the room.

"There is nothing standard about it! They are searching for the same mark this one here has, but I don't see her being forced to strip down." He glared at me.

I placed his face; the medical team. Of course he knew my body inside and out. They all did.

Susan stepped to his side. "The women went first, she was already inspected."

"Bullshit!" He reached underneath his shirt and produced a gun. It was cocked and pressed against Susan's forehead before any of us could move. "Get on your knees. Arms up and out to the side."

Susan did as she was told, moving slowly, looking the part of a perfect sacrificial lamb.

He glanced at me next. "What, no lightning strikes?"

I gritted my teeth. "Word travels fast."

"That would be my fault." Alex said, raising his hand in confession from across the room. I narrowed my eyes at him. "What?" he asked. "There is nothing else to do around here."

"Hence the drugs," Susan piped up.

"Shut up! Everybody shut up!" His finger tightened slightly around the trigger.

I looked at the only other man in the room for support, but he was more useless than any of us, huddled behind a large armchair.

I felt Micah just outside the door.

Stop! I commanded. *He has a gun to Susan's head and an itchy trigger finger.* Micah didn't respond but I felt him ease off the door handle.

Despite the jokes, heat crawled up my neck. There was no way I could let Susan get hurt - again. My emotions fed the weather outside and more wind crept in along my weaves, following the already established path.

The gunman allowed a small smile to creep onto his face. "I was warned about you; about some kind of power that is a part of you; runs in your veins. But I don't see it. I think there is nothing but fear there."

"You have no idea what is coursing through my veins." I was slowly stepping toward him as we spoke.

A strong gust of wind caused him to step forward. His face lost all its confidence, his eyes widening. "It doesn't matter. I was also told to use this to bring you back to him." He produced a knife, the athame Shawn used to scar me. "I wasn't planning on doing it just yet but it looks like my plans have changed."

I was just within reach for him to scrape the point of the knife along my neckline. The sensation sent chills down my spine and Shawn's smell invaded my senses, overpowering them. I was too scared, too helpless to do anything but stand there and shake.

My body froze, locked in a block of ice. Through blurred vision I could see the wind picking up. If it weren't for the non-existent ice I would have been knocked over. A muted choking fought its way through the wind. I blinked the forming tears away and realized it was the gunman. Still managing to hold the knife and the gun, his mouth worked furiously trying to expel something that wouldn't come up. As he slowly sank to his knees, Susan rose, chin lifted and eyes narrowed, concentrating on the man. She was drowning him; forcing the water particles carried in on my wind down his throat and into his lungs.

Micah was screaming in my head. *What happened? Talk to me!*

I tried to respond but only stutters and broken phrases were sent. Finally I managed to emit one clear word, *come.*

Two blurred bodies appeared. One tackled Susan, taking her out of the gun's sights. The other simultaneously tackled the gunman and both rolled away like tumbleweed in a windstorm. No longer at my neck, the knife dropped to the ground in front of me, and wavered slightly from the wind, giving it a life of its own. I couldn't take my eyes away, mesmerized.

Once everyone got to their feet, several heads came into view. Their very outlines wavered.

"What is wrong with her?" barked one voice.

Another voice squeaked, "It's the knife – hide it. Get it out of here!"

An old, wrinkled pair of hands covered the knife with a towel, wrapping it tightly without touching it and moved it away. Immediately the ice around me burst into liquid and I collapsed to the floor in a splash of water.

Chapter 17

More Questions than Answers

I lay on the ground shivering. I expected to be soaking wet, but my clothes were dry as a bone.

"What's wrong with her? She's ice cold." Micah leaned over me.

Cato started barking orders, "Get that man tied up and take him to the basement."

"You don't want him on the boat with the others?" One of the guards hesitated.

"No, we need to interrogate him. Micah – come on."

Micah spared a glance at Cato over his shoulder. "I'm not leaving her."

A moment of silence passed between the two. It seemed all at once Cato understood what our relationship was doing to the well-oiled machine of an operation he had worked hard to officiate his entire life.

"Fine. Alex, then."

Alex relinquished his hold of the gunman to the guards. He stopped at Susan as his eyes passed over her. She nodded, and Alex set out to follow Cato, shoulders squared.

I didn't have much say in what was going on; I couldn't have spoken had I wanted to. My teeth chattered too violently. Micah slid one arm under my shoulders and another under my knees, hoisting me to his chest. As he carried me out of the room I couldn't help but notice someone digging a bullet out of the wall.

Micah carried me straight to his room, and the private bathroom that accompanied it. He set me in the bathtub, supporting me with one arm and flipping on the hot water to the shower with the other. He plugged the drain and the water slowly began to build up, surrounding me in warmth, but the cold was set deep into my bones, clinging to me mercilessly.

He began to strip me of my clothes, then his. When he slid his body into the bathtub next to me I could only squeak in protest. He wrapped his body around me, forcing me to the top, letting the heat of the water raining down from above warm my front while his body warmed me from behind.

"Don't do this to me, baby," he whispered in my ear. "Fight it, you are stronger than this."

I had no idea how close I was to losing the battle until I heard the fear in his voice. Why was I losing? The more I thought about it, the more I panicked. My shivering started all over again despite the heat surrounding me. He held on to me tighter, resolved to bring me back.

"No. This isn't happening. I won't let it." His words were slipping away and seemed almost foreign, like they weren't part of my world. I felt a peace calling me, beckoning for me to join it and turn my back on all the fear, confusion, and anger that was my life.

I headed that direction but something was nagging at me; something not right. Some unfinished business; I was forgetting something. There was another life slipping away as well; a life undone too early. An even stronger feeling washed over me. It was two lives, not just one. I turned my attention back in the direction I had come. Micah and the baby were pulling me back – each one absorbing the cold for me. They were using themselves as bait, taunting the cold to join them. Micah took the majority of it, but the baby could access the numbing freeze set deep in my bones more easily.

That won't do, I thought to myself. I plunged myself back into my body, away from peace. *Peace will come another time. Just not now.*

My eyes flew open. I gasped, taking a desperately needed gulp of air. My body was sore, but the cold was no longer there. I felt Micah shivering behind me. I turned around to face him and began rubbing my hands up and down his arms and legs, willing the warmth back into him.

He seemed to be concentrating, and after a few moments let out a deep sigh of relief. He opened his eyes, and looked at me. "It's gone. I've released it far away from us. It won't be coming back."

Satisfied he was okay, my hands instinctively wrapped themselves around my belly. "The baby. She was helping. She was doing the same as you."

His hands quelled my worried fingers. "She's okay. I took it from her as soon as I could. She's safe, I promise."

"How could you know? We should call the doctor—"

"Kaitlyn. I felt her, just as I can feel you. Come here." He leaned me into him, forcing my belly under the rising water.

I let the complications sink in, and began to shake again, this time in tears. Micah rubbed my back, hushing me like child. Water overflowed, rushing out of the bathtub like a waterfall.

When my sobs turned to hiccups Micah turned the shower off with his foot and glanced at the floor. "We are going to have a hell of mess to clean up."

I laughed and pushed myself closer to him. He grew hard and my nipples responded, pushing back against his chest. Embarrassed for both of us, I reprimanded him, "You have to be kidding me. We just had a near death experience – all three of us."

"Sorry, just a natural response to our...present situation." He was silent for a few moments and then asked, "Why do you think that was?"

"What?"

"The near death experience. Why did that happen?"

"I don't know. I was just frozen with fear. Once I saw the knife, I couldn't move. But it wasn't like that before, even on the island with Shawn. I always responded with sarcasm. I was never frozen with fear."

"It's not just you that you're fighting for anymore." He rubbed my stomach. "There are two of you and your body knows that. Maybe the response of fear instead of anger is a protective instinct."

I nodded, agreeing with his point, but not liking it.

He went on, "There was something else, though. How come your body temperature dropped so much?"

I shrugged my shoulders. "I think it was the knife. It did something to me. As soon as Cato took it away whatever was happening stopped."

"It is possible Shawn put some kind of spell on it. If the wielder of the knife is being attacked by an element, as Susan was doing to the gunman, the same element turns against its intended target – you."

"I thought Shawn wanted to recruit me, not kill me."

"He does. But he could have enchanted the athame long ago for his own protection. He was always looking into magic that was beyond his responsibility with the group. Cato discouraged it as much as possible, but you know Shawn."

"Unfortunately, yes. I do know Shawn."

We both fell silent as we let Shawn come between us, as only he could.

"I'm sorry, Kaitlyn. I can't do this anymore." He looked down, gripping the sides of the bathtub tight.

I pushed myself off his chest, "Do what?"

"I can't just stand by, fending off attack after attack until finally one of these times he's successful."

I narrowed my eyes. "What do you mean?"

"I'm going after him, without you."

"The hell you are!" I pushed myself completely off of him, my movement causing even more water to splash out into the bathroom. "What do you intend to do without me there? Punch him to death?"

"If need be, yes."

"No. If you're going, I'm going." Though another personal encounter with Shawn was the last thing I wanted.

Micah picked up on my uncertainty. "You are not going anywhere. If I could handcuff you and lock you away in a safe while I was gone - I would."

"Well why don't you? Cause I'd have to use the bathroom?"

His eyes flitted around the bathroom as if he were considering the possibility.

"You bastard!" I swiped at his face with an open hand.

He stopped my swing, locking tightly onto my wrist. His other arm snaked around my waist. "I'm serious, Kaitlyn. If anything ever happened to you, I wouldn't survive it."

I relaxed into his hold and stared him down. "And what makes you think that doesn't go both ways?"

He lifted his chin and I saw understanding flood his eyes.

I shook my head, frustrated it had taken him this long to grasp the concept. I got out of the bathtub, slipping on the flooded floor the whole way to the door, and headed to my room after grabbing his robe to cover me.

I was stopped short in the hallway seeing Alex walking past. I reached out to him, hoping to gain an ally. My hand touched his shoulder and landed in liquid. I pulled my hand back sharply. It was red, all blood. And still warm. My eyes widened. "What happened?"

He turned toward me. His entire chest was covered, splotches even reaching his face. "It's not mine."

"What—?"

"Not now, Kaitlyn." He turned away and kept walking.

My blood-covered hand was still up in disbelief. Micah came up next to me and watched Alex disappear down the hallway.

"That was supposed to be my job," he said it softly to himself as he wiped off my hand in with his water-soaked shirt.

Cato passed next, his faded blue eyes were distant. Micah hurried to put on dry clothes and raced out the door. "Get dressed and meet us in the library."

His body rushing past sent a breeze through my hair and jolted me out of my shock. "What do you mean *your job*?" My question echoed down the hallway after him but he was already gone. I sighed and made my way to my room. Once again my head was filled with more questions than answers.

Chapter 18

States of Mind

My arrival was too late. By the time I got to the library, recent incidents had been discussed and further action was planned. Cato and Susan were on their way out, intent on their own list of things to do.

Micah followed behind them, nearly crashing into me at the doorway. "We're leaving tomorrow."

"We meaning...?"

"Meaning me, Cato, and Susan. Alex will be staying here with you."

I didn't respond, keeping my lips pressed together tight for fear of saying something we would both regret later.

He continued, "You have a few things to do while we're gone."

I remained silent.

"I want you to work on communicating with the baby. If I can do it, then you can. If something ever happens, it may be the only way to save her."

Finally trusting my voice, I said through gritted teeth, "What else?"

"Spend a lot of time with Alex. He can protect you while I'm gone and he's going to need you to help him work through this recent information-gathering episode Cato put him through. Stay close to him, just not...too close."

"Okay...anything else?"

"Yes. I feel a little awkward telling you this but..."

I couldn't take the pause. "What is it? Just spit it out already."

"We're putting a bunk bed in Alex's room – I want you to sleep there for now." He avoided my gaze.

"So, you don't want me to get too close to the man but you want me to sleep with him?"

"Don't be childish, Kaitlyn," he snapped. "I'm doing the best I can here. Just do what I ask and it will be easier for everybody."

"You mean easier for you."

His eyes flared with color; never a good sign. "This has to be done my way. There is no discussion about it. Don't fight me on this."

He was right; arguing would do no good, but hell if I would make it that easy. "I promise I will *consider* your requests," I said in a low, even tone.

He took a step closer so aggressively that I took a step back. I hit the wall and flinched as his fist went flying inches away from my face and through the drywall of the room. I gasped, looking at his arm trembling in anger beside me. He withdrew his arm from the wall and grabbed my chin. "Damn it, Kaitlyn! Don't you understand? I would hurt you in order to keep you safe!"

I didn't respond. I couldn't. It was one of the most romantically angering things anyone had ever said to me. I had never seen him so furious, yet there were tears forming in his eyes.

He briskly wiped them away with the back of his hand before the evidence of his emotions went spilling down his face. "God damn you, woman," he tilted my chin up further and took my mouth with his in a bruising display of force. I tried to wiggle out from in between him and the wall but he just responded by pressing in tighter, holding my body captive until he was done with it.

"Micah," I pleaded with him in between breaths. "You're hurting me."

He breathed in my words, then gave my lips a short reprieve in order to bite at my neck. His hands clawed themselves around my hips and down my thighs.

He stopped just as suddenly as he had started, and my feet hit the ground with a loud thud. I hadn't even realized they were off the floor. He kept his forehead pressed against mine, breathing hard, straining to regain control of himself. "Sleep in my bed tonight. I have a lot to do and won't be there until late, but I'll check in on you." He leaned in for what might have been another kiss, if you can call it that, but thought better of it and left the room abruptly.

I went to bed early, hoping to be asleep long before Micah came and long after he left. My dreams were chaotic; never once did I sense Micah beside me in bed but he was always there to pull me away from Shawn's tainted grasp. I woke up in a sweat, suddenly too aware of what Micah's absence would do to me. Who would save me from my nightmares? Certainly not Alex. He contained no more magic than a child's wizard play set.

I quickly dressed and left the room, thankful to be away from Micah's scent. It was too much to bear. I found Alex perched on a chair just outside the door with a magazine in one hand and a cup of coffee in another.

"Good grief, has it already begun?"

He looked at me, "Good morning to you, too, Sunshine."

"I'm sorry, Alex, but I don't agree with whatever Micah told you. I don't mind spending time with you. It will hurt our friendship, however, if I start to feel trapped."

He lowered his magazine and crossed his legs. "Ok. How about we just take this one hour at a time and see where it goes?"

I just looked at him.

"Come on, we'll start with breakfast." He stood, holding out his elbow for me. At least I didn't have to worry about morning breath around this one.

Halfway through a bowl of cereal I asked, "Has everyone left already?"

"Micah has. He went early to make sure there was a boat ready. Susan and Cato leave shortly. Cato wants to see you first."

"What for?"

He shrugged his shoulders, looking down. "Truthfully I've been trying to avoid him lately."

I put my hand over his. "I'm finished. Why don't you stay here while I hunt him down? He's probably in the library. I'll come right back here when I'm done." I made an invisible cross over my heart. "Promise."

Walking toward the library, I realized I would follow Micah's rules not because he asked me to, but because Alex needed me as much as I needed him, maybe more.

It could be worse, I thought. *I could be handcuffed to the toilet right now.*

I found Cato in his library, where he usually was. He regarded me with cool, calculating eyes. There was no sign of his usual warm gestures. I had no idea what brought on the change, but perhaps it was a good thing he was leaving for however long.

"You wanted to see me?"

"Yes. Follow me." He led me to one of the deepest corners of the library. "This section contains a lot of my personal notes on each of the Gaias we have had. We'll need you as knowledgeable, as strong, as possible. While we're gone, you should take some time and study these notes."

I peered closer at the scribbles on the spines of the ledgers and notepads. They appeared to be in chronological order, dating from, "1853?"

"Some of them were passed down from my predecessors."

I looked back, arms crossed. "Ok, I'll take a look. Thank you for showing them to me."

"Yes, well – they belong to all of us, really." He moved to another part of the room. "Over here are my notes on discovered 'hot-spots' around the world. It includes energy depleting areas as well as areas that intensify the energy. I though you could expand on my research there, look for patterns." He silently regarded his stacks of books and notes. I couldn't tell if he was avoiding looking at me or just lost in thought.

"What is the matter, Cato?" I blurted out before I could stop myself.

He let out a sigh and rubbed his temples. "Kaitlyn, you have to understand – up until a year ago everything was just as it should be. Then you came, and well, everything has turned upside down. I've lost Shawn, Micah is distracted, and no one is focused."

"You don't think Shawn would have done this even if I hadn't come along?"

"There is no telling what he would have done. He's no longer the son I thought I knew."

"And you aren't the Cato I thought I knew." I fixed him with my own cold stare. "What did you and Alex do yesterday to that worker?"

He crossed his arms. "We did what we had to in order to get the information we needed. It was no less than what we've done in the past."

I nodded my head, recognizing what kind of leader we truly operated under. "Maybe, Cato. Just maybe, your world has been upside down all along and it is just now righting itself." I left him. There was nothing more to say.

Alex was still waiting in the kitchen, taking advantage of my absence to finish off the last of our only package of toffee-nut cookies.

I offered a small smile. "I know you are going to save me one."

Before he could answer, Susan stood up from behind a counter where I hadn't seen her, "He won't, but I will." She snatched the last cookie out of his hand, stuck her tongue out at him, and surrendered the cookie to me.

"Aw, that's just not right," he complained. "I've got the worst sweet tooth today."

"And I'm eating for two over here," I said.

Susan held up my hand in triumph. "After one round, the winner by decision is Kaitlyn 'The Pregnant Gaia' Alder." She turned to look at me. "I'd put a victory belt around you but I don't think it would fit."

"Maybe she should lay off the cookies, then." Alex pouted.

We both stuck our tongues out at him. Susan put her arm around me and directed me a little way from Alex. "I have something for you." She handed me a notebook from the counter. "I have a friend who is sort of an expert in the dreaming world – she sends me advice and notes every now and then; all of which I keep in here. Micah thought you could use this while he was gone."

She flipped through the pages and stopped halfway through the book. "This may be of particular use to you."

I read the title, *Spell to Give Someone a Dream.*

"If you have a dream foretelling what Shawn might do or where he is, you can send it to Micah. Also, Alex knows how to get in touch with us using secure communications."

I closed the notebook and tucked it under my arm. "Thanks – I'll add it to the list of homework everyone else has given me to do while you are gone. How long will you be away?"

"We don't know – we hope to make it back before the baby is born."

I looked at her, and my jaw dropped thinking it might take that long. "You have to be back by then. I don't think I could do something like that by myself." Susan's presence truly would be missed during labor, even more so than Micah's.

She placed a reassuring hand on my arm. "We will do our best, Kaitlyn. In the meantime, stay safe. I mean it. I don't want to be left picking up the pieces of my brother."

"Okay." I looked down, suddenly finding myself fight back tears. I laughed nervously while I wiped them away. "I don't know why I'm crying."

She wrapped her arms around me, hugging tightly. "You've been through a lot lately. We all have. You are strong, Kaitlyn, and we can beat this. We can beat him."

I hugged her back, afraid, both for her and me. "Come back – all of you. Except maybe Cato. I could take him or leave him at this point."

It was her turn for a nervous laugh. We stood a few more moments comforting each other until she released me to say goodbye to Alex. Even across the kitchen I could see the awkward tension in their hug. I made a mental note to tease him about it later.

Susan's departure seemed to leave us at a loss. Alex and I looked at each other.

"What now?" I asked.

He pulled something from behind an oversized package of dates no one ever seemed to touch. "Now, we dive into that stash of toffee-nut cookies I hid—"

"You snake!"

"And I can give you a tour of some of the Chakra you have never seen," he finished, seemingly unperturbed by my name calling.

Chapter 19

With Pleasure

"And this is my room." Alex brushed cookie crumbs from his mouth. He remained in the doorway while I walked around, taking in my new sleeping arrangements.

"Small," I commented.

"Us non-magical types are low man on the totem pole around here. At least I'm not forced to have a roommate like most the others. Well, not until now anyway." He cleared his throat. "But I've always wanted a bunk bed. Now, thanks to you, I get one!" He took a running start and made a massive leap, "I get top bunk!"

"Glad I'm not a total inconvenience." I snorted at the apparently ten-year-old man with whom I was supposed to spend my nights. My eyes scanned the rest of the room. It was a little messy but no more than mine, and no foul odors crept in from the dark corners. It would do. I walked over to his shelves, eyeing bits and pieces of radio parts. "Bringing your work home with you?"

"Eh." He shrugged his shoulders from his perch. "I like tinkering around with communications equipment. I was a radio-man in the military you know."

"You were in the—" my line of questioning was interrupted by the most beautiful sight I had encountered in a long time. "A Nikon D3X!? You've been holding out on me." I picked up the top of the line camera carefully, treating it like gold. It practically was. The camera alone ran around $8,000, not counting the array of lenses, flashes, and filters he had laid out next to it.

"You know your cameras." He jumped down from the bed, taking a renewed interest in me.

"Well, yeah. I'm a photographer, or was anyway. I'm partial to Cannons, mainly because of price, but any digital SLR will do."

"Oh, Katie - this isn't just any SLR. It is 138 megabytes of 14 bit image files with a 24.5—"

"Megapixel format," I finished his sentence for him. "Like I said, I am a photographer. I know the industry equipment."

"Then you know it's not the cost of the equipment that counts, but how you use it." He slipped the camera strap around my neck.

"Are you serious?"

"You got something better to do?"

"I guess the rest of the tour could wait…" I stared at the camera.

"Then it's settled. Come on – there's nature out there that needs to be photographed."

We spent the rest of the day in the gardens, Alex giving me complete use of what I thought should be his most prized possession. I loved seeing the world through the cameras lens. It distanced me, somehow. Made me feel like I was merely a witness, instead of deeply involved – a nice change. I hadn't realized how much I'd missed it. I clicked away, able to capture all the beauty and magic nature had to offer in one mystical moment – to be halted for all time. When we got hungry, and had exhausted our cookie supply, I was too reluctant to leave my long lost passion behind so we satisfied ourselves with offerings from the fruit trees and continued on our, or my, photographic journey. I only forced myself indoors once twilight approached and the camera's battery was running low. Over dinner, in between awkward silences when other workers of the Chakra came in and then quickly left the kitchen after seeing me, I couldn't stop babbling about the day.

Alex seemed just as delighted to have someone to share his hobby with. "Tomorrow, I'll show you my darkroom."

"Get out! You have a darkroom?"

He nodded, "For my film cameras. I can't exactly run to a photo center down the block to print my images. Once I became a more permanent part of the family here Cato gave me a lot of space for what I said was necessary for my work. It is one advantage of being a techie, no one knows exactly what you need; they just go along with it."

The day had gone by faster than the Nikon's high-tech flash. I yawned and looked out the window, the corners of my mouth turning down as I realized it had grown pitch black. Days without Micah might be bearable, but sleep would still be hell when nightmares plagued me.

"What's the matter?" Alex asked.

"It's getting dark."

He raised his eyebrow, "And?"

I shrugged, "I get nightmares. Micah can help me avoid them, but now that he is gone…" I let my words trail off.

"What are you going to do? You can't just not sleep."

"Can't I?"

He paused, thinking. "What about the notebook Susan gave you?"

It was still sitting on the kitchen counter, where I left it. "I haven't had a chance to read it."

"There is no time like the present."

"Fine." I picked up the book and flipped through while Alex hunted down dessert, as if we hadn't been eating cookies all day. There were some notes in Susan's handwriting but the it also contained mailed letters from her friend and printed e-mails or cut outs of various magazine and newspaper articles. There were dream protection spells, instructions on how to make magical dream catchers and dream pillows, as well as spells for peaceful sleep.

I stopped on the short section that clumped together information about dream catchers. They were Native American in theory, but if I combined that by blessing the dream catcher with spells it just might work. "I'm going to need some things."

"Like what?"

"Thread, a metal ring, beads, and feathers."

"Easy enough. Except maybe the feathers."

"What about that owl's nest we saw today? There might be some feathers around the ground by that."

"You're not going to make me walk all the way back out there, are you?" Alex whined.

"No. I'm going to make you get me a flashlight so I can walk out there. You don't have to come."

Alex groaned again. "Micah would kill us both if I let you go traipsing around in the dark alone. I'll go get the flashlights."

Fifteen minutes later we were just below the owls nest. I could hear hooting in the distance. We found four feathers on the ground without too much trouble. I had my pick of those that were particularly ornate. On our way back, we passed the trail to the large boulder and I had an idea.

"Follow me," I called over my shoulder to Alex. He let out another grunt of disproval. Entering the cleared circle, I tried suppressing any bad memories and concentrated on my task. I got on my hands and knees, scanning the ground for bits of the lightening-shattered boulder to use instead of beads in my dream catcher. I wasn't finding any.

My knees stung. I hissed, "Who broke a bunch of glass here?"

Alex bent down to examine the ground next to me. "That's what happens when lightning hits rock – it melts and fuses the grains of the rock together. Fuller... fulg... fulgurite is what it's called."

I picked one up and examined it. It looked more like a root; hollow in places. Perfect for stringing them together. I grabbed a handful and we made our way back to the building, Alex thoroughly annoyed. He collected the rest of the supplies I needed while I retrieved some personal belongings from my room. I was about to pile my large comforter and more pillows in my arms until I thought better of it and stopped by Micah's room for them instead. No matter how angry I was with him I'd still find peace enveloped by his scent.

Alex set up a reading lamp for each bunk. In my cove, surrounded by Micah's blankets and pillows I weaved the dream catcher together while above Alex flipped through Susan's book.

Once the dream catcher was put together, complete with owl feathers and lightning rocks, I studied it and let out a dissatisfied sigh.

"What is it?" Alex hung his head over the side of the bed.

"Well doesn't it say it needs a charm or something in the middle? Something to act as the final filter?"

His head retreated and I heard him flipping through the pages. "Not exactly a physical charm, per say." He read the notes verbatim, "*As a final touch to your dream catcher, adorn it with a keepsake-like entity, either physical or spiritual in form.*"

My hand immediately went to my neck, wishing I still had the butterfly necklace. Alex peered over the side once again, helping me think. "What about the baby?"

"Huh?" I didn't make the connection.

"It's always with you and I can't think of a better, or more reliable, lucky charm."

My face brightened. "You know, for a non-magical type you're pretty good with this stuff."

Alex found a spell for me in the book, and I ad-libbed a little along the way:

During the mercy of the shadowcast
My eyes will close but remain open inside
Fear and danger surpassed
Enemy's intentions denied
To the Goddess of dreams, I pray that you
Bind my baby to my spirit and this catcher of dreams
And protect my soul while I slumber.

I rested the dream catcher against my belly as I said the chant two more times. I opened my eyes to find Alex staring at me, a wide grin on his face.

"What? Cheesier spells have worked for me in the past." I hung the dream catcher up above my head and rolled over, out of eyesight of his teasing stare. I tried changing the subject, "Are you going to spend all night reading that notebook?"

Finally, I heard him roll over and turn off his light. "I don't mind holding on to it; it smells like Susan." I heard the loud slap of his hand covering his mouth.

I shot up, nearly hitting my head on the top bunk. "You like her!"

"I wouldn't say it like *that*."

"You looove her!"

"Let's just say we've had our moments. Besides, it's not like there is a whole lot of choice around here."

"Oh, please. You get out often enough."

Alex didn't respond.

"Alex and Susan, sitting in a tree…"

"Kaitlyn…"

"K-I-S-S-I-N-G," I sang very softly.

"Kaitlyn!"

"First comes love, then comes marriage, then comes the baby in the baby carriage."

"Not always exactly in that order," he leaned over the edge of his bed to rub my belly, "Buddha, Buddha, Buddha!"

"Asshole!" I hit his face hard with one of my pillows.

He grabbed onto the pillow and caressed it with his face, "Hmmm, smells like Micah."

I took the pillow back and stuffed it behind me. "Give me back my Micah and go bury your nose in your Susan."

"With pleasure, Kaitlyn. With pleasure."

Chapter 20

Set and Match

The next week with Alex went smoothly. The empty feeling in my gut due to Micah's absence began to subside, for which I gave much credit to Alex. He kept me busy. It was better for both of us that way. In our down time I saw the shadows of pain and remorse creep into his face. He would start to flinch and jerk as painful memories surfaced. Then, suddenly, he'd jump up and announce another project for us to do. If not, I was more than ready to do it for him.

We quickly settled into a routine. In the mornings, Alex put me through a training routine similar to what I did with him before; exercise, various weapons training as well as martial arts. The only difference this time around was the doctor insisted on being present and stepped in when he thought the moves were too dangerous for a pregnant woman. In truth I was grateful, I didn't necessarily look forward to being thrown around on the hard floor or lifting heavy things. I was getting lazy in my old age.

We spent our afternoons playing with the camera or experimenting in the darkroom. If there was time left before dinner we retreated to Cato's library so I could research each of the subject areas suggested by Cato, Micah, and Susan. Alex always stayed close by, usually tinkering with his radios or some other type of equipment. Evenings were reserved for playtime; listening to music, playing card games, or going for walks were our usual modus operandi (a phrase often used by Alex).

We stayed up late each night, ensuring that by the time we went to bed we would be tired enough to fall asleep fast. It was a dangerous time of the day for us both, left in the dark with nothing but our own thoughts. My dream catcher was working, and thanks to my spell I often dreamt of my daughter. Sometimes she was a baby, but it was more fun to dream of her as a fully grown woman. Her face always changed; she looked like my mother, my grandmother, or even Susan.

But one new, somewhat unsettling aspect to my dreams occurred almost nightly. My dreams would vibrate, hum from some outside force. The vibrations started small, but each night they grew more intense. I knew it was Shawn, trying to force his way in. One of these nights he would succeed. I tried re-blessing the dream catcher, but Shawn was slowly feeling his way around my guards, prodding their weaknesses.

I spent more and more time in the afternoons in the library, anxiously studying the sleep cycle and dream phenomenon, hoping to be able to hold my own when Shawn finally did break through. Thumbing through pages of books related to symbolism, I came across a few detailing the purpose and uses of the athame. Intrigued with the idea of using Shawn's own weapon against him, I piled the books into my arms and plopped down at the base of the large tree in the library where Alex had a blanket spread out with various radio parts strewn all over.

"Make some room, will ya?" I frowned, pulling out a sharp, metal object from underneath me.

"Oh, Kaitlyn," Alex retorted while patting my belly. "The Chakra isn't large enough to make room for you."

I picked out the heaviest book I could find and bopped him on the head with it.

"Ow! What is this anyway?" He snatched the book from my hands and read the cover, "*Symbolism of Ritual Tools.*"

I took the book back. "Yeah, and any more remarks like that from you and I'll make a symbol out of you."

He gave me a look of disapproval. "You can do better than that."

I grumbled something about the lack of caffeine in my diet and buried my face in the large book, trying to ignore him. I opened it to the first chapter.

Whenever an athame is used in a ritual or spell, part of the energy wielded is absorbed into the handle through the blade. Thus, the athame slowly accumulates power, strengthening both itself and its owner. It is normally used to direct energy, command spirits and to make symbolic divisions.

The athame, along with the wand, are tools that mostly wield male energy as well as the element of air. In fact, the two are often interchangeable although the wand is used to manifest change on the physical plane while the athame is used to manifest change on the higher or spiritual planes. These two realms can be interrelated.

I pictured Shawn and Vayu side by side on a battlefield. Shawn with his athame, Vayu with his wand; an unstoppable team covering all of the dimensions. Other books contained instructions on how to use an athame, how to purify it, and how to absorb the energy from it.

Alex poked his head between the book and me. "What'ya reading?"

I quickly slammed the book shut. I didn't want him to know just yet what my plans were. He certainly wouldn't agree. The subject had to be brought up delicately. "Nothing." I looked around for a distraction. "You have your little radio put together?"

"I'll have you know my *little radio*, as you so affectionately put it, is an HF, frequency-hopping, encrypted communications systems."

Distraction achieved.

"Meaning...?"

"Meaning that you can talk to Micah, even if he is thousands of miles away and it will be completely secure. More secure than our satellite communications anyway. Shawn might still have access to our satellite and even though he might not be able to decrypt it, we don't want to take any chances." He handed me the handset. "Want to try?"

"Oh, um. Not right now. Can we maybe try tomorrow?" I wasn't prepared for a conversation with Micah yet. Knowing him, he'd be able to tell I was hiding things from him just by the tone of my voice.

"Sure." He shrugged his shoulders and replaced the handset, face disappointed; maybe he was hoping to talk to Susan.

There was a momentary silence, and my eyes scanned his radio. Military classification markings were stamped on most of the parts. "Where did you get that anyway?"

"You'd be amazed at how much stuff you can walk away from the military with. Especially if you are the corporal in charge of the gear."

"Okay, corporal. What else did you walk away with?"

Alex's eyes lit up in a smirk. "Come on, I'll show you."

He led me back to the long hall of basement rooms. Some doors had security locks, others stood wide open.

He stopped at one particularly heavy steel door, punched in a code, and pushed it open. My eyes went wide. The room was packed full of more radios and their various parts, but also had gas masks, batteries, all kinds of guns and ammunition, military uniforms, scuba gear and more. "Tell me you didn't steal all of this!"

"No, only a few things. The rest I got at military surplus stores and gun shops." Alex puttered around the room, pulling out and displaying his most prized possessions. "Some things might have been acquired by less than legal means. Cato has a few nefarious connections."

"Now that, I believe." Legal or not, there was some comfort in knowing we had a small arsenal a few floors under us.

We exited the room and as he punched in the code to activate the lock, I looked at some of the other doors. "What are all these other rooms?"

"Everyone has a personal lab." He pointed as we walked past. "Susan's room. She does experiments and testing with water in there. She keeps it locked saying it protects the validity of her experiments. Micah's room. Never been used. And this is Vayu's room. He didn't ever lock it. Want to check it out?"

Alex pushed open the door, not waiting for my answer, and flipped on the lights. Mostly the room was filled with pamphlets; half of them packed away in boxes. I picked one up and began leafing through it while Alex looked at a series of papers on a clipboard.

"Looks like advertisements on how individuals can decrease air pollution." I began to read some of the hints and tips aloud skipping over the details, "Participate in utility energy conservation programs, choose products that say 'low VOC', buy local produce... it says here that driving with your air conditioner on increases fuel consumption, but only at lower speeds. Windows down at high speeds makes A/C a better option, fuel-wise. Did Vayu put all this together himself?"

Alex nodded yes. "Some of our Elementals choose to advocate their cause to politicians and environmental organizations. Others aim their efforts at the general population. Looks like Vayu was getting this all ready to ship out. He has mailing labels, packing lists, and everything is already postmarked."

I picked up another brochure that talked about decreasing air pollutants inside homes by using certain plants. *NASA recommends 15 samples of a variety of plants for a house under 2,000 square feet to improve the air quality. Some of the best plants for this include aloe vera, English ivy, fig trees, spider plants, bamboo, lilies, pot mums, daisies, and mother-in-law's tongue.* "I think we should finish the job for him."

Alex thought for a moment then agreed, "I don't see the harm in it. Besides, what else is there to do?"

We both knew the real reason; night was coming. We'd put off sleep as long as we could. We got to work following Vayu's packing lists. The boxes were heading out to health clinics, schools, libraries, and localized environmental advocates. Vayu's organization made it easy and we were done in a matter of two hours.

As Alex taped up the last box, I mention, "Tomorrow is Sunday."

"So?"

"So, I thought maybe we could take a break from our usual routine and try something different." I traced my finger around one of the shipping labels, trying to look as casual as possible.

He frowned. "Tomorrow's supposed to be the obstacle course. The doctor and I made a few adjustments to accommodate mommy-to-be."

"Push it back a day."

He crossed his arms over his chest and looked at me with narrowed eyes. "What did you have in mind for tomorrow, exactly?"

"I came across some spells I want to try, but I need you there in case something goes wrong."

"Kaitlyn, if something has the potential of going wrong then we shouldn't do it."

"Oh, you mean like the rope swing? Or the wall climb? Or are you talking about the stairway to heaven? Belay and safety nets or not, you can't deny something could possibly go wrong with those."

He hung his head in defeat. "Point taken."

"Good. There is something I'll need; maybe you know where it is."

"What?"

"Shawn's athame."

"Oh, no." He shook his head. "We are *not* messing with that thing. I saw what happened last time and you weren't even touching it."

"That's just because I wasn't prepared. And I wasn't the wielder. It wouldn't do that if I controlled it."

"Micah would have both our heads."

"Micah doesn't have to know. Besides, he isn't here to help me and I can feel Shawn getting closer and closer. That athame has powers. I need that power to protect myself. I need to be one step ahead of him."

Alex rubbed his chin, "And if I don't help?"

"Then I tear this house apart, one brick at a time until I find the damn thing."

He sighed. "Ugh, fine. Come on, Stubborn McGee."

Set one goes to Kaitlyn.

Leading me to the living room, Alex started inspecting the paneling on an otherwise bare wall. "There is a small notch in here somewhere – if I can just remember where it is..." He searched for a few seconds. "Ah-ha!" He pushed on part of the wall and a giant section opened outward. A large steel door appeared when he pulled away the paneling. He typed a code on a keypad, and the door swung outward to reveal a room about the same size as mine. I stepped in. The shelves on the walls were lined with non-perishable foods and first aid equipment.

"What is this?"

"It's a panic room." Alex began rooting around for something on the floor.

"And no one thought this would be a good thing for me to know?"

He shrugged his shoulders as he prodded along the floor. "Micah thinks if we're under attack by someone using elemental powers, a panic room could be more of a trap. Ah, here it is." I heard a quiet *pop* and a small compartment in the floor opened up. He pulled out a large, folded white blanket. "If we are going to do this, we do this my way."

"Fine." *Set two to Alex.*

He put the wrapped athame aside and started to close the door.

"Wait, what else do you have hidden in here?" Sitting in the compartment was Shawn's document which found its way to me via human sacrifice. I shuddered as I picked it up, remembering the not-so-good times Australia had to offer, then set it aside. I began pawing through the other contents of the safe. It had a few stacks of hundred dollar bills, traveler's checks and other denominations from various countries. Shuffling the money aside, several manila envelopes, each marked with names of the team members, came into view. I pulled out Micah's envelope and dumped the contents on the floor. Passports in different names from different countries, as well as several birth certificates and other identifying documents, scattered.

"Which is his real one?" I asked Alex, holding up three birth certificates.

"This one." He pointed to one of them.

I turned it over to read, pursing my lips. "Texas. Never would have pegged him as a cowboy."

Next, I took out Cato's envelope. He had the same assortment of documents in his, plus a few pictures. I slid them out. Cato was easily identifiable, even as a younger man, with his striking blue eyes. One picture was taken in front of the Chakra with Cato and a small boy about the age of five or so. I felt a small chill run through me as I studied Shawn as a boy. Even then he didn't look so innocent. "How old was Shawn when Cato adopted him?"

Alex leaned over to look at the picture. "I don't know." He went silent as the resemblance between the two struck him. He argued aloud with himself, which only went further to verify the assumption. "But we were all adopted. Cato didn't have any children of his own."

I flipped to the next picture, "Or so you thought."

Young Cato stood next to a hospital bed alongside a woman and newborn child.

"No…." Alex muttered, without much confidence at all.

"Look here –a birth certificate with Cato as the father. Micah just has adoption papers with Cato's name."

Alex seemed stunned into silence.

Set and match to Cato.

Alex kept the athame with him as we locked the panic room; I kept Shawn's birth certificate.

Chapter 21

Whatever Momma Wants

She opened her eyes, and gasped at what she saw. Never before had she witnessed such beauty. The world before her was pristine. A clear, blue sky reigned over rolling green hills. Pink flowers dominated the valleys, and large trees flourished, stretching up into the sky. The sun, bright and intense, glimmered over everything.

On top of her hill, she could command what part of the world was brought before her. She saw the mountains, with clear blue waterfalls and streams. She inhaled the fresh scent of pine, and reveled in the animals frolicking on the stony landscape. She saw large cities around the world. Structures of steel replaced by planted trees, and those left standing covered in vines and flowers.

She smiled, proud because she knew this accomplishment was partly hers to claim. Someone squeezed her hand. She looked beside her, and saw Shawn standing there, with the same proud smile on his face. She flinched, but his hand on hers was steady and warm.

She studied him as he studied the landscape. His eyes were a bright blue that matched the sky, framed by long lashes. She had never noticed his eyelashes before. His face was tanned and smooth, free from imperfections. He had a strong, square jaw, and when he smiled, his teeth showed two rows of perfect, gleaming white teeth.

The world continued to move before them in vibrant colors, blanketed by clear, fresh air, and adorned by pristine flowing waters. The pair of them stood on top of the hill, admiring their kingdom. Shawn turned and motioned for her to look behind them. She did.

The valley behind them was filled with dead bodies, many half burnt. The stink of scorched human flesh filled her nostrils. The blood ran bright, just as vibrant as the red leaves in the mountain trees. Dead mothers clutched their children, frozen stiff in the terror of their last moment. Severed body parts littered the mass grave, which had no ending in site. She looked left and right, far out in front of her, and the bodies just continued.

"Our gift to the world." Shawn said, squeezing her hand tightly.

She smiled. "It's beautiful, Shawn."

* * *

I woke up, sweating, with Alex leaning over me. From the sting on my cheek I was almost positive he had slapped me.

"Are you ok? Kaitlyn! Can you hear me?" he yelled.

"Yes, yes. The whole damn Chakra can hear you." I propped myself up and rubbed my cheek.

The smell of something burning was still with me. I turned to look at the headboard behind me, "Oh my God." The dream catcher was singed. All the twine blackened or gone, the falagmite had fallen and was scattered around my bed. Nothing but stem was left of the owl feathers.

My heart started to pound. "The baby was tied to this. Get the doctor, quick! I need to check on her!"

Alex raced out the door and down the hall to the doctor's room. I made my way to the lab. Shielding my eyes from the fluorescent lights, I stumbled around, hands in front of me, turning on every machine I came across. The room whirred to life.

Alex pushed the doctor into the lab, making the man stumble as he rubbed the sleep from his eyes.

The doctor blinked, looking at me. "What happened?"

"I need you to check on the baby. Heartbeat, size, and do another ultrasound. I need to see her."

I was starting to hyperventilate. Why would I do something so stupid? Binding the baby to something that was under constant attack?

"Oh, God." I slumped to the floor, hugging my knees.

"Calm down, Kaitlyn." The doctor pulled me upright and led me to his table. "Lay down and take deep breaths. Alex – come hold her hand while I prep."

Alex loomed over me, his familiar face helped ground me. "I'm sorry, Kaitlyn. It was my suggestion to use the baby. I shouldn't have said it."

I shook my head. "We were both being stupid. I have a long way to go before I hit my stride as a mother." I looked at the doctor. "What's taking so long?"

He turned from where he stood at the sink washing his hands to glare at me. He dried his hands, slowly, then pushed the ultrasound machine toward the table, turning off a variety of machines I turned on in my panic, including a blender. "I don't think we'll be needing this today."

After a thorough examination, the doctor announced everything was fine. The baby kicked hard, right into my kidney as if to agree. I rubbed my belly. "I'm sorry, Peanut. No more adventures for you. From now on we play it nice and safe."

I looked at Alex with one eyebrow raised, forcing a nod of agreement out of him. The doctor gave us both something close to a glare, excusing himself for the night.

"What time is it?" I squinted at a clock hanging high on the wall on the other side of the room.

"Four-thirty."

I shook my head. "I can't go back to sleep. That was too close."

"I know. Do you wanna try contacting Micah? Susan said you may want to send him your dreams."

"Maybe." I looked down, playing with the hem of my nightgown. "I'm not sure if I want to share this one. I don't know what good it would do."

"Well, let's go get some breakfast and think about it."

"Pancakes and hash browns?" My eyes lit up.

He laughed. "Whatever momma wants momma gets."

By dawn, we had decided on completing the athame absorption right away, without contacting Micah. I felt a little guilty, letting almost a month go by without speaking to him even though I had the means. Alex checked in with them occasionally but I always found a convenient excuse to avoid being present.

We seated ourselves in the living room, clearing a large space of furniture. The doctor sat on one side of the room, as Alex insisted he be present. He had me tethered to his equipment in order to monitor the baby's heartbeat, my pulse, and my blood pressure. It was all very high tech compared to the equipment I brought; a bowl of salt, a bowl of water, incense, and a candle.

"Okay." Alex laid the rolled-up blanket out in front of us. "Let's just take this one small step at a time."

I could see the doctor lean forward anxiously out of the corner of my eyes and I huffed in annoyance.

Alex slowly unrolled the blanket revealing Shawn's athame. I held my breath, waiting for the icy chill, but nothing happened. I studied it closer. It looked older than I thought; aged well past Shawn's years. Spots on the black handle were worn thin enough to reveal the wood underneath.

Satisfied that we were as prepared as we were going to get, at least without any boy scouts present, Alex handed me the knife, handle first. I gripped it, squeezing tight, hoping to exude a sense of control.

I chanted a spell I found in one of the books, "I consecrate you, my athame, with Earth, that you may provide me with the protection of the Great Mother." I waved the knife over the dish of salt three times.

"I consecrate you, my athame, with Air that you may provide me with knowledge of infinite places." Next I waved it through the incense smoke three times.

"I consecrate you, my athame, with Fire, so that I may be empowered with the strength of the Fire that burns in the core of the Earth." I passed the athame over the lit candle three times.

"I consecrate you, my athame, with Water so that understanding and wisdom of great mysteries will be mine." I passed the athame three times over the bowl of water.

I finished the ceremony, declaring, "I consecrate this athame with Spirit so it may hold my magical energy."

Everyone in the room grew silent. I raised my eyebrows at Alex as if to ask him if he were ready. He nodded his head once. With as much strength and force as I could muster, I thrust the knife upward into the air and cried out, "Now share with me your magical energy!" The knife quivered in my hand. I touched the flat side of the blade to my forehead and nose.

My body fell forward into Alex's arms, unconscious. Another part of me fell backwards, and didn't stop at the floor. I kept falling back until the light from above disappeared and was replaced by a cavernous black of nothing but empty space. I flailed my arms and legs, trying to slow my fall. Nothing seemed to work, I couldn't even call upon the elements. It was as though they couldn't hear me. I fell until I lost track of time. It wasn't until I had accepted my fate and even embraced it by forcing my body into a dive, willing myself to take control simply by letting go, that a deep pool of crystal clear water rushed up to meet me.

I began my frantic swim and broke the surface, gasping. I tried to take in my surroundings, my efforts impeded by the splashing and loud conversations of a multitude of women surrounding me. They weren't human, more like balls of gas.

They were fighting, each jockeying for position on a flight of stairs carved into the side of the cave. I followed the stairs up and saw a small platform at the top, jutting out over the pool. One woman in her full physical form stood there alone. Strength and energy emanated from her in waves, shrouding her in a misty gold smoke. When I concentrated, I could actually hear her having a conversation with Alex. She constantly struggled to maintain her position on the ledge, fighting back the other women. Finally, she was overpowered and thrown from the ledge. She came splashing down in the water dangerously close to me. She resurfaced and joined the fight on the stairs once again, this time at the bottom.

The next closest to the ledge took her position. I closed my eyes, concentrating on my physical body. This one didn't bother to talk. Instead, she ran, fleeing from Alex. Last time I ran from Alex we both ended up in an icy lake. I needed to get my body back before something bad happened.

The shift of consciousness sparked a mad frenzy. Women saw their chance to be heard, to be real once again. I was shoved back down into the water amidst the struggle, pushed deeper and deeper until I thought there was no hope for return. Underneath, there were more gaseous forms. I swam over to a clear spot against the cave wall, taking a position next to one of the gaseous forms. Her face emerged, smiling. Next a hand formed and she reached out for mine. The physical connection joined us mentally.

I need air, I conveyed to her desperately.

No, she sent back. *Breathe in, your body will remember*.

I frowned, but had no choice; the bodies above me were thick, impossible to fight through.

Giving into the fall helped, I told myself. *Maybe this is no different.* I closed my eyes and took a deep breath. I panicked at the water rushing into my body. After a moment of painful squeezing, my lungs contracted, then relaxed. The being next to me communicated again. *This is your body. Should you will it, you can have control once again. Encourage the cave to work with you. It will give you an advantage over all else.*

I nodded my head.

Wait. She squeezed my hand tighter. *Take my knowledge with you.*

My body tingled with energy, starting at my hand and moving through my veins. She was a former Elemental, her specialty wind and air just like Vayu. I looked around and it dawned on me. They were all Elementals or Gaias, probably those who had been touched by the knife. She released my hand and I felt the knowledge of air manipulation course through my brain as if it had been there all along.

I bowed my head to thank her, then swam to the surface, scaling the cave wall as I went. My lungs shifted back to breathing air with ease. When I surfaced, I had to duck back under to avoid a fireball. Each of the four elements raged throughout the cave. There was no way I was going to fight my way up the stairs, battling all those elements at once. I needed a different route; one that could approach the ledge undetected. I felt the cave wall shiver slightly, and a small grip emerged. I looked around but no one else seemed to notice. As soon as I grasped it another grip emerged a few feet above. I learned quickly, directing where each one was created. I went as fast as a pregnant rock climber could, before anyone noticed. They were all so focused on the stairs and the ledge it didn't seem to matter.

I made my way to a lip jutting out from the cave wall I hoisted myself onto it in order to plan out my next move. Hoisting myself up, I stood at the entrance to a large hole. I peered in. Something shimmered, as if a gaseous form was retreating further back, out of my sight. My gut told me to leave it alone. I backed away, and almost fell off the lip.

After steadying myself, I turned to face my goal. The ledge over which everyone fought was level with me, but still too far away to jump. I had to make this part quick; no mistakes. I put my hand against the wall, communicating my desire to the cave. A long but thin ridge emerged, all the way to just above my goal. I began to run, relying on the cave to give me more room on the ridge when I needed it. As I passed over it, the ridge behind me cracked apart and splashed into the water. My movements and the splashing was attracting attention. Faces emerged, watching me. The woman on the ledge was still focused on running from Alex.

Once close enough, I planted one foot and took a diving leap at her. I knocked her off with such force that I almost went over myself. I turned, scrambling to get a grip on the slick ledge. The women on the stairs stilled in a moment of shock, then came to life as soon as they realized I was at a disadvantage. I stopped my frantic clawing and closed my eyes, concentrating. A wall shot up all around the ledge, effectively blocking them out and throwing me just inside it. Once the wall was tall enough to give me peace of mind, I lifted my arms into the air. A blinding light greeted me, raising me up to join my consciousness with my physical body once again.

"Esther, listen to me. I'm not going to hurt you – I'm here to help." Alex was on top of me, pinning me down with his weight.

"Alex, get off of me."

He opened his eyes in surprise, then narrowed them as if he didn't fully trust me. "Kaitlyn?"

"Yes, it's me. Why are you talking to me like I'm a child?"

He hoisted himself up, then me, not quite releasing his grasp on my wrist. "Esther is a child, or was, from what I could gather. Probably one of the youngest Elementals we've ever had."

"You knew her?"

"No, I think she was from somewhere in the 1800s, before electricity was invented. The lights inside the house scared her. Are you okay? What happened? Did you absorb the knife's energy?" Alex wasn't waiting for me to answer any of his questions.

I brushed myself off and looked around. We were somewhere in the gardens. "Kind of. The knife holds knowledge and the essence of each woman it has touched. I think I absorbed them, but their information still has to be shared willingly."

"So now you have a bunch of women trapped inside of you?" His forehead crinkled with confusion.

"As long as the knife is close, I should be able to access them. Which way is home?"

Alex pointed in one direction and I started walking. He followed.

"So why exactly are you suddenly inflicted with Multiple Personality Disorder?"

"I believe the PC term is Dissociative Identity Disorder."

He rolled his eyes.

I continued, "It seems as though some of these personalities are anxious to have control; which makes sense seeing as how the athame represents strength, action and consciousness – or so the books say." I stopped suddenly, causing Alex to bump into me. "Why women?"

"What?" He frowned.

"Why were there only women? The knife obviously touched Vayu, and probably other men as well." I started to walk again, the Chakra now in sight.

Alex offered and answer first, "Maybe the athame, being a male symbol, only absorbs female power. It could be its natural way of balancing itself out as you all claim the world does."

I turned around and pinched his cheek. "Look at the big brains on Alex."

He leaned back to escape my assault. "Look at the time. I promised Micah *we'd* call in today." With the added emphasis, I got the distinct feeling I wasn't getting out of it this time. I grumbled the rest of the way into the Chakra.

Chapter 22

Kilo-what?

Alex collected his radio equipment, the maps and notes I had been working on, and sat us both in the library. No chances to disappear on him this time. It took him a good ten minutes of fiddling with the radio, trying to connect to the team. Just as I was getting ready to walk, citing the ten minute rule, the radio crackled to life. Cato's voice flooded the library. I swear the books stood up straighter and leaves on the large tree in the center of the room went just a little greener.

"This is Charlie Brown, we read you loud and clear Alpha Dog." I detected a small hint of pride in the code names. No doubt Cato's idea.

"Alpha Dog going secure, stand by." Alex flipped another switch and a series of beeps mixed with static ensued. "Come in, Charlie Brown. Confirm you are secure."

"Affirmative."

Alex relaxed both his posture and his radio etiquette. "Where are you guys?"

Cato replied, "Southern Australia. We are getting some strong reactions to the elements here and have tracked Shawn to a local airport. He was departing but we were unable to find out where."

"We may have some information that can help you. I have Kaitlyn here with me, she's been working hard."

"Welcome, Kaitlyn!" Cato said. "On our unsecure communications, I dub you kilo.... kilo... kilo-something."

"Our call names are matched to our first initials, in the phonetic alphabet. A – Alpha, B – Brave, C – Charlie…" Alex explained as Cato continued to stutter.

"Um…" Cato paused. "Well, let me think on it a bit. Passing the reigns over to the Reich of Mike."

Micah's voice came over the airwaves. He sounded distant, even more so than Cato. "What do you have for us, Kaitlyn?"

I cleared my throat, taking the handset from Alex. "Okay, so I've mapped out known hot spots all over the world and compared them to volcanoes, heat flows, and magnetic strips. Most volcanoes occur on or near hotspots and tend to line up with magnetic strips. Heat flows also follow the course of magnetic strips. There appears to be a correlation between each of these natural phenomena and known energy depleting or energy giving locations. For example, Galapagos, the Chakra, and Yellowstone all sit on top of volcanoes. The Chakra, along with our newly planted forest, and Yellowstone sit over lower than average heat flows while the Galapagos Islands have a higher than average heat flow." I released the handheld and took a breath.

Micah jumped in, "So you think anything that is energy depleting for you and energy giving to Shawn will be in an area with a higher than average heat flow?"

"Right – if you guys are at the southern tip of Australia..." I unfolded my map, "there's a hotspot close with slightly above average heat flows. However, just west of you, smack dab in the middle of the ocean the heat flow gets as high as they can get, *and* there is a hotspot."

"Under an island?"

"Two island sets, as a matter of fact. Both fairly close together." I paused while I flipped through my maps. "One is the French Southern and Antarctic Lands and the other is Heard and McDonald Islands."

"So which one is it?"

I gave an annoyed grunt before clicking the handset back on. "I don't know – this isn't an exact science."

Alex grabbed the handset. "Give us some time to research both and we'll get back to you. In the meantime, this isn't all Kaitlyn has been up to. She has more news."

"What?" Even over the radio, I could detect the suspicion in Micah's voice.

What? Like, what did Kaitlyn do now? Like, she does nothing but screw things up?

I snatched the entire radio and walked away with it. "How about asking how the baby is? Or how I am for that matter? Aren't you a little curious to know, seeing as how you went gallivanting off like a cowboy to protect us – leaving us vulnerable and fending for ourselves?"

In my anger, my body inadvertently brushed against the radio, flipping switches on and off.

Alex jumped up, sticking his face in front of the handset. "Be advised, we are no longer secure! Cease communications. Do you copy?"

"Oh, cease this!" I wove a quick net, wrapping Alex up in a cocoon of wind. I tied off the weaves and he stood there with his arms across his chest, unable to move against the invisible force. Only his hair and the extra skin on his face, rippling against the wind, gave away what held him captive.

Picking up the handset once again, I forced a measure of control into my voice and said, "Don't you dare disconnect."

"Listen to me, Kilo-*watt*," Micah said.

I was too upset to acknowledge his clever way of using the very word that set me off to create my radio call name.

Micah continued, "You forget that Johnnie *Bravo*..."

I did a quick thought process in my head, *Bravo for B – B for baby, ok got it,*

"...and I have a certain connection. I know probably better than you that Bravo is fine. *And* I know you're under constant attack when you sleep. I'm doing my best to help her ward off the attacks. So get off your high horse and give me a little credit here. Now, *what* have you done?"

I glanced at Alex; my wind weaves were holding up surprisingly well. "Nothing."

Alex's eyes went wide. Sooner or later he'd have to be released and would fess up.

I sighed, "I had a dream that might be of help. I'll use a spell to send it to you."

"Right now?" Micah asked.

"I need an hour."

"I'll stand by. Anything else?"

Alex began shouting something about the athame; most of his voice carried off by the wind. Annoyed, I flipped my hand toward the wind cocoon and released the weaves. He slumped down to the floor, but didn't move toward me. He waited patiently for me to break the news myself.

"Not sure if I should say everything over unsecure lines."

"I can fix that." Alex took the radio from me and went through the same procedure. Once Micah verified his end was secure, Alex handed me the handset.

"Here goes nothing." I pushed down the handset switch to activate it and gave my confession as quickly as possible, saying it all in one breath, "I absorbed the athame's power and energy. Now I have a bunch of women inside me trying to claw their way out." I paused. "Sometimes they succeed."

Nothing but dead silence responded.

I hesitated, wondering if we had lost the connection. "Are you there?"

Cato's voice came over the radio. "Yes, we are here. Micah is, well, Micah is still absorbing this new information."

A muffled flurry of curse words came from the background and the handset on the other end was disengaged. Alex and I gave each other a hopeless look. We were both in big trouble.

Alex took the handset, and clicked it on. "I think, in light of all this, it may be time for us to regroup."

"We've had an issue with Susan's passport," Cato sounded less and less happy with his crew. "It will most likely take us a few days to resolve. We are stuck here until then."

"That's ok," Alex said. "We'll figure out which islands we're headed for by then."

"Sounds good. And Alex – no more experiments with Kaitlyn until we are reunited."

"Read you loud and clear." Alex seemed relieved the order was given by Cato, as if I would be any more inclined to obey. "Alpha Dog and Kilowatt out."

He broke the connection before any more drama ensued, and turned to me, "Well, Kaitlyn, looks like we have some work to do. You need to send that dream to Micah, and I'll start researching both islands."

"After lunch?"

He rolled his eyes, "Is nothing more important to you than food?"

"At the moment, no."

Chapter 23

Cause and Effect

I was in the kitchen alone, staring at the athame on the table in front of me. Alex had run off, excited to plan for a trip that would finally take him away from his island prison.

I carefully laid out the same set up I had used for the consecration spell; a bowl of salt, a bowl of water, burning incense, and a lit candle. This time, according to the dream book, I had to be careful to set each element toward their direction of power: salt representing earth sat to the North, incense representing air sat to the East, fire to the South, and water to the West. I crawled onto the table, positioning myself in the middle of the circle of elements.

I relived my nightmare, including every gory detail, hoping Micah may catch some clues that I missed. Shawn had been very clever about the dream. I had no idea what was happening until it was already over. All my research and preparations on dreaming hadn't even mattered. I gasped for air as I reached the end of the dream; sweat dripped down my face. I wiped off with the sleeve of my shirt and started on the spell, "Give me the ability to send forth this dream, across the Earth or water's bound, whether Micah be in the sky or on the ground. By the powers of fire to let it shine bright, by the powers of earth and air to send it tonight, by the powers of water to sweep within dream's door, and by the power of me shall Micah remember it evermore."

I squinted one eye open. He wouldn't receive the dream until he slept again, but surely I should have some inkling that the spell worked.

You're doing it wrong.

I heard the voice as clear as day. When I swiveled my head around scanning the kitchen, no one was there.

"Who is that?" I called.

Silence.

I tried again. *Who is that?*

Come inside and find out.

Now I understood. One of the women had figured out a way to communicate with me. Was it a trap? I considered waiting for Alex in case something went wrong, but then again, he would probably refuse to let me do it in the first place.

A quick in and out, I told myself.

I picked up the athame, closed my eyes, and recreated the sensation of falling back into the cave without moving my physical body. The fall went quick this time, now that I knew what to do. Instead of diving into the water I hit my ledge with a soft thud, right in the center of the sturdy walls I built. I looked around cautiously, ready to raise my hands to welcome the light and bring me out at the first sign of danger.

There were no sudden movements, no gaseous forms, and no flickers of energy to indicate trouble. I faced the wall where I knew the stairs lay just on the other side and waved my hand, turning the hard rock to crystal. It went translucent. On the other side was one lone ball of being, which took shape into human form as soon as it saw me. She was pretty, with long black hair and clothed in a homemade dress that looked straight from the medieval ages.

She approached the wall, drinking in the sight of the Gaia who had caused all the commotion. Other gaseous forms floated behind her. None approached, but several let their faces emerge momentarily, looking at me curiously. We each placed one hand on the stone, the crystal carrying our voices through to one another.

"I am Arianna, and I was Gaia long before your time." She took another second to look me over. "You are strong; commanding the athame's powers like none has before."

"The energy of the athame, and all of you, have been drawn into my body. Because this place is in my physical form, I will always have the advantage." I let my voice carry, echoing through the cave and deep into the water. Hopefully deterring anyone from trying to take control again. A few on the stairs actually shrank back, but Arianna met my gaze, steady and strong. I swallowed. "What do you mean I'm doing it wrong?"

"During my time as Gaia, I grew strong with Akasha, the fifth element that binds all others – the eternal source of all energy. Akasha binds the material and spiritual worlds. It can most easily be called upon when meditating or dreaming. I know about dreaming spells."

I was growing impatient. I didn't want to overstay my welcome.

She caught on without me saying so. "I will hurry. Our dreams are normally a mirror image of our thoughts, but sometimes things get mixed up in transfer. Those cause the unexplainable happenings in our dreams. I can tell you what you have done wrong in your spell, but I want something in return."

Ah, and there was the rub. "What?"

"I want control, for just a few minutes. You can name the amount of time."

"Why?"

"This form I am, that we are, isn't me – my spirit has long since joined with the earth. I am just Arianna's memories, her essence. Still I want to feel human again, for however short a time."

"That's not a fair trade. I'll just as easily share my dream another way without having to risking losing myself to you."

"You are right." She pursed her lips in thought. "I will share my knowledge of Akasha and dreams with you as well."

Tempting, but still dangerous. The question was, was it more dangerous than approaching Shawn and all his minions unprepared? I knew the answer before the question was complete. "Fine, but this is how it will work. You tell me what went wrong in my spell. Then I return to my body and complete the spell. I will also alert my friend to what I'm about to do. When I do give you control over my body, your hands will be bound. You will promise not to cause physical harm to me or anyone else, nor practice any of your powers. I will decide when it is time for you to return. Once you do, you will share the rest of your knowledge."

A slow smile formed across her face.

"What?" I asked.

"Nothing. That was just easier than I thought it would be."

Warning buzzers went off in my head. "How do I know you'll keep your word?"

"How do I know you'll keep yours? After all, this is your body, not mine." She patted the wall of the cave and chills went down my spine. She was right, it was my body and they were all trapped inside; free to do whatever damage they pleased. I had to find some way to make peace with them. I had a feeling this wasn't the only time I would have to barter away control.

"All right, all right. I get your point. I need just one more thing from you – I need you to let me know about the other personalities in here, who would be best to target for certain spells, powers, all that."

She nodded in agreement.

"Let's get this over with." I waved away a small sliver of the wall, just large enough for her to fit through, then quickly closed it again behind her as a surge of gaseous forms rushed for their opportunity to take over the ledge. Those to hit the wall first actually bounced back and I could hear a few whimpers of disappointment. "Tell me how to complete the spell."

"Like I said, the dream or spiritual world is a mirror image of our world. When you are working with energy meant to be transferred in that world, even your tools should be a mirror image. So your salt, instead of sitting North, should sit South. Your fire should be North."

I gritted my teeth to find the fix that simple, but I probably would have never figured it out otherwise. "Fine, I want you to wait here until I get back. Don't try anything funny."

She agreed, "Do not be gone too long."

I turned the wall solid again, the other personalities disappearing from view, and lifted my arms, only making the ascent to join my body once I was sure I didn't have any unwanted stowaways. I opened my eyes, and found Alex staring at me.

"You were doing it again, weren't you?"

"Doing what?" I set the athame down on the table and gave him an innocent look.

It didn't work. He put his hands on his hips, glaring at me.

"Yes but it was necessary. The dream spell wasn't working." He held out his hand to help me down from the table. "But now I know what to do."

"Cato said—"

"Cato said no more experiments," I interrupted. "This isn't experimenting. I know what I'm doing."

He stood, arms crossed, looking down his nose at me. "So what is the consequence now?"

"Consequence?" I moved toward the refrigerator, keeping my walk casual and my gaze downcast to avoid looking him in the eye.

He came up behind me and shut the door as soon as I opened it. "Yes. Consequence. Results of a previous action. Cause and effect. There's always an effect that comes along with the things you do, and most of the time they're unpleasant. So out with it."

"Fine. I agreed to let one of them have control of my body for a short, short amount of time in exchange for some information." Before he could protest I quickly gave orders, "So, help me back up on the table so I can finish this spell. Then you can go get some handcuffs."

"Why handcuffs?"

"We can't have someone running off with my body now, can we?"

The glare faltered slightly. At least he seemed satisfied I was taking precautions.

Once back on the table, I reversed each element, recalled the dreaded dream once again and chanted the spell. After finishing, I felt a significant vibration in the energy around me.

It will stay with you until you sleep again.

"Well thank you very much, Miss Arianna," I mumbled.

I met Alex in the hallway and we made our way to the living room together.

"Selling your body for favors –" he mumbled, binding my hands and feet. "Technically you've become a prostitute."

The comment should've earned him a slap in the face, but seeing as how my hands were rendered immobile I settled for an equally belittling retort, "And that makes you a pimp."

"Touché." He tightened the handcuffs around my ankles extra hard, looking somewhat satisfied to have emitted a squeak of pain from me. "Okay, we're ready to go. Do your thing."

"I'll only be gone a couple of minutes. Just don't answer too many of her questions, and for both our sake's keep her under control."

He nodded and I took a trip back inside myself for the second time that day. Arianna still stood inside the circle of stone, waiting, not that she had much of a choice.

"It worked," she said.

"What? The dream spell? I'll find out after tonight."

"Trust me, it worked. Now it's my turn." She lifted her arms as I had, and disappeared into the blinding light that emerged. If I concentrated I could hear her talking to Alex. I gave her several minutes, careful to pay attention to the tone of her voice and the energy in the cave, relying on it to tell me if something was wrong. Once I grew tired of straining to hear her, I briefly crystallized the wall and was shocked to find dozens of gaseous forms just on the other side, feeling for a way in. When they saw the wall change, a quick surge of both physical and not-so-physical bodies pressed against it. I quickly solidified it and called

Arianna back. She didn't answer right away. She just continued talking. I fumed, but didn't dare try calling the light for fear of what two bodies accessing the same consciousness at once might do. After about the fifth call, she finally came and I made room for her in the tiny space.

"That was exhilarating!"

"Yeah, well just come back when called next time," I scolded her with my hands on my hips. "It's time for you to finish your part of the bargain."

"In a hurry to get somewhere? You won't be going far with all Alex has done. Are you sure you are not a prisoner there?"

"Alex and I have an agreement, don't worry about me." I held up my hand for her to take. She hesitated only briefly, and then consented. Just as with the Air Elemental, I felt my body tingling with energy starting at my hand and moving through my veins. I could feel the knowledge in her mind and sensed it becoming a part of me. I allowed myself to explore, finding memories and powers she wasn't necessarily transferring to me willingly. Finally I reached a barrier. She dropped my hand.

"You're holding back," I said.

She shrugged. "If I gave you everything now, what else would I have to bargain with?"

Smart woman.

It didn't matter, I felt sufficiently overloaded as it was. I would need time to practice with my new powers, before absorbing more. "Fine. It's time for you to go. I'll call you when I come back, but in the meantime, stay out of my head. Next time I want to talk to one of you...you –"

"Shades," she interrupted.

I paused. "Shades?"

"We call ourselves Shades – like shadows, spirits, or apparitions."

"Ok. Next time I'd like to talk to a Shade who knows all about the one who controls the Gaias powers."

"You mean the Rais, or maybe the Ardwyad?"

"The Medwin, the one who controls the merging of powers between Elementals and the Gaia; the one who can add or subtract to the Gaias energy." I was referring to Shawn.

"Oh. Not every Gaia has one of those—"

"Lucky me," I mumbled, interrupting.

"But there are a few in here who might know. I will find out."

I began ushering her to the wall opposite the stairs.

She paused as she realized which way we were facing, "The stairs are on the other side."

"I know. That side is, well, let's just say temporarily closed." Before she knew what I was doing, I waved open a large slit in the wall and pushed her off the ledge. I quickly closed the wall, even before I heard the loud splash down below. She wasn't going to be too happy with me, but there had been no other choice. I waited for the chatter and heightened energy coming from the rest of the Shades to subside. I wouldn't want them to take that momentum and find some way to push themselves into my protected ledge. Once satisfied, I lifted my arms and found Alex staring me down.

"Took you long enough."

"I had a few more items of business to take care of." I held my cuffed hands out to him, "Mind releasing me?"

"I'm tempted to leave you just like that. It would be far less trouble for me."

"Just curious, did you see me use my hands when I created that fun little wind cocoon around you?"   My threat was obviously worse than his, because my hands and feet were freed in seconds. "That's better. Now, tell me what you've found out about the islands."

Chapter 24

Sun Tzu - It

"Both the Heard and McDonald Islands and the Southern and Antarctic Lands sit smack dab in-between Australia, Africa, and Antarctica." Alex assumed the position of an important lecturer, using the kitchen counter as his podium, looking down his nose at his only pupil – me. "Recent satellite imagery, and communications I've been able to collect from each of the islands, show no indications that Shawn is there. If he is, he's covering his tracks extremely well."

In our usual custom of working until we were dead tired, we were still at it by one a.m. He continued, raising his voice over the noise of our second pot of coffee brewing. "In fact, I don't think we will know quite where Shawn is until we get there. In any case, we have few options as far as transportation. A French oceanographic ship travels to each island set four times a year from Reunion, another island just east of Madagascar."

I groaned, "Not a boat..." Seasickness plus seven months pregnant was not a good combination.

"The next ship is scheduled to leave in four weeks."

Make that eight months pregnant. Alex ignored my griping. He was getting good at that as of late.

He babbled on, "The islands are uninhabitable and barren, and there is no permanent population."

My ears perked up. "No people - sounds like my kind of place."

"Sounds like *Shawn's* kind of place," Alex retorted. "At least one where he can plan, run operations, and conduct experiments in relative peace. It's a nature reserve. The islands are bleak, rocky, ice-covered, and actively volcanic."

I flashed back to the Galapagos, another nature reserve with very little population. "I'd bet you anything Shawn set up shop there."

"Ok then. We have about a week and a half to prep before travelling to Reunion. That will give us two weeks to find a way onto the boat leaving for the islands."

I narrowed my eyes. "And what, exactly, does 'prep' consist of?"

"Well, I need to take inventory of gear we'll need, clean and service it, pack, arrange our travel plans…"

"Ok," I said, "And what will I be doing?"

"You, my dear, will be doing your thing."

"My *thing*?"

"You know, your magical thing. Practice. We should expect to be at a major disadvantage. We will be outnumbered, probably more inexperienced, and we'll be on their turf. You need to prepare yourself for every possible magical scenario. Be able to defend against any attack. And, you need to find a weakness. Find something he won't be expecting. This will be a no-hostages mission, Kaitlyn. If we go, we go to take him out. If we fail, we keep going until the last man is standing, and then we go again. You need to be ready."

His words resonated through my mind but the one phrase that stuck out was 'major disadvantage'. He was so right. I needed to prepare and I knew just how to do it. I whipped into action, heading for the door. "Call Micah and let him know the plan."

"Where are you going?" He called after me.

"I need some privacy."

"Your own room tonight?"

I stopped and turned around in the doorway. "No – my own head."

He started to disagree.

I stopped him short, "I need to do this, Alex. It will be the only way we can win. I need knowledge and experience, fast. The only way I can get it is through those women. They'll help us fight the battle. They'll give us the numbers and Shawn won't be expecting it."

He eyed me carefully weighing the consequences, but the strategist in him prevailed. "Ok, Sun Tzu. But I will be checking in on you, and not a word of this to the others until they need to know."

"Agreed."

"Agreed," he said more hesitantly.

We parted ways. Before heading to our shared room, I stopped to help myself to the only computer with internet access at the Chakra. Located in a dark, closet-sized office next to the guard's room, I knew access was spotty at best. Still, I had to make plans for myself and for my baby. It took some time with the slow connection. For days, I had made sure to take several rolls of photographs, claiming I was documenting changes in each element after magic was used.

"Why can't you develop them?" Alex had asked.

"Sorry. Doctor's orders. The chemicals are bad for the baby, and I don't want to bog down the computer with images from the digital camera," I'd answered.

It might've even been true. Sounded logical enough to me. He didn't check with the doctor, and he didn't know I spent just a couple of minutes each day producing 40 or more pictures of puddles, rocks, leaves, and whatever else was on my way to my training spot for the day. Rarely did I even take the time to look through the eyepiece before I clicked away. And so, I had extra time during the day to practice and time in the evening on the computer when I could be sure Alex was locked away in the darkroom.

I was only interrupted when the doctor came by wanting to play internet poker. The first time he caught me I had looked like a bumbling idiot, trying to come up with some reason I was on the computer. Every time thereafter I always left a screen up on a baby naming website that I could quickly switch to.

"What have you come up with so far?"

Speak of the devil... the doctor stood in the doorway, once again interrupting valuable prep time. I released a tense breath. "What do you mean?"

He sat down in the large armchair that took up half the office and crossed his legs. "Names. For the baby."

"Oh, right. Well, um, we have some ideas but we're not sharing. We don't want, you know, opinions and that kind of stuff."

He stayed silent, with his hands folded in his lap. He wasn't leaving.

"I mean, not that we don't trust or respect anyone's opinion, or *your* opinion, for that matter, but Micah and I just want to keep the debate between us. For now."

The doctor nodded his head once. It gave no indication he agreed, was annoyed, or even that he cared. He definitely wasn't leaving.

I feigned a yawn. "Well, maybe I'd better turn in for the night."

"Yes, yes." The doctor jumped on the chance to encourage me to leave. "You need your rest, of course."

I said good night, and mouse clicks could be heard once I barely made it out of the room. Annoying.

Chapter 25

The Black Mamba

This was going to be a rough night. Pouring over Shawn's manual was not my idea of fun. I had put it away for the past month, keeping it hidden in a box in Alex's closet, under a pile of foul-smelling boots. Not that I was trying to hide it from anyone – well, except maybe myself - but every time I entered the room, I could feel it. Its tainted energy oozed out from the crack at the bottom of the door and crept toward me. It never quite reached me, but it certainly beckoned, following me like a sunflower follows the sun.

Tonight I asked Alex to retrieve it while I set up an area in the grass just outside the sliding glass doors. I wanted to be at my strongest, surrounded by the elements that worked with me. Piles of soft, tilled dirt from the garden, buckets of water from the Chakra well, lighted candles – enough that they provided ample reading light – and last but not least, air. Tonight it smelled fresh, with the slightest hint of sweet fruit. I looked around, satisfied. No tricks tonight – not by Shawn, not by the manual or any of his other tools, and not by the Shades inside me. I sat down inside the circle and reached for a toffee nut cookie, by far another necessity to face the battle ahead of us.

I braced myself as Alex entered the elemental circle with the manual.

"Geez, you'd think I'd just presented you with an angry black mamba."

"You don't know what's in that thing."

He threw it at my feet. It landed silently.

Memories of what I had read so far were already causing the bile to rise in my throat.

Alex took a deep breath. "You don't have to do this."

I looked at him – Alex was going to do it anyway, with or without me. We needed to finish the document and understand Shawn's intentions. It was the best way to fight him. I smiled, good old Alex, stuck in some sort of crazy time warp where he was constantly preparing. I looked back at the document. We were safer going at it together. Go team.

"Ok." I touched the streaks of ash left by the dying man who gave the document to me, shuddered, and then opened it quickly. I skimmed the table of contents, spotting our target for the night and opened it to that page. The title read, *One Less*.

Alex leaned over. A quick scan of the summary at the top, and Alex muttered, "Dear God."

A list of the largest manmade disasters that had occurred over the last century filled the page, accompanied by documented evidence of natural disasters taking hundreds of human lives that occurred shortly thereafter. Shawn was seeking a connection. He studied the distance between each manmade and natural disaster, both in time and in space. Correlations regarding intensity and methods were analyzed. Residual effects after each disaster were recorded.

"How long has he been working on this?" Alex asked, obviously appalled.

"At least since Sarah – possibly before." I looked up at him. "Did you know Sarah?"

Alex shook his head. "Not very well. We didn't really end up working together a lot. Shawn kept her to himself."

"Well, let's just get through this. Look here." I pointed at the next page. "April 1986. Chernobyl. The nuclear meltdown in Russia. It released 400 times the amount of radiation than the Hiroshima bomb."

Alex tracked my progress. "In August of that same year, Lake Nyos in Cameroon released 1.6 million tons of carbon dioxide that had been trapped under it. It suffocated 1700 people. Shawn thinks it was the planet's reaction to Chernobyl."

"What caused the release of toxins? Maybe a manmade accident?"

"No. Says here possibly triggered by a landslide or earthquake. Some think a heavy rainstorm the day before had something to do with it. All of that was natural. This was the first known large-scale asphyxiation caused by a natural event."

I leaned back, away from the document to think. "It's like the planet reacted to a release of a chemical compound with another release of a chemical compound. Only this time it targeted humans."

Alex nodded. "Could happen again – he included a report that documents the natural barrier there, the dike, is weakening. If it gives way it will flood villages in Nigeria and release even more carbon dioxide into the air. Lake Kivu in Congo, 2,000 times larger than Lake Nyos, has the potential for the same event."

"Where is Chernobyl compared to Cameroon?" I asked.

Alex ran inside to retrieve a world map. "The location isn't the same, but Chernobyl and Cameroon are close to the same longitude line."

We were silent.

Finally I spoke, "Let's move on, maybe the other connections aren't as viable."

Alex read now, "Another air pollution event. In June 2003, the al-Mishraq fire in Mosul, Iraq. 1.3 billion tons of sulfur dioxide released into the atmosphere."

"What was the planet's response?" I asked.

He went back to scanning the page. "A heat wave in Europe that same summer was responsible for 40,000 deaths. That was the hottest summer on record in the area since 1540. All of the countries in Europe were affected, even some outside of it. There were extensive forest fires in Portugal, 1,500 heat-related deaths in the Netherlands, and melting glaciers in the Alps caused avalanches and flash floods in Switzerland. 2,000 people in England, Scotland, Wales, and Ireland died from the heat that summer, too."

"Again, the events didn't occur in the same place, but they weren't all the way across the world from each other either. Next." I prodded Alex on, not wanting to look at the manual.

"The Exxon Valdez. In March of 1989, 11 million gallons of crude oil spilled into Alaska's waters. There wasn't one massive event in response, but rather several small flooding events in the U.S. All happened in 1989; the Texas flood in May, Louisiana flooding in November, and Tropical Storm Allison in June which caused severe flooding in the southern U.S. Casualty numbers weren't high but damage to infrastructure, crops, and businesses were extensive."

"But what about all the manmade disasters that didn't evoke a reaction from the planet? Like here –" I leaned over to him, pointing. "1984. A chemical plant in Bhopal, India. A tank holding the toxic compound methyl isocynate overheated and released it. It was heavier than air so it rolled along the city like a fog. It was a poisonous avalanche that killed 20,000 people or more. There are no massive natural disasters recorded that same year or the next."

Alex looked at me. "20,000 people? Not to mention those that survived and probably have hideous health problems? I don't know Katie - sometimes our own disasters are enough punishment."

I took the papers from him, giving him a break. "Here is another one without consequence. The Centralia, Pennsylvania underground coal fire doesn't show any reported natural disaster afterward." I scanned ahead "Oh. Shawn attributed this to the fact that perhaps the coal fire was fanned by the planet. In 1962, local fireman set fire to a landfill, a common practice at the time. The landfill sat on top of an abandoned strip mine, but somehow, veins of coal retained the heat even after the fire was put out, and continued to smolder for two decades. Eventually, a fire underground flared up, and left untended, opened up a 150-foot sinkhole in the small town in 1981. It has been burning ever since."

"But if the planet was planning revenge because we burned landfills, why did it wait so long?" Alex asked.

"I don't know – maybe it was keeping the possibility on standby. Just in case we did something else fucked up."

We both paused.

"Do you realize what's happening?" Alex asked.

"Yeah. We're buying into his theories."

"Yeah."

I closed the manual. We both reached for the last cookie at the same time. I raised my eyebrow at him then casually glanced down at my protruding belly.

"Oh, fine." He growled in defeat. "I'll go get the other box."

I finished my cookie slowly, repeating a calming chant, keeping Shawn's manual from terrorizing my mind. A flicker of light caught my eye. One of the candles flared.

I smiled in response and said as I heard Alex approaching, "See – maybe the planet is on our side."

"What does it mean?" he asked, keeping a wary eye on the flaring candle.

"I think it wants us to burn the document."

"Agreed."

Alex held the papers up while I touched the edges lightly with the flame. "Satisfied?" he asked.

I answered with a big yawn, "For now."

"Hallelujah."

I began crawling around the circle, blowing out candles. The buckets and dirt could wait until tomorrow. I glanced at him. "Do you believe in God, Alex?"

He shrugged. "Practically my whole family is staunch Catholic. I grew up with religion in the forefront, common sense in the rear."

"So I'll take that as a no?"

"You should take that as an 'I don't believe in religion', but God is a different story." He turned the tables. "What about you?"

"I have begun to realize, that my parents were somewhat Wiccan in their beliefs. Nature was their God. We celebrated a lot of the religious holidays only because they were derived from pagan traditions back in the day."

"But you admit there is something more to life than just the Earth and humans."

"Sure," I held up the half-eaten toffee-nut deliciousness. "There are cookies!"

Alex rolled his eyes. "You know what I mean..."

"What?" I played with him.

He cleared his throat, picked up a candle, and held it like a microphone. "There is magic in the air..."

"Stop!" I laughed. "And don't quit your day job."

"Why? My day job sucks."

I crossed my arms and let out a squeak of protest, since his day job mostly consisted of me.

"Well, I mean – look at the perks." He looked at me. "Oh, that's right. There are no perks." He winked at me.

I picked up one of the smaller buckets of water, and before he could react, doused him with it. "Just 'cause Susan's not here, doesn't mean I need to be concerned with your 'perk'."

"You little..."

I squeaked again and ran. I didn't get far; a few steps later I tripped over a pile of dirt which was obscured from my view by my bulging midsection.

Thankfully, Alex caught me mid-fall, hoisting me back on me feet. "Damn, Katie. You've gotten heavy."

I steadied myself. "Wow, you are just full of compliments tonight, aren't you?"

"Yep – I certainly have my way with women. Come on; let's get you to bed before I get my ass kicked."

I took his arm, letting him lead me in. I looked back. The ashes of the burned document were still there. I waived my hand, and weaved a small net of wind, scattering the ashes into the air and out of my view.

Chapter 26

Ready or Not

The next week flew by. It had barely felt like a couple days when Alex announced our departure for the following week. I had spent every waking moment in a not-so-awake state, conferring with Arianna, my newly appointed second in command. Together we built a team of strong Shades, each with a specialized power. Every one of those Shades had a second team consisting of at least two, sometimes more, other Shades as backup. Moreover, I was given knowledge willingly by almost every Shade inside the athame. There were a few who refused, but I didn't push them. I had enough to learn as it was.

Today was fire day. I had prepped as best I could by ensuring Alex knew where all the fire extinguishers were, and that they had been recently inspected. I took several with me to the most open field I could find, well away from the Chakra and anything even remotely flammable. I even took the liberty of removing all my clothes.

Once inside, Arianna explained I would need a fire Shade and a former Gaia to help.

"Why a Gaia too?" I asked as we floated down the stairs. The Shades were calm today, lazily floating about, giving me a sense of security that no hijackings were going to occur. I glanced up at the crevice in the cave that always gave me an uneasy feeling. Someone was in there still, but she was inactive, staying well out of sight.

"Because the element of fire, although considered to be the purest element – resistant to pollution – also relies on the magic of the other elements to be effective. Usually Fire Elementals have some abilities with the other elements, and could even potentially take over as Gaia if necessary."

We approached two women sitting on a small island in the lake of the cave.

Arianna sat me down with them. "This is Aideen, a Gaia, and well, we don't know this one's name." Arianna gestured to the other woman. "She doesn't talk much, and doesn't speak any of our languages."

"What's the *craic*?" Aideen asked with a strong Irish accent as she shook my hand.

"I'm sorry, the...?" I was never any good with accents.

She rolled her eyes. "Effin' yank. What I mean to say is 'what is up'?" She managed in her version of an American accent.

"Oh. I'm good." I turned to the other Shade and extended my hand to her. She shrank back.

"She nae like to touch." Aideen informed me.

"Sorry." I waved at her instead.

She narrowed her eyes back.

"Well, I'll leave you three to it, then." Arianna said with a nod, disappearing into the water surrounding our small island.

I shook my head as I watched her gaseous form sink into the depths of the pool. "I will never get used to this place."

Aideen shrugged. "Ye kin only piss wit da cock ye got."

I laughed, "I don't know about you, but I'm sort of lacking in that department."

The fire Shade spared a horrified glance toward Aideen and her phrasing. It was only a split second, but I caught it. She could definitely understand us.

"Ok, let's start. I've done fire before, but only on a small scale."

"Aye. No wonder. Ye got to use air to fuel it, if ye want to make something of it."

She started her weaves, forming a small fireball that floated in between the three of us. She gestured with her hands, more so than I'd seen anyone do. When the ball of fire was steady, she held it in place with one hand and started another weave of air with her other hand.

"It's like knittin', ye know. Make yer weaves, but use a needle to fuck with it." Her free hand constructed a tight, narrow wind tunnel, no bigger than her hand. With her brows furrowed and tongue creeping out the side of her mouth in concentration, she poked and prodded at her fireball. Each time she did, it either grew in size or intensity. Just as the heat grew to be so much we all three had to lean away from it, Aideen reversed her wind tunnel and the fireball shrank.

"Now ye can tie it off."

I watched her force her weaves around each other in tight knots. Even though she still had to expend a small amount of energy, the fireball for the most part was self-sustaining, and required little concentration.

I couldn't resist, I reached behind me into the pool of deep water, used a little energy to gather a small puddle in my hand, then forced it at the fireball, effectively extinguishing it and soaking my two partners all at once. Aideen laughed, but the other freaked. She changed into her gaseous form and flew straight up and then in circles, faster and faster until droplets of water shot out, drying herself as effectively as the spin cycle of a washing machine.

Aideen leaned toward me. "She's one dem fires, ye know? Doesna like water."

After enough spinning that would have caused my stomach to empty, the fire Shade resumed her place in our circle, giving me a pointed stare. I could almost see flames in her eyes. Trying not to burn bridges, literally or figuratively, I apologized with another wave and friendly smile.

She crossed her arms.

"Okay," I tried brushing the incident off, "let me give it a try." I copied Aideen's weaves and accomplished the fireball in no time at all, then attempted the air needle. At the first poke the ball nearly blew up in our faces. It took more precision than I cared to try. But I did, and after several hours I had the control I needed. If we weren't so ethereal, we'd all be sweating from the heat.

Aideen showed me how to mix earth with fire, effectively creating a type of lava, slow moving and deadly.

The Fire Elemental took over, and gave me a detailed show of the different types of fire and how to create them. Her flames changed from yellow-orange to red to blue depending on their intensity. Then she manipulated, or dispersed, the gasses and vapor created by the fire.

Even Aideen seemed to pick up a few pointers from the lesson. The fire Shade, either still bitter about my water or pretending she didn't understand us, effectively ignored all of my questions. Didn't matter; I had gotten what I needed from her.

Finally, she resumed crossing her arms and shrank back as far as our little island would go.

"I think she is done." I looked at Aideen.

"Aye."

I looked up at my walls protecting the platform that led to control of my body. No forms floated around the walls for the time being, or even on the stairwells. Still, I needed Arianna to escort me back, to watch my back while I entered the platform, but she was nowhere in sight.

I turned my attention back to Aideen.

"So, when were you a Gaia?"

"Early 18th century. But only for a year, 'til they found another."

"Oh. You mean they…"

"Aye. They burnt me. A circle of them Fires." She gestured toward the Fire Shade.

The frankness shocked me.

"'Tis no matter. Painful at first, but over quick. I think 'twas harder on me ma."

"She knew?"

"She was one o' them Fires."

A sick bile crept its way up my throat. "Your mom helped to kill you?"

Aideen shrugged her shoulders. "Cried buckets, she did. But the decision was made. 'Twas for the good of the Earth, aye?"

The bile formed a large lump and refused to go back down. "Is your mom here?"

She shook her head. "Ne'er was marked by the knife."

"Ready to go?" Arianna interrupted the horror story unfolding before my eyes.

I jumped. "Yes, please. Let's get out of here." I didn't want to know any more. I looked at Aideen, "Thank you so much for your help. And I'm sorry for your, your...well I'm sorry for what happened to you."

We hugged, and I attempted to wave goodbye to the Fire Shade, but her back was already to me. Arianna and I made our way up the steps. I didn't talk, didn't even turn around to look at her before I weakened the wall barrier. I needed to get out before I broke down.

Hindsight, I probably should have taken better security measures. In my hurry to leave, I didn't consider an attack. The intense heat grew behind me until I had to cower down. And then nothing but blackness.

* * *

When I came to, I found myself buck naked, dancing around a large bonfire in the middle of the night.

It had been afternoon when I left my body.

Immediately I backed away from the searing heat of the fire; most of my skin had turned cherry red with what must have been hours next to my, or her, creation. I bumped into Alex.

Head turned away, he quickly wrapped his coat around me. Feet quickly shuffled and I looked around to find several men, most of whom I recognized as the Chakra staff, hurry away carrying fire extinguishers, and in one man's case what I could have sworn was a bag of popcorn. "What in the..."

"Hell. Yes. This is my own personal hell. I've had to watch them watch you dancing around that fire like some sort of crazed witch for hours. It was like watching porn and discovering your sister's the main character. Your pregnant sister. Ew." Alex shook to rid himself of whatever chills crawled up his spine in memory of my performance.

"Why didn't you turn them away? Or stop her?"

"Her?"

"Well it wasn't me putting on that show!"

"Could have fooled me." Alex crossed his arms. "Anyway, we tried. And several men had to be sent to the doc to get treated for second-degree burns. I kept the rest here in case the fire got out of hand. But once we left you alone, you just sort of…did your thing."

"Great. Just great. Well, she's off the team, believe me."

"Team?"

"No time to explain. I have to get back. There's more work to do."

"No, you need to rest. We leave tomorrow afternoon."

"Tomorrow! I won't be ready by tomorrow."

"Ready or not, here we go." Alex walked me back to our room and saw to my packing.

"This is pointless." I threw down the shirts I was stuffing into my bag. "None of this matters."

"None of what matters?"

"These! Shirts, clothes…shampoo!" I took out bottles and threw them across the room. "These things mean nothing right now! What matters is my baby's life, and mine. I need to practice!"

"Quit delaying the inevitable, Katie. We leave on that boat whether you've had time to pack your shampoo or not."

He picked up my bottles and shirts, placing everything in the bag for me. I looked at it with disgust, as if it was the very first step to my defeat. I sat down on the bed and sighed.

Alex did the same. "You look exhausted. Maybe try to get some rest on the plane?"

I shook my head, managing to hold back the tears threatening to flood my eyes but my quivering lips gave me away. "I can't. I have more work to do. I need to be prepared for him."

"True. But none of that work will matter if you're too tired to stay on your feet for the battle." Alex put his arm around me. "I'll make you a deal. Sleep for half the trip and work for half. And if you're still too tired to stand for the battle I will hold you up."

"And if I falter because I have not trained enough?"

"Then I will step in front of you and protect you with my life."

I looked up into his eyes and read truth there. He would die for me. And that was the problem. It wasn't just my life and the baby's I had to worry about. It was Alex with his goofy ways of making me laugh, and Micah whose arms are the only place I've ever truly longed to be. Then there was Susan with enough confidence to fill a room, and Cato, and the staff, and the rest of humanity for that matter. I broke down as the enormity of our undertaking hit me for the first time. I cried on Alex's shoulder. My wailing soon turned to sobbing and hiccupping which in turn became snorting and uneven, labored breaths.

I woke when it was still dark – sprawled out on my bed. My breakdown led to some much needed sleep, but that few hours of missed training could mean defeat. I found my suitcase neatly packed and Alex staring at me from the doorway with an arched eyebrow, assessing me.

I cleared the sleepiness from my throat and made an attempt to smooth out my hair. "I hope you know that counts as my half of the bargain."

He snorted in response. "Truck leaves in three hours."

"Just enough time for one more session."

He looked me over, no doubt taking into account the dark bags under my eyes. "Fine – a quick one."

I sat up in bed, careful to wake up fully before I attempted to stand. "I need some air."

"Want me to go with?" Alex picked up my suitcase.

"No – I'll just be out in the gardens. Come get me when you're ready to leave." I needed some practice using the earth element, having rarely used it except in the case of extreme agitation. Once against Shawn, once against a plant seed.

I walked away under Alex's watchful eye, and went outside toward the gardens. Stepping into the vegetable section, I saw it was now in full bloom with ripe tomatoes, carrots, cabbage, and potatoes.

I made my way to the center of the garden, plucking a cherry-red tomato from its vine as I passed. I chose a freshly tilled spot, the smell of dirt still strong in the air. Tomorrow everyone would be pitching in to plant new herbs, except Alex and me. We would be long gone. But tonight, the only thing that would be planted here was my butt. I sat down in the dirt, cross-legged, and sank in slightly. Biting down slowly on the tomato, it burst open in my mouth, sending squirts of juice running down my chin. I hummed in pleasure.

Sufficiently relaxed, I sank deep down into my subconscious, landing on the protected cave shelf with a barely audible thump. *I'm getting good at this.* Arianna, sensing my presence was just on the outside of the protective wall before I could call for her. She was a good lieutenant.

"Got an Earth Shade picked out yet?" I asked her as I stepped through the wall. I kept a wary eye out for that Fire Shade.

"Don't worry, we've got her blocked." Arianna gestured to the same island in the middle of the cave lake, where four Shades surrounded her; keeping her paralyzed by a strong weave.

"What if one of them needs a break?"

Arianna forced her human face out of her gaseous cloud to roll her eyes at me. "We don't take breaks. We are Shades. We don't sleep, we don't pee, and we don't eat tomatoes."

I immediately checked my chin for tomato dribble before I realized I wasn't exactly in human form down here either.

"You look fine, Kaitlyn. Spittle and all."

I laughed.

"Come on, I did find an Earth for you, but this one wants to do an exchange."

"Sorry, can't right now – I only have a little bit of time… But at least let me meet her. Maybe she can give me something."

Arianna led me down the staircase, introducing me to a form sitting at the bottom. "Here she is."

"English?"

"No, Chinese."

I looked at Arianna. "We're going to have some serious communication issues. Maybe we should focus on English speakers only."

Arianna moved closer to me, nudging my shoulder, "Oh, Kaitlyn. We all speak the same language. The language of magic."

I tried to push Arianna away but my semi-solid arm went right through her translucent body. I huffed in frustration and sat down next to my non-English speaking Earth Shade.

Arianna sat next to me.

"You gonna stick around this time?"

"Thought it would be safer. Besides, you need a translator."

"You speak Chinese?"

She shook her head. "No. *Magic.*"

I looked at the Chinese Shade. She wavered, then took shape. Showing what was once their human form seemed to be a sign of respect, or maybe at least a sign of introduction. She was very beautiful. Large brown eyes and smooth olive skin. Her shiny black hair was pulled back into a tight bun. Two apparatuses that reminded me of chopsticks ran straight through her bun. I refrained from making a joke about the Chinese food the cave had to offer.

She wore a traditional Chinese dress. Bright red flowers on a yellow background circled the fabric. Raising her dainty hands, she began a series of motions. Dust and dirt that littered the cave walls and floors flew to her. She gathered them up until a large mound of earth materialized in front of us, shaped like a tiny mountain. The mountain moved, slowly sending waves of itself back and forth.

"The earth element is the most dependable." Arianna watched with me. "Steady and practical. Earth magic operates at a slower rate, but it is more likely to persist and endure."

Next, the Chinese Shade took out the two sticks holding her bun together. Her hair flowed down to her waist in a beautiful black straight line. With her sticks, she began drawing designs into the dirt pile. Her weaves and designs were easy to follow and commit to memory. Arianna was right, it was slow going but some of the steadiest weaves I had ever seen. Once done, she laid down her sticks and pushed her arms forward. The symbols sank until they disappeared.

"Tracing signs or patterns in the earth can make spells more effective. The same can be done by burying symbolic items in the ground," Arianna said.

Suddenly, the pile of dirt burst outward, spraying the entire cave with its contents, effectively returning each grain back where it had come from.

When Arianna and I emerged from cowering below our raised arms, the Chinese Shade had her hair back up in a neat bun, chopsticks in place, without a speck of dirt on her.

I brushed the dust and grime off of me. "Thanks for the demonstration. It was helpful. I'll return again tomorrow and I can loan you some time with my body."

She immediately shook her head.

"Why not?"

She spoke again in her soft voice, then laid one hand on my belly.

Arianna leaned forward, whispering in my ear, "The earth element above all values fertility and the cycle of life. Giving back to the earth what once was taken, and celebrating new life."

The Chinese Shade smiled.

I smiled back. "Thank you."

She bowed, then gracefully returned to her gaseous form.

Chapter 27

Reunion

My stomach was the topic of the day. Once the doctor, Alex, and I had made it to the airport in Jakarta, I was drawing all sorts of attention. I was a white, unveiled woman in a Muslim country being escorted by two men. I was almost eight months pregnant, and I was in a bad enough mood to enter a staring contest with anyone who dared look my way. Which was pretty much everyone.

"Baby in there?" the attendant had the nerve to ask as we handed him our passports and plane tickets.

"No. I'm smuggling a basketball."

Temporary confusion lit his face.

I didn't back down for a moment, "You know, Magic Johnson, Larry Bird, dunk, swish, layup?"

"I sorry, I no understand."

"Ah. Not as good with the English language as we thought we were, I see."

Alex pushed me aside, trying to appease the upset attendant. I didn't care if we never got on that plane. The thought of seeing Micah again was making my stomach flip.

I turned to look at the plane that would carry me straight to Madagascar, and to him. Maybe I could create some unfortunate weather. My protruding stomach brushed against the doctor's arm. He gave me a dirty look.

Target acquired, and...fire.

"You know, you don't seem especially sympathetic toward pregnant women."

He rubbed at his temples. "Truth be told, I perform far more abortions than I do deliveries."

My shock nearly snapped me out of my bad mood. "What?"

He spared a glance at Alex, who was now challenging what was and wasn't airline policy regarding third trimester women. The doctor looked back at me. "Many find what you do to be a difficult life. They either can't be bothered with a baby, don't want to risk watching the Seven dispatch of their child, or wholly believe they are making an ultimate sacrifice to control population numbers."

"You mean like 'one less'?" I tested him. I don't know why it had never occurred to me that he could be another one of Shawn's implants until now.

He rubbed his temples again. "Huh? Listen, I don't encourage them one way or another; I just do what I'm asked. I don't get paid enough for it anyway."

I nodded. "Thus the poker habit."

"Hmph," was his only response.

"How many children have you delivered, exactly?"

He crossed his arms, defending his professional competency. "Enough."

"How. Many." I crossed my arms right back.

He considered me for a moment, probably wondering if he should tell me the truth. He really didn't know the extent of my magical powers; never bothered to ask. He was, in fact, as uninterested in me as a person could get – disturbingly so.

Finally, he gave in. He dropped his arms and his shoulders sagged. It wasn't even worth the fight to him. "Two. One baby died, the other survived. But the mother didn't."

I scoffed. "Wow. Just wow."

"I miss Vegas. Damn these Muslim countries!" With that, he turned his back, obviously done with the conversation.

Alex, having won the argument with the airline, picked up my carry-on bag. "Come on, guys! Thanks to Buddha belly here we all got first class seats."

The doctor blew past Alex, bumping shoulders with him as he passed. "Get me out of here. And I will most likely not be returning." His loud statement echoed down the long hallway to the plane.

Alex narrowed his eyes at me. "What did you say to him?"

"Don't look at me; he's the one with the gambling problem."

We followed the doctor down the hall toward the plane, still ranting about the country. I silently wondered if he had already started a gambling pool on my delivery date. Then cursed, because if he had, he might very well be inclined to cheat.

* * *

Our connecting flight from Madagascar to Reunion almost left without us. I hardly had the chance to see the airport. People, bags, and cultural trinkets on display whizzed by in our rush to catch the next flight. The airport in Reunion didn't make up for it. It could hardly be called an airport at all. The runway wasn't even paved. The bumpy landing prompted an emergency run to the bathroom. Where a flight attendant on a proper flight might have forced me to sit down, here I only had chickens and toddlers lining the aisle to contend with. By the time I emerged, everyone had debarked, leaving behind several feathers and the

God-awful stench of – I turned right back around into the bathroom.

Things were quiet when I came out a second time, and Alex and the doctor both looked more than mildly annoyed. I was getting used to that. I stumbled my way to the front of plane, my stomach knocking against chairs in the narrow aisle.

Stepping into the humid air, I spotted Micah and Susan immediately. They looked beautiful. They were tan and fit, with matching green eyes that almost took my breath away even from a distance. I was the antithesis; large and frumpy, with disheveled hair – and to top it all off, my shirt smelled of vomit. We made our way down the steep stairs, the doctor in front of me, holding one of my hands and bracing the whole way down to catch me should I fall.

Now he cares. I rolled my eyes. Quite the attitude change when his boss was present.

Alex was behind me, keeping a tight grip on the back of my shirt. The attendants were unloading luggage from underneath the plane. I spotted my large, black duffel bag and silently willed them to be careful with it. My life literally depended on that bag.

Micah walked forward as we came down the last few steps, and I felt the sudden urge to run. He couldn't see me like this; why would he want anyone that looked like this? Especially when he was so used to seeing beautiful women like Susan. Not that she was competition, of course, but she probably, almost certainly, raised his expectations.

Inevitably, Alex's grip on the back of my shirt tightened. He couldn't read my thoughts, but he absolutely knew me well enough by now to know given the choice I'd run away. Bastard.

As soon as our feet hit the ground, the doctor began talking, "Well, Micah, I've kept her in good health for—"

Micah shoved past him, taking me into his arms right then and there, planting a long, slow kiss on my lips, making good use of both of our tongues. Sparks zipped through my already overheated body, but I didn't mind. Every part of me needed this. The doctors 'ahems' barely even registered.

Eventually his mouth moved from my lips to my forehead, and he planted kisses there while squeezing me tightly. As soon as he stopped kissing, Susan pushed him out of the way and one hug was replaced by another.

Hers was quick. She stepped away. "You smell like throw up."

"Thanks for noticing."

She looked me over critically. "And you've been making your own clothes."

I looked down at the sorry threads that barely held my outfit together.

Micah came to my defense. "She looks beautiful."

I blushed. He wasn't looking at my clothes.

"It doesn't matter." She stepped forward again and put her hand on my stomach. Susan pulled back sharply, and glared at the doctor. "Are you aware her amniotic fluid is low?"

He immediately crossed his arms and glowered at her. "Of course, I've been monitoring it. It is not low enough yet to warrant any type of intervention, we just need keep checking it," he huffed.

It was the first I had heard about it. I turned to Micah. "We need to have a serious talk about your hiring practices."

The doctor's disgruntled look turned shell-shocked. "Well, I never...you don't have any right..."

I raised my eyebrow, daring him to challenge me. With the information he shared in Indonesia, he had no leg to stand on.

He puffed out his chest and pulled his shoulders back. "You know what? I don't have to take this. I quit."

He turned on his heel, walked over the pile of luggage, grabbed his two large bags and wheeled them toward the airport. Micah and Alex started after him, but I grabbed both their arms. "No. We don't need him. He is not good enough for me or the baby."

Susan piped up, "She's right. I never did trust him. We can find someone else."

"And if we can't?" Micah asked.

"Then we can handle it ourselves." Susan squared her shoulders with his, pulling herself up to her full height.

I joined her. This was not up for negotiation.

Micah turned, watching the doctor enter the airport. "Goddamn it." He scratched his head in agitation, then glared at me. "Two minutes, Kaitlyn. Two minutes. After months apart, I finally see you, and in the first two minutes you have all my plans turned upside down." He sighed, rubbing his chin in thought. "I love you."

My eyes widened. Bracing for another fight, I hadn't expected that. Before I had a chance to respond, he was down on one knee, producing a small box. "Will you marry me?"

Susan hissed at her brother, "Not here, you idiot! On the tarmac of an airport? Could you be any less romantic?"

He didn't flinch at her insults. He looked at me, waiting for an answer.

I stammered, "It hasn't been a year and day."

"I don't care. I know what I want." He rose, removed the ring from the box, and placed it on my left ring finger. "Don't you?"

I nodded, not bothering to hold back the tears. The bathroom truck was emptying contents from the plane. The air reeked of gas as the fuel truck operator made a sloppy time of his work. The noise from a jet taking off caused us to cover our ears. Susan was wrong, I couldn't possibly think of a more romantic place.

Alex and Susan gathered up our luggage, and Micah took my arm as we walked toward the airport to get a cab. I looked up at him, forcing a smile. Truth was, I did know what I wanted.

Chapter 28

The Competition

Reunion is a small island in the Indian Ocean that sits to the east of Madagascar. The territory is an overseas region of France, but settled by Africans, Chinese, Malays, and Indians, giving the island an ethnic mix that would rival the United Nations. Reunion holds the record for the most rainfall in a 24-hour period ever recorded on Earth.

Today was sunny and bright. The only evidence of heavy rainfall was the lush tropical life all around the island. It wasn't an overly-touristy, mega-resort kind of place. Instead, it was one of the most diverse areas I had ever seen. A rugged interior, full of majestic mountains gave way to the dozens of miles of warm, sandy beaches.

We drove past a group of young, muscular men toting their surfboards and coolers to the beach. Teenage girls wearing less-than-string bikinis followed closely after.

"Um, I don't think I'll be going anywhere near the beaches." I looked longingly at the locals, soaking up the sun with every inch of skin. My skin at the moment was full of stretch marks and in no condition for a swimsuit.

Micah put his arm around me. "And I won't be going anywhere without you."

That made me smile. But I was all too aware of how unattractive I looked. My eyes drifted back to the beaches.

He took my chin in his hand. "Don't worry, we won't be anywhere near the beaches. I have a small cabin rented in the mountains. There's a 30 foot waterfall visible from the back deck."

"What about everyone else?"

"They are staying on the beach, but we won't see them much until we leave again. I've had my fill of Susan and Cato."

"What about Alex?"

"What about Alex?" he asked, looking at me suspiciously.

"He's kind of your brother, well, adopted brother – don't you want to see him?"

"No. I don't want to chance him getting in the way of my view."

I laughed, shaking my head as he continued to look at me. "Don't worry, you would be hard pressed to find someone that could block my profile." I stuck my stomach out further.

"I know. I can't believe how big she must be getting in there." He placed his hands on my belly, and was rewarded with a small kick.

"Oh my God, I felt her! That is so awesome!"

"Awesome?" I groaned. "She is sitting directly on top of my bladder, using my kidney as a punching bag and head-butting my ribs."

"That's my girl!" He rubbed my belly proudly.

"No taking sides! Not until you can see her face!"

Micah kissed me square on the lips again.

"What was that for?"

"I don't know." He looked just as confused as me. "I guess I'm just, so happy."

I punched him in the shoulder.

"Ow!" He rubbed at it. "What was *that* for?"

"Because. All it took was for us to separate for like, four months, for you to be happy."

He sighed. "Just for the record, I was miserable for those four months. And – it will not be happening again."

"You say that now – but that's not always under your control." I leaned back in the seat, crossing my arms; that small motion was even becoming difficult to do.

The taxi turned onto an unpaved, rocky road, leading up to a row of houses. Driving through the island, there seemed to be a wide gap in income level. We had passed scores of shantytowns, full of wood shacks packed together, that would border the property of large mansions. Luckily, this row of houses was neither. They were traditional Creole houses; modest, cozy-looking, and best of all – private. A small grove of trees sat between each house, blocking one another from view. A steep, red-tiled roof sat on top of a cream-colored house. Vines grew up the stony sides. The small white porch with wicker rocking chairs leading up to the house all looked very inviting but at the same time sturdy and safe, built to withstand season after season of the relentless cyclones known to plague the area.

"It's perfect, Micah."

"Thanks. Susan didn't like it so much. Not close enough to the water for her tastes."

"I would turn down the whole damn shoreline for this. I could live here the rest of my life."

Micah laughed. "Let's say we look inside before declaring plans for the rest of our lives, huh?"

I was undeterred even after a tour of the small home. Sporting two cozy bedrooms upstairs, one much larger than the other, both with slanted ceilings from the rooftop; I couldn't help but think how perfect it was. The small room could make a great nursery.

The rest of the house sat on the main floor. A living room, a kitchen with windows on three sides – all with breath-taking views of the surrounding mountains – and a small dining area. The house was modestly furnished, but had all of the basic necessities.

"I can rearrange the furniture if you don't like it the way it is," Micah said.

"What do you mean? We shouldn't be moving around the owner's furniture."

Micah took a deep breath. "We are the owners."

It took me a moment to process it. "What?"

"I, or rather *we*, bought the place. Your name's on the title too."

I looked around, awestruck that I actually owned something this great. Well, half of something, technically.

"I hope you're not mad," Micah continued. "I just loved it so much, and I was so excited to see you and actually start our life together. I thought we were close enough to the Chakra, but in a somewhat private place, away from— "

"Shh." I put my finger up to his lips. "Shut up and let me think."

He couldn't shut up. "If you don't like it just say so. It would sell easily enough. I was supposed to propose to you here – Susan had it all planned out."

"Micah. Shut. Up." I don't think I had ever heard him talk so much in the span of two minutes since I had known him. I closed my eyes and took a deep breath. The sweet and tangy scent of hibiscus drifted in through the windows, but it was the scent of ginger that made me smile. It smelled like home. More than home. It felt like everything I imagined heaven to be.

I felt tears gathering under my lids, and when I opened my eyes they brimmed over. "I love it, Micah. Everything's perfect. Thank you." I hugged him. It was awkward, with the baby in-between us.

"Wait. The baby." I suddenly remembered. "What are the hospitals like here?"

"Not the best. Which is why I was expecting the doctor to stay…"

"Oh, please. That doctor would have killed one of us, if not both."

"What?"

"Don't you do background checks on the people that you hire? I mean, first Vayu – then Doctor Mengele."

"Ok, ok – ease up. Vayu was well established within the organization; been with us almost as long as I have. No one saw him coming—"

"Not even with all that glitter?" I raised an eyebrow.

Micah ignored my interruption. "And the doctor was Cato's doing. It was my impression he was well ensconced within our community and at the very least maintains our secrets."

My lower back was starting to ache. I rubbed it. "What you guys need is an HR department."

"Want the job?" Micah moved behind me, pushed away my hands, and did a much better job of alleviating the pain.

I hummed in pleasure, and let my head fall back on his chest. "No way. I'd spend all my time dealing with sexual harassment claims against you."

"What?"

"The ones I'd be filing. You know, because of inappropriate touching..." His hands were kneading lower and lower, working out the non-existent kinks in my buttocks. "Lewd comments..." He leaned forward, licking my ear and commented on how big my breasts were getting. "And sexual advances." His hands snaked around to grab hold of my hips, pulling me back into him. I rubbed up against him, then angled my head back, mouth open, hungrier for him than I ever had been.

We kissed again. His lips were so soft, and his tongue so insistent. For the first time in months, I felt the urgent tingling inside and yearned for him to push me back on the couch, spread my legs and...

Knock, knock.

"Damn it! Someone's here." When he let go of me, I had to work to steady myself. He looked back at me as he went to answer the door. "There are drinks and snacks in the kitchen. See if there is anything you like."

As I scoured the refrigerator and came out with orange juice and yogurt, giggling floated in from the living room. I straightened, back and shoulders going stiff with anger. Female giggling, the fake, flirty kind that was too high pitched and forced. The kind that told the receiving end, *I am totally into you and would suck your...* Jesus, what was wrong with me?

I closed my eyes and summoned Arianna.

Is someone interfering? I asked. *Someone who can't keep their hormones in check?*

No, Kaitlyn. She answered almost immediately. *That is all you.*

More giggling, but this time inside my head.

Great, no one to blame but myself. Much harder to deal with your faults when you couldn't pin it on anyone else.

"Kaitlyn – are you ok?" Micah was in the doorway to the kitchen, his brows furrowed. "Your face is going red."

"*Qu'avez-vous dit?*" The culprit moved next to Micah, placing one hand on the bulge of his bicep. Her eyes went slightly wider with pleasure as she pawed his arm. She held a feather duster in her other hand.

I squeezed the yogurt cup so hard, the lid popped off, hitting me in the face and squirting yogurt down the front of my shirt. The heat in my face increased, embarrassment heaped on top of anger.

She turned at the noise and gasped seeing me, removing her hand so quickly from Micah's arm you'd have thought he was on fire. Which he would be, if he didn't choose his next words carefully.

"Kaitlyn, this is Marie, the maid. I forgot she was coming today."

"I see. And just how often does she...come?" I breathed through gritted teeth.

"Once a week." He kept his voice soothing, like he was trying to talk down a stomping rhino.

"*Qui est-elle*, Micah?" The way she said his name, *Mee-ka*, the last syllable stressed with an extra high pitch, caused me to bring back my yogurt-wielding arm, taking aim for her face.

"Kaitlyn!"

I looked at him, confused. "What?"

"What's the matter with you?"

"What is the matter with me? With me?? Oh, I don't know. Maybe I'm upset because while I was stuck at the Chakra, pregnant, under constant attack, trying to figure out whatever is going on inside me with these Shades - you are gallivanting around, getting feathered by French maids."

"You're being ridiculous."

"No," I looked down at myself. "I am being a pregnant, stressed out woman, covered in vomit and yogurt, and now I have to compete with the likes of her?"

The air around us crackled with electricity. I felt my hair rising up and out in reaction to the static. I straightened, arms puffing out and the little French puff, still standing next to Micah, shrank back in fear.

Micah stepped toward me, holding out his arms as if to intercept me should I go for her. "There is no competition, Kaitlyn. Look at your left hand. Who's wearing the ring?"

I looked down, and smiled. "You are right, dear. All the better to hit her with." I curled my hand into a fist, intending to use the ring like a set of brass knuckles.

The tart let out a scream, turned tail, and ran for the front door. I whirled my right hand in a circle, lassoing what air would come to me in that quick few seconds, and hurled it her way, effectively pushing her the last few steps out of the house. The last thing I saw before the door slammed shut behind her was the tiny, pink thong that disappeared between her butt cheeks under her too short skirt, as she went sprawling face first down the porch steps.

Suddenly quiet after the maelstrom of yelling and wind, I looked at Micah, smoothed out my hair, and said, "I need a shower."

His mouth was open, somewhat in shock, but he pointed. "Bathroom's upstairs, towels in the closet."

"Great."

When I came back down the stairs, toweling off my wet hair, Micah was standing on a stool, dusting off the top of the living room fan with the instrument left behind by the maid in her haste to leave. Smells of a roasting chicken drifted in from the kitchen.

He stepped down from the stool and looked at me, wary. "Better?"

I considered the scene. He could have very well followed her out the door, but instead, he chose to stay behind, cleaning where she left off and making me dinner. I smiled. "Much."

He sighed in relief.

So did I.

Chapter 29

The White Elephant

That evening, after dinner and a few games of cards, Micah suggested we go to bed. I was suddenly nervous. I was much, much larger than the last time we had seen each other, and I wasn't sure if I'd be comfortable sharing my awkward body with him. Judging by his subtle touches, romance was definitely on his mind.

"Don't be nervous," he said when I curled into myself at his touch. "Here, let me give you a massage."

I rolled over on my side in bed, away from him, relieved I could hide my face, which was flushed with embarrassment.

His fingers kneaded into my lower back, smoothing out kinks that had been long-time residents. Slowly but surely, his hands worked their way lower and lower, then around to the front.

I stopped him there. "I'm sorry – I don't think I can do this."

I could hear the frown in his voice. "What's the matter?"

"Don't be mad."

He almost sounded exasperated, "I'm not mad. Just tell me what is wrong."

"I want to…do this with you, but I don't think – I mean—"

He stopped me with a kiss. A quick peck on the forehead. "If you aren't comfortable, it's fine. I can wait."

"Really? You can turn it off just like that?"

"Well, no. But I'll survive."

I relaxed back into the pillows and smiled. "Not if you keep inviting that maid over."

He laughed. "I don't think she'd come over again if I promised her a million dollars."

"That's debatable."

Our conversation petered off, but our wakefulness did not. I tossed and turned for what seemed like hours.

"I need to sit up."

"More pillows?" Micah stacked them all behind me and to my sides.

I frowned, guilty at keeping him awake. "What about you?"

"Trust me, I've slept in worse places – and with worse pillows."

A few minutes of silence and he asked, "Can you sleep?"

"No."

"Do you want to talk?"

No I didn't. "About what?"

"Maybe about Shawn's manual. Alex said you guys finished going through it."

Automatically bile began rising in my throat. I thought of all of Shawn's correlations between manmade disasters and the planet's attempt at avenging them, and how scarily spot-on some of his assumptions were. I thought of how he had planned to continue the depopulation effect, and then I thought of my dream, hand in hand with Shawn, standing on a mountain of dead bodies.

My fists squeezed into tight balls of white, my fingernails cutting into my palms. "No, I can't – I can't talk about it."

"It's ok." He stroked my hair. "I'll get what I need from Alex."

We fell silent again while I tried to relax, concentrating on the strange hum of exotic insects outside. The walls of the house did nothing to block outside sounds. I thought of my Seattle apartment, and how quiet it was. Delivery trucks and loud pedestrians right outside were never heard unless I had the windows open. My apartment sat on top of a bakery. The smell of donuts and fresh bread drifted up to me by five a.m. every morning, but I never heard a sound. I wondered whom the apartment had been leased to after I left, and I couldn't help but wonder how perfect the place might have been to bring home a new baby.

Just me and her, in our private, quiet, dark little place - safe from the world.

"I love you, Kaitlyn." Micah said rubbing my belly, reminding me he was a very large part of this equation.

"I love you, too," I responded. "Go to sleep, Micah."

I stroked his hair and waited for the steady, deep breaths of sleep. I snuck out of bed. Sleep wasn't going to come any time soon, and there was nothing more frustrating to me, even now, than being unproductive.

A trip to the bathroom, a small snack of dinner leftovers, and a quick rummage around the living room for reading material left me bored out of my mind. I walked out onto the back deck and breathed in the humid air. The scent of ginger came to me again, along with the sound of the waterfall from across the darkness. I looked in its direction, squinting. Once my eyes adjusted, I could spot it. The blue of the water glowed slightly, beckoning me. I couldn't resist.

I took the steps down from the deck and started on the path toward the waterfall, wearing nothing but my thin, wispy nightgown. The weather was fine, but shoes would have been a smart choice. After the second time stepping on a sharp rock, I cursed loud enough to illicit a return response from a wild monkey high in the trees above. I turned back to the house to retrieve footwear.

I was stopped short by Micah's glowing green eyes, and nearly jumped out of my skin. "Jesus fuck you scared me!"

He didn't respond.

"I was just going for a walk."

His eyes glowed so bright in the dark it was unnerving.

"Are you mad?"

Finally, he shook his head and said something.

I repressed the urge to shout out 'hallelujah'.

"Kaitlyn, please. It could be dangerous out here. What if something happened?"

"Not in our neighborhood, sweetie." I tried to lighten the mood. I took his hand and pointed at the waterfall. "Look. If you saw that you would be doing the same."

He finally smiled. "Yes, but I'm not eight months pregnant, emotionally unstable, and capable of creating large-scale natural disasters."

"Hey! I'm not emotionally unstable!" I withdrew my hand and attempted to cross my arms. My difficulty ruined the desired effect. I threw my arms down at my sides and huffed in frustration.

"Case in point…"

"Oh, shut up."

"Come on, if you want to see the waterfall, let's see it together." He took my arm in his and led me down the path, footwear forgotten for the moment on both our parts.

The walk there was more taxing than I cared to admit, but it was beautiful in the dark. Reunion was a whole new world once the sun left the sky. The nocturnal animals and insects were out in force, and perhaps noisier than their daytime counterparts.

We stopped as a chameleon made its way lazily across the path. "I thought those things were supposed to blend in. There's no way we would've missed that."

Micah shrugged. "If it was blending in – we would've stepped on it. Mother Nature has a way of looking out for herself."

I immediately thought of Shawn's theories, wondering if Micah would ever buy into them.

Micah clapped his hand at the chameleon to hurry it along. It paused, turned one beady eye toward him, the other still looking forward, then continued at his slow pace once again, clearly unconcerned.

I laughed. "Look at that. My big bad wolf throws down with a lizard one-tenth his size, and loses."

"Ha, ha," Micah retorted. "Just keep a look out for the bats."

I froze. "Bats?"

"Flying foxes. Oh, and the rats."

I hunched my shoulders up around my neck and put my hands over my head as if the creatures would join forces and attack at any moment. "Ok. Not looking so much like paradise anymore."

"Oh, look at the big bad Gaia." His turn to mock me. "Wielder of flame, commander of water, Queen to the air, and ruler of earth. But throw a rodent her way and—"

I punched him in the arm.

"Oh, come on. There's nothing really that dangerous out here." He put his arm protectively around me and left it there for the rest of our walk.

Being that close to him was once again causing a stir within my body. While the air around us smelled of sweet, tropical spices, Micah smelled like campfires and pine trees. My stomach suddenly rumbled. I really could have gone for some smores.

Trying to keep my mind off of food, I asked, "Have you researched the geography and topography of the island much? I mean, does it lie on a hotspot like the Chakra or Galapagos?"

"Yep. Got that covered." He tapped his temple as if having already thought of it made him the smartest man in the world. "This place is a neutral zone, so to speak. For you, it doesn't take away energy but it doesn't add to it, either. But the same goes for me – or Shawn. No one gets an advantage here."

"Might be best, not knowing who the baby will take after." I stopped short, realizing my mistake. "I didn't mean – "

"I know," he said a little too quickly. "It's fine."

But it wasn't. Micah was trying to build a perfect future, and the perfect picture of a family, but the truth of the matter was the baby might not even be his. This was our white elephant.

I leaned in closer to him, squeezing his arm, trying to let him know I was there for him as much as he was there for me. The waterfall was getting louder, and we could feel the light mist before the falls even came into view.

We rounded a grove of short trees and thick bushes, and emerged into a small open area. Going forward, the path ended abruptly in a steep cliff to the base of the falls, leaving us about halfway up the waterfall.

The scene took my breath away. The water seemed to come out of nowhere; the dark cliff blended in with the night sky. It was like the water was emerging from a black hole, a different world altogether. The intensity and speed at which the water fell was frightening, but air blew up at us in gentle, brief puffs, as if to calm our fears.

"This is a popular dive spot," Micah said loudly enough so I could hear him over the water.

I took a step toward the edge of our spot, extended my neck and peeked over. The white, churning water in the pool below, bright compared with the dark surrounding cliffs and sky, almost looked luminescent.

Micah pulled me back, "Come on, there's something even better than that."

He took my hand and led me back down the path, but took a sharp left turn into the thick forest. Although the falls temporarily left our view, I could still hear them getting louder and louder. Micah parted an especially thick hedge and we ran smack up against the waterfall, still about midway up it. He turned to me, yelling, but it was completely impossible to hear anything over the water.

A small ledge up against the cliff led from the forest's edge straight under the waterfall. The waterfall itself was pouring over it, offering an awfully slippery rock and an equally treacherous fall.

I pulled back at him, giving him my best 'are you effin' insane?' look. He insisted, pulling me forward and pointing to something in the cliff wall. Notches had been drilled out and outfitted with a thick braided rope. The rope was new, although wet. A quick scan showed no frays, and it wasn't dirty from the overuse of grimy hands. Something told me Micah had installed it himself, wanting to create our own private cove amidst the wilds of Reunion Island. His beaming smile was the only confirmation I needed.

Still, this could have probably waited until after I had given birth and the baby was safe in someone's arms. Maybe Susan's. She would make a good babysitter. I wonder if she had a permanent place down by the beach.

Micah's insistent tug brought me back to reality and the rushing waterfall of death. Going into the thick of it, it didn't nearly look so majestic. Just treacherous. I angled my body away from the wall of the cliff, since my belly was far too big to face in, and holding Micah with one hand and the rope with the other, I began to shimmy my way across. The ledge wasn't nearly as slick as it looked. Being barefoot actually helped. My feet formed into the rough rocks, grabbing onto them more easily than I could have in shoes. Micah's grip was as solid as the rock formation behind me, which seemed to be pushing me further and further out onto the ledge. Micah gave one final insistent tug, and we were inside a cave. Impenetrable rock surrounded us on three sides; rushing water greeted us on the fourth.

Although we were right next to the waterfall, the sound of the water hitting the pool seemed suddenly blocked by the wall of water itself. At most, it was white noise, slightly amplified, bouncing around off the cave walls. We still couldn't talk, but we didn't need to. Just enough light was let in to discern Micah's silhouette, the faint outline of his face and of course his green eyes, which studied me so intensely I had to look away.

Grabbing my chin, he pulled my face back into his and kissed me, hard. His hands worked their way up my body, missing nothing. My thin nightgown was soaked with mist. I could feel the pads of his fingers as if they were touching me bare.

Within the cocoon, my senses were all out of whack. The colors were surreal, almost fantastical. What light that did come through the wall of water gave everything else a luminescent blue-green hue. Although the cave was dark, as my eyes adjusted, I could start to make out tiny shards of silver dotting the walls, ceiling, and ground.

The scents of Reunion Island ceased to exist in the tiny cave. I could only smell Micah, gruff and woodsy.

My will succumbed and my hands returned the favor, pressing into his chest, pushing against a wall that wouldn't move, wanting me too badly. We undressed each other, having no pity on anything that stood between us. He knelt down and sucked at my breast until they were rock hard and aching for him to continue. I grew warm in between my legs and seconds later climaxed; sharp spasms taking me, and probably him, by surprise.

He raised his eyes to me in question. I was too impatient to answer. Instead, I returned the favor, kneeling down and giving him generous one-on-one time with my mouth. His legs and buttocks tightened in response. I wanted him, all of him. I was hungrier for him than I ever had been before.

When he could stand it no longer, he lifted me to my feet, turned me around and pushed me forward into one of the walls. He spread my legs with his own foot, then felt for my opening with his hands. Though he meant to only get bearing, the feel of him touching me there was too good to let pass. I reached down and forced his hand further into me. He obliged, peppering my neck and ears with kisses. I couldn't get enough.

In one swift motion, he withdrew his hand. I arched my back to follow him and he returned, thrusting himself into me with a vengeance. His hands held my hips in place. Months without him left me tight, but I was slicker than the ledge we came in on, and I needed him. I needed this.

I willed my body to relax into him. As soon as he felt me give in, he began thrusting again, slowly, steadily. I braced myself by putting my hands up against the rough cave wall. It was sharp, I'd have cuts to contend with in the morning, but for now it felt good.

He leaned forward, yelling in my ear so I could hear, "Use the elements. Make them pleasure you."

I turned my head in question and he nodded his encouragement. I turned back around and concentrated. No way I could top the pleasure Micah was pouring into me, but what if…

I called the tiniest bit of wind in through gaps the water left. It blew gently in my ear, and I tilted the side of my head to allow it access. I called for a little bit more, weaving in bits of heat to warm it. I wrapped our bodies in a warm breeze, then in a selfish gesture, focused it and sent it below, in between my legs. The pure sensation of warm air, with Micah pushing into me, was better than anything I'd ever felt. After only a few seconds, I had to move it away. I didn't want to come again quite yet.

But I didn't let the air go completely. I kept it close, encircling my breasts and pinching at my nipples as if it were Micah's fingers.

I wondered briefly, about what witches say; magic coming back to you three-fold. I hope to hell it did.

Micah broke off a larger piece of rock from the cave wall. He presented it to me as if to ask for my permission. I nodded, quickly and urgently.

He reached around and placed it between my legs. I sent tiny tremors into the rock, then tied off the weaves. It buzzed in response. I was paralyzed with the shooting sensations running through my body. I could only stand there, mouth open. I wasn't even sure if I was moaning anymore. Micah continued to grind into me with a fury. I climaxed – then held still while he finished. It didn't take long. One final, deep thrust and he went lax.

All of the built up energy and elemental power still coursed throughout my veins. I let go, releasing it back into the ecosystem. The cave walls buzzed in response to the blast of power. Finally, the wall of water burst outward - the energy had nowhere else to go. The moonlit forest was revealed for a fraction of a second, until the water resumed its constant, steady fall over the entrance to the cave.

We collapsed together, exhausted, but in pure bliss. He sank down with me, until we were both lying down, catching our breath. The rocky floor scraped me, pressing into my back. I didn't care. I would pay that price time and time again if only I got to experience that every day. I looked at Micah. I *could* experience it every day. This was the life he had planned for us.

Chapter 30

Ready for Battle

The life Micah planned for us, the life on Reunion, wasn't ours yet. Two days of peace and then we were on a boat, headed for the battle of our lives. My stomach cramped on and off all night. The seasickness, combined with the lack of sleep and energy, put me in a strange place. Literally. I unwillingly bounced back and forth between consciousness and my secret cave of women, who were all just as antsy over the looming battle. With each nautical mile covered, I could feel the heightened energy coming from the islands. The Shades could too. Many cowered in fear, retreating to the darkest corners and watery depths of the cave. Part of me wanted to go with them. But there was more than just me at stake. I had no other choice but to rally my teams, purposely surrounding myself with the strongest and most trustworthy Shades, trying to force confidence into them and myself.

When dawn's first light poked through the small porthole of my room, I dressed in the warm snow gear Micah purchased for me and opened my door. Micah was already missing from bed, no doubt attending to some pertinent task on the fishing trawler.

I made my way to the captain's bridge. Everyone was there; Cato, Susan, Alex, Micah, and the French captain. With the exception of the captain, who kept his eyes glued on his sonar machine, everyone looked at me.

I frowned. "What?"

Simultaneously, four pairs of eyes traveled to my now extremely large belly. I covered it protectively with my hands. "What?!"

"Sorry." Micah walked over to me and put his hand around my shoulders.

I shrugged it off, already annoyed at the extra weight. Only a couple minutes out of bed, my lower back was already screaming in pain.

Micah repositioned himself with what dignity he could muster and cleared his throat. "We have some bad news."

I waited for him to continue. Whatever it was, it couldn't be worse than my still-cramping stomach.

"Susan senses no less than three Nerinas on the islands."

I moved to sit down in the stool, massaging my lower back with one hand.

Alex stepped forward. "Reports I could get my hands on at Reunion before we left show four departures leaving for the islands in the past three months, carrying a grand total of at least 20 people. None have returned."

My kneading hands move to my temples. "Which means what?"

"Which means, Kaitlyn, that we are grossly outnumbered." Cato took the podium now. "If there are at least three Elementals for each fire, water, earth, and air, plus Shawn, even if their powers are miniscule compared to ours, they could still overpower us."

My rubbing stopped. "We aren't outnumbered."

An especially strong cramp gripped my midsection. I leaned over, putting my head between my knees. I could barely tune into what Cato was saying,

"…schizophrenic tendencies. Our battle plan cannot be…just you."

"I've got it handled," I tried to reassure the crew from fetal position.

"Are you ok, Kaitlyn?" Micah knelt down beside me so he could feel my forehead.

"Yes. It's just seasickness. I need to take a walk outside. I'm sure it will be fine."

"I'll go with her." Susan stepped over to help me up.

I tilted dangerously, trying to navigate the narrow doorways of a boat with a midsection that looked like I was smuggling melons and balance that was decreasing by the day.

She helped my awkward body without a problem, perfectly at ease on the swaying ship, red high heels and all.

She helped me make a couple of rounds on the outside decks until I felt well enough to stop. We watched the islands come into view.

"Are you ready for this?" she asked quietly.

I touched the waterproof case strapped to my body underneath my clothes, then to my protruding belly. "I have everything I need right here."

She nodded. "I am going to stay on the boat with the captain. Everyone else will accompany you ashore. We have no way of knowing what to expect when we get there. Satellite imagery for the last few months of the islands is distorted. We think that was Shawn's doing."

I nodded. "He is smarter than you guys give him credit for."

She turned to me suddenly. "No matter what happens, Kaitlyn, I'm here for you. I have a feeling the Seven is about to go in a whole new direction. As far as

I'm concerned, some of their archaic practices are about to come to an end. You won't go anywhere, no matter what. You're our Gaia – our family. You and yours..." she laid her hand over mine on top of my belly. "...are protected."

I smiled up at her, wishing that some sort of outcome where we could stay with Susan, after the battle, was possible. I knew it wasn't. And for that, I cried.

She hugged me, cooing over and over, "It's ok. It's ok."

I pulled myself together, and my sobbing stopped.

"Now," she wiped a tear from my eye. "Are you ready?"

I laughed. I was eight months pregnant, seasick, and crying. I was the very antithesis of being ready for battle.

"Yes," I said with resolution, because there was no other choice. Just like the Shades, the team here had to believe in me. Otherwise all was lost before we could even get started.

Chapter 31

My Kryptonite

Less than half an hour later, I came to an abrupt realization that I didn't have it all handled. A giant wall of spinning, white, harsh water raced toward our tiny fishing charter. I watched, paralyzed with shock, my death approaching at an alarming rate.

Susan ran to the bow of the boat, dispersing the wave in large chunks, diverting water left and right before it could slam into us. Knowing her, she'd prepared for this specific event. It was our downfall in Spain. She had probably been practicing how to handle this exact scenario ad nauseum ever since. I wished I'd thought of that.

Still, there was wave left over by the time it reached us. The ship reeled to the left. The flimsy glass windows on the captain's deck proved no match for my weight. I went crashing through. A brief, heart-stopping free fall ended in a hard landing. I braced for the icy cold waters of the Southern Ocean, but got the deck of the fishing trawler. The cold water came shortly afterwards, spraying from above.

"Kaitlyn!" Micah's panicked voice came to me before he did. "Are you ok?"

"I think so." I attempted to get up but a sharp, stabbing pain in my back stopped me. "Ow."

"Don't move..." Another lurch of the boat sent Micah and me sprawling into the railing. We gave a whole new meaning to 'manning the rails'. I lay motionless, afraid to discover what damage my body incurred. From my new position I spotted Susan, still at the bow of the ship, working her hands and chanting.

The ocean responded to her, but the attacks kept coming.

I gathered energy to help, I could still do something lying prone on the deck, but a voice inside my head spoke.

No. Don't!

I ignored it, summoning more energy from the ocean surrounding us. Suddenly, I felt blocked. It was weak, eerily similar to one of Shawn's walls, but it was coming distinctly from within myself. From the Shades.

I could break through, easily. But they had never done that before.

This is a diversion. Save your energy for the real fight.

They were right. Shawn was attempting to drain me before I could even get close to him. I reached toward Micah, who was picking himself off the floor. "Get me out of here."

He looked at his sister, doing her best to fight off the attacks, but understood. "Alex, Cato – get to the raft!"

"Grab my duffel bag!" I yelled after Cato. He didn't acknowledge me, no time for that, but he made the diversion below deck.

Micah picked me up, carrying me to the small, rubber lifeboat tethered to the back of the trawler. He lowered me down to Alex; the entire process sending more jolts of pain up and down my body.

Amidst the chaos of the sea, we made progress away from the fishing boat, circumnavigating the island, and approaching it from the other side. Our little engine did what it could, but it couldn't move quickly. The constant up and down and side to side motion actually worked out the kinks in my back, though, leaving behind only a dull ache.

Despite that, the ride was hell. The constant spray of ice cold water showered us as we tried to hold on for dear life. When the small rubber boat finally ran itself up on the land, no one moved. I'm not sure I could have. My fingers felt frozen to the small rope loops running along the inside. My clothes were soaking wet and stiff from the cold. I attempted to move my legs and heard my pants crackle, as if they had already turned to ice.

"Well this sucks."

A few groans answered my statement. I made no effort to do anything. The land was draining me. The Galapagos flashed through my mind. I forced it away. Eventually, a small warmth, starting at my toes, made its way up my body. I tested each limb as it became unfrozen, and realized Alex and Micah were doing the same. I was still exhausted, but I could move now.

Finally, I looked over at Cato. He had been the source of the heat. Dark, heavy bags circled his eyes and his wrinkles, as many as there were, seemed especially deep. He lifted his eyelids slowly and managed a small smile. "I'm done for, Kaitlyn. I can't handle this lack of energy in my old age. I'll do what I can from here, but you'll have to go on without me."

I nodded, understanding exactly. I pulled myself toward the duffel bag Cato still clutched, pried his icy fingers off, and pulled out a few essentials to leave with him.

"What's this?"

"A blanket, made from all natural materials from the Chakra; plus boots and a hat. It will help mask you from the island."

"That's my girl." Cato nodded approvingly.

I beamed with pride until Micah grabbed my arm and judiciously pulled me out of the raft and dumped me on the sand. As soon as my feet hit the ground, I froze.

"What?" Micah asked.

"If this place is anything like Galapagos, I can't move. The island will react."

"Ok." Micah paused. "Well, that kind of puts us at a disadvantage."

"No. Alex – hand me a blanket out of that bag."

He obliged and in short order had me dressed in the same attire as Cato; blanket wrapped around me like a cape, boots and a hat.

"Lovely," Micah remarked.

The blanket felt heavier than it should have been. I looked down and inside at the portion hanging over my front.

"I added a few touches of my own," Alex said.

Concealed inside was a row of lightweight throwing knifes, angled and leveled to be at the perfect height to be retrieved by my throwing hand. Shawn's athame, my one link to the Shades as long as the knife was close enough, was there, too.

"Aw, thanks! It's almost like…like you brought me flowers."

Micah cleared his throat.

I raised my eyebrow. "And you?"

"Sorry. No flowers."

I rolled my eyes. "No. I mean, do you feel that energy loss?"

He paused, taking a deep breath then exhaling slowly. "No. I feel, actually a little more powerful."

I nodded. "That's how it is with Shawn. Take a few steps in front of me."

Micah obliged, walking in a straight line, then stopping and turning. "Are we done with the sobriety check, officer?"

Nothing had happened. He moved but the island didn't. Now it was my turn. I took a deep breath in, and held it. No gust of wind. One step forward. No earthquake. As a final test, I closed my eyes and conjured the element of fire, lighting it without preamble. There was no explosion on the island, no volcano eruption. I was satisfied.

"Ok, I am good to move, but I still feel drained. If this turns into an extended fight; I'm not sure I'll last. These Goddamned places are like my kryptonite."

We started walking toward the center of the island.

"I think I can help there, Kaitlyn. I might be able to block some of energy-depleting sources for you," Micah said.

I shrugged, too tired to consider it more. "Ok – shield me."

Instantly I felt a protective barrier slide over me. I wasn't more powerful, but I was at least back to normal. It wavered slightly as Micah tripped over a rock, and the ill effects of the island managed to creep through, but he quickly solidified the barrier again.

For the second time that day, I beamed in pride, only this time it was pride in Micah. "It works!"

I extended my hand out and practiced a small weave of air. My magic still worked through the shield. "This is very, very good."

Back up to my normal strength, my confidence rose. It still may not be enough, but a weakened Gaia was something Shawn was probably counting on.

We continued moving toward the middle of the island. I glanced back at the boat, and Cato, watching them slowly disappear as we moved up and over a hill.

"Okay. This island is mostly barren. No trees. The wind can be harsh." Alex looked at Micah as he briefed him on the terrain. "No one lives here permanently; it is mostly just visited by scientists and researchers. They tend to take refuge in the underground caves. I couldn't find much information about the caves. They're numerous, but I'm not sure they're connected. Also, there's an active volcano. It's how the island was formed."

Micah nodded. "Got it. Kaitlyn – I think you should concentrate on the water and air elements. Those are your strongest. Use what the island has to offer, then just add to that or manipulate it. If Shawn's team is hiding out in caves, wind and water will be able to penetrate them without causing us too many problems." He turned back to Alex. "Are there any civilians on the island now?"

Alex shrugged. "Couldn't find any official research teams scheduled to be here."

"That is good enough for me."

We were heading uphill now. The icy air, combined with the exertion of climbing, was getting to me. I panted, breaths coming short, and my leg muscles felt ready to give out. Micah reached for my hand and pulled me along, forcing me to the top of the hill. When we crested, our jaws dropped. There must have been a hundred people in the valley, all spaced evenly apart. At first it looked like a random pattern but after taking a step back, and taking in the design as a whole, I realized the formation was shaped like Shawn's mark.

Whether or not positioning his people like that increased their strength, it certainly put the fear of God into me. Or the fear of the Devil.

"Just a scare tactic," Alex mumbled, but I could tell he was shaken as well.

"Yeah. It's working," I replied.

Micah agreed.

I looked at him, shocked. He was supposed to be our fearless leader, knowing the perfect thing to say to boost our confidence in this situation. I punched him in the arm, hard.

"Ow." He rubbed the spot, then pulled himself together under my glowering stare. "I mean…okay. I think we should break up the formation, just in case."

I followed his gaze to the far end, and could just make out three women directing weaves away from us and toward the ocean; toward Susan. Their strength was amplified by two men standing on each side of them. They were Shus, using air to expand and push the weaves out further to the fishing trawler. Together, the five of them formed the upper lip of the seditious smile in Shawn's mark.

"So we've got Waters and Airs there." As Micah spoke I followed his pointing. "And Earths in the lower lip. The outer circle doesn't look like Elementals at all; just guards."

Alex reached in his backpack and pulled out binoculars. "Yep. Maybe fifty of them; each with automatics and plenty of ammunition."

"Great," I mumbled. Magic I could handle; bullets I could not. I'd practiced redirecting bullets with wind, but never managed to throw them off their mark. They were just too fast.

Inside the outer circle was a triangle, then a square. Micah borrowed Alex's binoculars and confirmed, "Fires then Earths again; each intermixed with Air Elementals."

"It's still missing something. Wait, let me check." Micah stepped behind me, lifted the blanket off my shoulder then pulled down my coat and shirt, studying Shawn's mark.

"Glad I didn't forget the map."

He didn't acknowledge my snide remark. "It's missing the inner circle."

"Look closer. I bet Shawn is in the middle – being the entire circle himself," I said.

Micah lifted the binoculars to his eyes, "Oh, you're right." He snorted. "Tool."

"Okay – I say we start with the Water Elementals. They are the fewest and that would free up Susan to help us."

Alex kneeled and began digging through his backpack. "I'm going to branch off; start taking out the guards." He pulled out a sniper rifle and connected a high-powered scope, one of our more sophisticated weapons. After me, that is.

"Why not just take out Shawn, first?" I asked.

"No," Micah said. "I feel his wall. He's protected somehow. I'm sure he's thought of bullets as well. You can try but that would probably just alert him to your position. The wall is thick and concentrated; he has to keep it small. It doesn't extend to the guards so you can still take them out."

"Right." Alex popped in a magazine with a snap and turned off the safety. "I'm about to go sniper on their asses."

Micah and I watched Alex slink away, blending in with the terrain almost immediately. He would watch our backs, but who would be watching his?

Chapter 32

Now or Never

"And then there were two." Micah looked at me and smiled.

I reached for his hand, and we connected. I could feel the familiar spark of energy jump from his hand to mine. His shield around me strengthened. Our eyes widened as we acknowledged it. We were much, much stronger together.

Finally, I understood what he was trying to say back at the rock, right after Vayu was lifted into the air. I squeezed his hand in confirmation.

"Come on, we'll take them from the east. Susan has the north, Alex went west, and Cato – for what good he is – is south."

We made our way over the terrain, circling around hidden caves that seemed to open up out of nowhere in the ground. I took care, not quite trusting my back yet, scared I might stumble over some rocks and take a hard hit to the belly.

Micah's grip was solid, as was his shield that moved with me. We took our places east of the formation without incident. We weren't even sure if they knew we were on the island yet. Squinting, we could just make out body forms all the way around the valley. Including Shawn standing dead center, barking out orders to his minions. His attention was focused on the Nerinas, weaving their flows straight toward Susan.

Suddenly, his head whipped around toward his guards at the west. Two lay sprawled out on the ground, the third quick to follow. Alex fired, each shot dead on. After the fourth went down they finally returned fire.

But they were shooting blind; no one could spot Alex in the rocky hills, or even the flash of his muzzle in the broad daylight. In fact, they were squinting into the sun, giving Alex even more of an advantage. As the only non-magical being on our side, he was going to need it.

"Now, Kaitlyn! While they are distracted!"

I pulled my eyes away from the distorted bodies on the ground, now numbering in the double digits, and looked to the three Nerinas, down to our left. Why Shawn had picked a valley to stage his troops was beyond me. So far we had the upper hand.

I closed my eyes, cautiously summoning energy held within the ground below my feet, unsure of how the island, or I, would react. It was neutral energy, slightly tainted by the volcanic ash, but with enough of my influence, it could still work with me. I released a breath. This island was not nearly as potent as the Galapagos.

I used the net Vayu taught me in Australia, constructing it with tight weaves, just big enough to cover the span of the three women. I sent it out, fast and hard, but kept it low, right above the heads of everyone else in the formation. You could see their hair flip up as the wave of air passed over each one. It needed to take the women by surprise, before their Shus detected it.

Success. The net dipped down in front of them and I pulled back, drawing it in tight. The three women went crashing back. I angled my pull, using them to take out two of the Earth Elementals and a guard standing behind them on the lower lip of the smile.

"Hah!" Micah cried out, putting an arm around my waist in a tight hug. "Good job! A few more like that and we'll be home in time for supper!"

The ocean calmed almost immediately. Hopefully Susan had made it through ok. The Elementals I took out were now sprawled on the ground, not moving. No way to tell if I had killed them. I shrugged it off, instantly recalling the cruel lack of sympathy from Shawn when we lost Juan. "One less," I whispered to myself.

Shawn's eyes shot to me. I froze, paralyzed. I had tunnel vision, and he was standing at the end. He smiled, as though he knew what I had just said. The nightmare came back to me all at once and I felt my physical body fall directly into Micah's arms.

There was a brief struggle. Something was wrong, inside. The rock wall inside the cave to protect the entrance to my conscious body from Shades had disintegrated. Instead of disappearing in a puff of magic, the hard rock had shattered. Pieces of it littered the ground and the stairs, and other pieces shot around the cave like deadly missiles. The Shades roared, battling each other. I felt Arianna and some of the team we put together – they had the clear advantage of numbers – but they were distracted. I was exposed.

My presence was barely noticed, except by the one true entity I should have been more careful with. I watched her gaseous form emerge from the crevice halfway up the cave. I knew she was there all this time, but I mistook her aloofness for apathy. I was wrong. She was only biding her time, watching, learning, planning her attack.

She floated forward, hurling energy bolts to clear her path, not caring who she hit – those fighting for or against her were effectively removed from the battle, left attempting to piece themselves back together.

Now she aimed her weapon at me. Not having had enough practice inside myself, I rolled, dodging them physically. I was at a loss for what kind of magic to use. I looked desperately for Arianna – for anyone to help. In my moment of distraction, the enemy Shade lunged at me, knocking me back off of my platform. I gripped the slippery ledge. My grasp was precarious as the rest of my body dangled over the distant water.

I tried telling myself I was just a Shade here, too. I could just float up and away; I didn't have to fall. But fear and panic paralyzed my brain. Maybe it was that pesky self-preservation instinct.

She landed hard on the ledge, barely glancing down at me – but her evil half-smile told me everything. I watched as she shot up to take command of my body. I reached for her, using what energy I had to try to lasso her and bring her back.

I connected, and part of me was dragged up with her while the other part was left behind.

I opened my eyes. While I had fought inside, the battle on the islands had continued. A familiar looking wall of water had formed far out into the ocean, and was now heading for the island. It had Susan's magical signature all over it.

Several holes had opened up around the perimeter of the valley, and more Elementals came out, previously hidden in the caves. How did we not know? I thought back to my recent experience in a cave with Micah. When I had let my powers go; they bounced off the walls. They couldn't get out. Caves were like a natural barrier to our powers. Nothing entered, nothing left. Shawn had known that all along.

I would like to say all hell broke loose. Hell I could handle. But this...this was an organized battle, well planned. Sun Tzu would be proud. Shawn barked out more orders. Air Elementals broke formation and ran toward Susan's tsunami, fighting back the monstrous wave with their own wall of air. The guards grouped, and began to charge the hill. Half kept Alex pinned down with gunfire, while the other half moved forward. Soon his fight would become point blank shots or hand to hand combat, and he was grossly outnumbered. The Earth and Fire Elementals formed a tight circle, Shawn in the middle. Simultaneously, they turned and faced me.

I did the unexpected. I broke the bond with Micah and ran straight to Shawn. I heard Micah yelling after me, struggling to keep the shield intact, but he couldn't. His energy was drained, and combined with the distance I was putting between us, it was too much for him. The shield disintegrated. I expected a full on attack from Shawn and his lackeys, even felt myself flinch in anticipation, but it didn't come.

Yet, I moved forward. Panic reached me. I wasn't controlling my body. The Shade had taken full control.

I could see what was happening. I could feel my body. Cold from the icy ground was creeping up into my legs. My lips were burning and chapped from the constant wind. But it was her body, not mine. She continued to walk forward, awkwardly. She had a slight limp caused by stiff leg. Maybe an old injury. Her left hip jutted out in an unintentional sexy sway.

It was that sway which stopped Shawn from attacking. Vayu, nearly out of the cave, saw me coming and raised his wand. Shawn put a hand up to stop him.

Vayu looked thoroughly disappointed.

Somehow, Shawn had just become my protector.

He is protecting me, bitch, the Shade spoke to me.

Hmmm, I answered. *We'll see about that.*

"Sarah?" Shawn's voice carried straight through to me.

"Hey, baby." Sarah stepped up to Shawn, kissing his cheek.

He stepped back in amazement. "It... How?"

"Your athame," she said. "That bitch absorbed all the Shades you had in there. Well, all the female Shades."

"Sarah!" He picked her up and swung her around. A foreign happiness lit up his face.

I took advantage of the distraction, trying to regain control. The temporary struggle brought my body to its knees. I gripped my head with my hands and screamed with frustration.

She won, again. But I was a lot closer to breaking through this time.

"Sorry about that, babe." She straightened again. "She's trying to win back her body. I don't know why. It's so damn...frumpy."

Shawn and Sarah turned to face Micah, and holding hands, began their attack. It was the very image my nightmare had conjured. Me and Shawn, side by side, doing his bidding. Destroying the population in order to save the planet.

And we had our sights set on Micah.

Fire and Earth Elementals combined their energy. The ground around Micah shook. It began bubbling, releasing steam, and cracking open. Together, the Elementals were turning the ground beneath his feet into molten lava.

"One last chance to join us, bro. Kaitlyn is gone anyway," Shawn called. "Sarah's too strong to let her come back."

I panicked, silent and helpless in my little cave. The Shades picked up my mood, and most started skittering about anxiously. The rogues by now were subdued, and my team of Shades made their own attempts at taking over my body. Sarah fought back, pulling at her hair and screaming at herself.

This could go very bad. My body was still carrying my baby. I couldn't do anything to let her harm it.

"Stop!" My command carried throughout the cave, and everyone instantly obeyed. "Form your circles; join hands. Make sure each circle has a Water, a Fire, an Earth, and an Air. Gaias in the middle. That is not just my body she is holding hostage – it is my baby."

A few gasps, some moans, but then they were all business. Every single Shade joined hands, creating circles, even if they weren't part of one before. It takes a village to save a child.

The strongest of the circles, the two I trained with, stood on the platform at the top of the stairs, waiting for the chance to elevate me back into my own body.

One of the Shades gave instructions in how to detain Sarah once she was returned to the cave.

We started chanting.

Above it all I could hear Sarah, "Now they're all acting up. Let's take care of Micah; then we can fix this little problem together."

The power of Shawn's circle increased exponentially, and the ground rolled up around Micah in waves. He could barely hold on. One misstep and he would be burned alive.

Micah watched me and Shawn hold hands, working together against him.

I chanted louder, encouraging the rest to put everything they had into it.

"Shut up, shut up!" I could hear Sarah yelling.

"Sarah? Are you still there – is everything ok?" Shawn's voice was worried. She was losing it.

I began to take control again; little pieces of the real world came through to me, then shot away as Sarah resisted. But I was getting through, and each time I managed to stay a little bit longer. I focused on the wall around Shawn. Micah was right; it was thick, impenetrable. There were several flattened bullets lying just outside; Alex had been taking shots when he could. It was difficult to comprehend; I could see weaves of all four elements, but it was too hard to distinguish where just one began or ended. They were working as one, melding into the perfect armor.

"Enough!" Sarah shouted, pushing me back down into the cave once again. "I'm going to put an end to this right now." She reached into the blanket, still fastened around me like a cape, and withdrew the athame. A smile lit up her face; I could feel my lips cracking as they were stretched impossibly wide, as she slowly lowered the knife to my stomach.

"No!" The cry was so loud, it echoed through my little cave, and throughout the valley. I realized, with sudden clarity, that it wasn't an echo. It was my cry combined with Micah's, but also Shawn's.

Sarah looked at him in shock. "Losing the baby would break her. It's the only way to ensure she doesn't come back. Don't worry, baby, you can heal the scars later."

"It's not that, Sarah." Shawn stumbled. "The baby…it might be mine."

Sarah's eyes widened even further, and he corrected himself, "Ours. The baby could be ours. Yours and mine. You will finish carrying it and we could raise it together, just like we always talked about."

"You…and her?" She took a step away from him, holding the knife in front of her.

"No. It wasn't like that. It was…"

"Rape," I answered. I managed to sneak in for a split second, just in time to get out that word.

"What?" Shawn frowned; he didn't know who was speaking.

Sarah was back now. "You raped her? Why? We had a plan. Even if I couldn't carry it out – something like *that* was never part of it."

"It wasn't necessarily like that," Shawn said.

"Necessarily? Tell me, Shawn - did you enjoy it? The feel of another women? Did she give you something me and my limp leg never could?" Sarah practically shook with anger.

Quickly I started relaying instructions to my circles. "…and after you do that, if she comes down do not detain her. Leave her loose."

They hummed in confusion.

"Do it. I'm going to need her. Okay, get ready. Here we go."

The elevation this time was rapid. Quicker than it ever had been before. And the takeover was easy. Sarah didn't fight it.

I blinked, adjusting to my body.

Shawn was still trying to talk Sarah down. As soon as I felt the Shades pulling apart the weaves of his shield, I rushed forward. The athame was in my hands. The hole was small; I would have to be exact. One step, a lunge, and I thrust my hand out, through the hole, and into Shawn's stomach.

Right before the knife entered his body, I felt a surge of power. The final thrust incapacitated Shawn instantly. I knew it was Sarah. Hell hath no fury like a woman scorned. It was just a matter of putting that scorn to good use.

Shawn and I collapsed together on the ground. The hilt of the knife dug into my side, pushing the blade further into him.

I clutched my side; it hurt but no skin was broken. To make matters worse, my back was acting up again. The pain there was arching around my sides and to my front, sending cramps all throughout my lower stomach, intense enough to blur my vision.

I pushed myself to my feet, and was face to face with Vayu. He peered into my eyes. There was no fooling him; Sarah was gone and I was back. I made a net in front of him, pushing it toward him and wrapping it around. He managed to unravel it. Before he could completely finish the job, I called the rolling ground from Micah and sent it toward Vayu. The Shades inside were helping; their magic flowed freely through my hands.

Vayu looked in fear at the wave of earth barreling toward him, and it got us both. We went flying. I slammed into a Fire Elemental. Grabbing a knife from my blanket, I shoved it into his throat before he could react. I threw another at a Fire Elemental, charging me. The Earth Elementals were busy battling the still rolling ground. I heard Alex's rounds whizzing by me. One caught a Fire Elemental as he threw a small fireball my way. I managed to duck under it, but it singed my hair. I looked back at Alex, still shooting and running down the hill toward me. He left several dead guards behind, but plenty more were chasing him. Things were not looking up for our small team.

The Water Shades inside of me joining their power with Susan. The wall of water appeared in a flash, looming over the valley.

The cleansing effect of the tsunami took us all out. By the time I made it back on my feet, I could spot several people out at sea, pulled away by the water. I searched frantically for Micah and Alex. They coughed and sputtered, luckily still with us. Unfortunately, so were Vayu, Shawn, and three other Elementals. The knife still protruded from Shawn's stomach, blood leaking out to replace what had been washed away. He gurgled, conscious, but he wasn't going anywhere.

With most of his army carried away, his shield was down. I reached out for earth again, and the ground rolled and pitched at my beckoning. But before it could affect Shawn, Vayu and the three remaining Elementals joined powers and formed a protective circle around him.

Twin tornados, identical in size and intensity, formed on either side of the valley. They sucked in snow, ice, and rock from the island, turning them an eerie silver color, shining almost unnaturally. Ice and rock shot out from each tornado, making deadly missiles.

"Look familiar?" Vayu yelled at me.

I furrowed my brow in confusion, trying to imagine what he was talking about…until a certain newspaper clipping I kept hidden in a box under my bed came to mind. It was a tornado that had taken my parent's life; the tragic story of a couple gone, and the daughter they left behind. It was a freak storm. Two twisters merged to form a super tornado; a whirlwind force that took everything in its path, including my parents.

"It was too easy, catching them by surprise like that." Vayu turned back to study his fabrications. He began to direct them together.

I stared at the creation that killed my parents, and worse, the man that created them.

"They were on to us, working to take apart the organization while it was barely in its planning stages. They knew too much. Had to go."

I looked at Shawn. He moved his lips as if to speak, then leaned forward, toward me, but pain won him over. He grimaced and fell back onto the ground, curling around the weapon Sarah and I shoved into him.

Micah, I called telepathically, *I need you.*

Alex and Micah ran to join me.

"Shoot him!" I shouted at Alex. He was taking aim before the words were out of my mouth, but Vayu was faster. Alex went flying back, caught up in a vortex of wind; his sniper rifle flew off in another direction.

Vayu conjured more wind, making it difficult for Micah and me to stay upright.

"Kaitlyn!" Micah yelled, his voice barely discernible above the wind tunnel.

I shook my head to indicate I didn't understand. He made a circling motion with his hands. Finally, his words got through to me, "Create your own circle!"

Susan was north, Cato south. I nodded and immediately ran for the east side of the valley – Micah ran west. Using their magic, with the help of the Shades inside me, I could create my own circle. We had the entire battlefield covered.

I stopped, turned, and raised my hands. My flows joined with Micah, and then we reached out to Susan.

She was quick on the uptake. The Shades help was fading noticeably. I was too far from the athame. But they did their best to compensate fire for Micah. Next, the three of us sought a connection to Cato. Hopefully he was conscious.

He was less than conscious. He wasn't even there.

Chapter 33

Found and Lost

Our flows wavered in confusion. The circle was not complete. I lowered my arms and looked at our enemy. Vayu, understanding what happened, smiled in triumph. Our last chance failed.

Another round of cramping had me holding my sides in distress. The wind still raged all around us; whipping my hair in front of my face, making it difficult to see, but something caught my eye. Cato, half-crawling, half-dragging himself toward Vayu and Shawn. He had made his way into the valley undetected until now.

Vayu started to direct the wind to overtake Cato, but the old man was obviously no threat. Micah and Alex started toward Cato. *No – let him*. I directed my thoughts toward Micah and he put one arm up to stop Alex as well.

Why? Micah asked.

Shawn is his son. His birth son.

With our telepathic communication, I was hoping Shawn could hear, like he could on the Galapagos.

He heard. Shawn lifted himself up on one elbow, grimaced, looked at me, then to Cato. With his slow crawl, Cato finally made his way to Shawn.

Cato began fiddling with the blanket I had left; still wrapped around him. I took a few steps closer but Vayu blocked my path with his strongest winds. I eased off. I wasn't looking to attack with Cato in the thick of the enemy.

Cato chewed a bit of the blanket, mixed it with dirt and began applying it to Shawn's wound. Cato was healing him.

As soon as Micah and Alex realized what was happening, they rushed in. But Vayu was on top of his game and sent them flying back, well clear of the group.

Micah reached out to me mentally. *We have no chance.*

I looked at Shawn. Cato withdrew the knife. Shawn grunted in pain. A small, half-smile lit his face. He had heard Micah too and knew he was right.

No, I thought. I had come too far. I had recruited and trained an army. I had increased my magical ability with months of hard training; all the while fighting off Shawn's dream attacks. I had done it all without my one true partner, Micah. And I had done it all pregnant.

Shawn began to lift himself to his feet. Cato, exhausted as he was, still lying prone on the ground, turned his attention to Vayu.

Vayu didn't miss a thing. With military precision, he sent out an air net, scooping up a stray pistol and brought it back to him. It fell into his hands, the safety came off, and he shot Cato through the head. Blood splattered over Shawn and Vayu. Shawn looked at Vayu in shock.

Vayu laughed, his gleaming white smile looking oddly misplaced on his blood-streaked face.

NO! The word screamed in my head, the mental push strong enough to command the attention of Micah and Shawn. I looked again at Cato's frail, withered body. Vayu had been responsible for my parent's death, and now my Godfather.

NO! I screamed again, louder this time. Everyone in the valley cowered, covering their ears, unsuccessfully blocking out the shriek that rang inside their heads.

With everyone incapacitated, the Shades inside pushed me to act. I closed my eyes, asking the Earth Shades for help. We needed to reveal the caves underneath us; all of them. My trusty friends obliged. Together, we sent our weaves into the earth, finding the air pockets and expanding out until the large caverns revealed themselves. We forced the energy upward.

Large chunks of ground burst open. Shawn and his circle, who stood over one, went flying up, and then back down into the cave. Unfortunately, so did Micah.

With the wind now non-existent, Alex and I ran to the open mouth of the cavern that swallowed Micah. "I'm okay!" he called up to us.

He was maybe only twenty feet down; I hoped Shawn had fallen further.

A sudden burst of pain shot through my midsection. It caused me to sink to my knees, clutching my round belly. I was broken, sapped of energy. The fight took everything out of me. The Shades inside were not using their own energy for weaves; they were using mine. It was more than my body could bear and the ecosystem had little more to offer. With so much magic and energy-hungry souls, the battle had robbed the entire area.

Alex pulled a rope out of his backpack, but it wasn't long enough to reach Micah. It would be some time before we could get him out. The blast of pain eased out of my midsection, but it was coming in cycles now. It would be back.

If I was going to follow through with my plan, it would have to be now.

Chapter 34

Fair Winds

Two hours. Alex probably had Micah out of the hole by now. Hopefully they would have enough sense to ensure Shawn was gone before they came after me. That would give me at least a little extra time.

More than 2,000 miles away lay my first destination; Perth, Western Australia. There was a bank waiting for me, where I arranged to have enough cash in a security deposit box to get me underground, and to stay there for a long time. I had to be off the grid; undetectable not only to the international and federal connections Alex had, but also to the magical connections of both Shawn, if he survived, and Micah. No one would have the chance to touch my daughter.

After the battle, I had expected to use the same wind tunnel Vayu and Shawn used to extract Vayu from the Chakra, but I had not expected to be completely void of energy, and in intense pain. Plan two consisted, oddly enough, of Shawn's plan. I was counting on using his escape if I had to. Since we arrived from the west, I looked to the east.

I went as fast as my body would carry me, away from the setting sun. Pulling the blanket tight continued to mask me from the island. Besides, it was freezing without Micah and his shield.

Cresting another hill, I let out a sigh of relief at the newly built, makeshift port jutting out into the ocean. When I saw the boat sitting at the end, I sprinted for it. Slightly smaller than our fishing trawler, it looked faster. I stopped and dropped to my knees as an extra strong cramp made me double over. I endured it, and then got up again. My escape was in sight. I had to keep going.

Once on the boat, I ran for the captain's bridge. I became a tornado myself, a force flurrying to push buttons and pull levers. The engine roared to life. It was a beautiful sound. I bent over with another cramp. As it built up, climaxed, then faded, I suddenly realized – I was in labor, one month early.

The pain was low in my stomach. I felt my muscles contract involuntarily in response to it. The scariest part was, I had no control over it. My body rode wave after wave, the same cycle each time. Swelling, peaking, flowing out. It was coming in regular intervals now; I counted 500 seconds in between. Roughly eight minutes. The doctor hadn't prepared me much for labor, planning to take care of everything himself. And now I was headed resolutely in the opposite direction of anyone that could help; Micah, Alex, Susan, and even the Shades. I knew the exact moment when my link to them disappeared. The distance between me and the athame was too far, and our connection snapped like a piece of string pulled too tight.

I was truly alone. No sense in wallowing in self-pity; I needed to prepare. I set the boat on course for Perth, and flipped on the auto-pilot. At this rate, I'd be arriving in the middle of the next night. Maybe I could sneak in undetected – that is if I didn't have a crying baby at my breast by then.

I made my way below deck and started searching the rooms, frantic to find general supplies. Opening the door to the first room below deck, Shawn's odor hit me hard. I took a deep, calming breath and forced myself in, rummaging through dresser drawers and boxes. Several copies of his manifesto, a few clothes, some knifes. That was it. I leaned down to look under the cot when I felt the waves of pain coming back. I buried my face in his bed spread, kneeling down, and endured. It was the worst yet, with Shawn surrounding me; his scent, the feel of his bed, even the salty taste of one of his pillows as I bit down. The contractions were getting more difficult to breathe through.

After it was over, I stumbled back into the hallway. Just opposite me was a very clean, white room. It had a bed, retractable at the feet; stirrups protruding from the end. On one wall were shelves lined with clean towels, antiseptic, and swabs. There was also a row of books. I walked over and ran my finger along their spines. *Natural Childbirth, Labor and Delivery, Birthing at Home…* I gasped. Shawn was planning on bringing me here, and delivering the baby himself. I pulled out a folder, full of notes. Scrawl in his handwriting filled each page. Information on how to perform a C-section… I closed it quick and stuffed it back on the shelf.

Further up, I saw stacks of newborn diapers, formula, bottles, baby clothes, and blankets. He was planning on keeping my baby. No evidence on what he had planned to do with me. My resolve to go underground deepened. I whipped into action. I couldn't stay in this room; I needed to be at the captain's bridge to steer the boat and monitor the equipment. Everything I needed would have to come with me. I started packing supplies in the small basinet I found in the corner of the room. I spent the next two hours ferrying books, towels, medicine, and baby supplies to the captain's deck. The time spent was made significantly longer; I had to stop every six to seven minutes now to ride out the contractions.

Sweating profusely, I made a bed in the corner of the captain's bridge using a thin twin mattress, blankets, and pillows. I lay down recovering from my many treks up and down the stairs; another contraction. They were four minutes apart, lasting up to 45 seconds each. I had done some reading of my own; this was the point you were supposed to go to the hospital.

After the contraction, I uncoiled from the fetal position, slowly lifting myself to my feet, and hobbled over to the steering wheel, flipping off auto-pilot. Icebergs crossed my mind. I peered through the large windows in front of me. There was a full moon gleaming off the frothy blue sea.

"I am in labor. I am alone in the middle of the Southern Ocean." I looked back at my makeshift hospital room. I took a deep breath in. The oxygen flowed into my body, slowing my heartbeat and replenishing my muscles. "I am about to meet my beautiful baby girl."

I smiled. I had never felt so in control.

Micah pulled himself up the last few feet of rope. The pulling had stopped, but the rope hadn't been let go of altogether. *What is Alex doing up there?* Micah crested the top of the deep cavern. A hand appeared; it was strong, firm, and familiar. It yanked back, pulling the rest of Micah's tired body over. He pushed himself to a standing position, and looked up, right into Shawn's bright blue eyes.

Micah did a double take, nearly falling back into the hole. Alex was still at the rope, confused into inaction. The very man they had just been battling, had tried to kill, was standing before them, helping them, and looking just as worse for the wear.

Micah reached for his gun, but it was no longer there. Alex had apparently done the same, giving Micah a sympathetic 'been there, done that' grimace. Both their weapons had been blown away by the Air Elementals under Shawn's command.

"Where's Kaitlyn?" Her absence was suddenly very noticeable among the maelstrom of male ego.

"Gone." Shawn replied. His hand was at his side, blood seeping through his wound made worse by helping Micah.

"What did you do to her?" Micah, fatigue momentarily forgotten, lunged for Shawn. He didn't give him a chance to answer. They were both on the ground, wrestling about as effectively as four year olds.

Alex broke up his adoptive brothers easily. "Micah – he didn't do anything to her. She was with me, and then just disappeared while I was pulling you up. She left on her own!"

Alex took an inadvertent kick to his stomach, "Damn it, stop!" He yanked first Micah, then Shawn to their feet, and watched them double over, breathing hard.

Alex didn't have abilities like everyone else – no energy was spent on magic. Most of the time, he was just squeezing a trigger. Fat lot of good that did him now; the enemy was still standing right before him, playing WWF with Micah.

Shawn straightened first, "Can't you feel her? She's headed east; fast. Probably took my boat."

Micah closed his eyes and concentrated, "Yes, actually I can." He narrowed his eyes at Shawn, "I've never been able to do that before.

Shawn lifted up his shirt to inspect his wound, "It's this place. Same as the Galapagos and a few others I've found. Gives us stronger powers – some abilities we wouldn't have at all elsewhere."

All three of them turned east, looking at the storm in the sky that most likely followed her. Their main reason for being there, for all three of them, gone, they had a moment of unspoken truce. They turned back to face the battlefield. Bodies were everywhere, some dead, some perhaps just unconscious, and several moving around, slowly, calling for help with their various injuries. There were guards and Elementals both; all humbled by pain whether they had magic in them or not.

Most of the guns, and probably more bodies, had disappeared when the ground began opening up to the caves underneath. Still more washed away, out to sea with Susan's tidal wave.

There, in the middle of the aftermath, lay Cato's still body.

"Was he really my birth father?" Shawn asked quietly.

"Yes," said Alex. We found the paperwork in a safe at the Chakra."

"Could have been faked," Shawn suggested.

"There were pictures." Alex said.

There would have been no need for Cato to fake pictures. Shawn knew that.

"She's eight months pregnant; I need to get her back." Micah said.

"It could be my kid," Shawn responded.

"Regardless, it will be me raising it." Micah turned, springing the direction Kaitlyn went, preparing to beat Shawn to her.

Alex stopped Micah, "Just wait a minute, Micah. He has something we don't."

"What?" Micah turned to face them.

Shawn reached behind him and pulled his athame out of his back pocket. "This." The sharp edge caught the sun, sending flashes of light across Micah's face.

Micah reached for it, Shawn pulled it back, but it was Alex that stopped them both. "Don't touch it, Micah. We don't know what it might do to us."

Shawn re-sheathed the knife before anyone else felt brave. "Although I didn't realize what it could do before, I know now. There are more than a hundred souls in here…"

"It wasn't their souls; more like their essences," said Alex. "They call themselves Shades."

Shawn sent a sideways glance to Alex then resumed lecturing Micah, "Ok. The Shades spent significant time with Kaitlyn. Maybe they helped her plan the escape."

Micah matched Shawn's cocky tone, "I doubt she planned this. We had a life together. She wouldn't have run away unless something spooked her. Like you."

"Whatever the case may be, truce until we find her?" Shawn stuck out his hand toward Micah.

Micah narrowed his eyes, then looked back at Shawn, and took his hand, shaking it. "Truce?" Micah slapped a pair of handcuffs on Shawn's wrist. Shawn's smile faded. "Hardly," Micah said.

'Fire, Book Three of the Akasha Series' is now available across all platforms!

About the Author

Terra is author of the eco-fantasy novels in the Akasha Series; 'Water', 'Air', 'Fire', and 'Earth'. The first book in The Painted Maidens Trilogy, 'The Rising', is also now available.

Terra was born and raised in Colorado but has since lived in California, Texas, Utah, North Carolina, and Virginia. Terra has served a 5½ year enlistment in the Marine Corp, has earned her bachelor's and master's degree and presently runs the language services division of a small business.

Terra currently lives in a suburb of Washington, DC with her husband of fourteen years and three children.

Connect with Terra:

E-mail: terra.harmony11@gmail.com
Facebook: www.facebook.com/terraharmony
Blog: www.harmonylit.wordpress.com
Twitter: @harmonygirlit

Discover Other Titles by Terra:

The Rising

Book One of the Painted Maidens Trilogy

Fifteen-year-old Serena is the youngest member of a dying race. The increasing acidity of the ocean is destroying her home, slowly eating away at the once thriving underwater landscape. But since the night of Serena's birth, it is an outside force that most threatens their dwindling population. Werewolves, who once served as protectors for mermaids in the Kingdom of the Undine, now seek to eliminate all who dwell in the ocean—and Serena is about to find herself right in the middle of the deadly conflict.

Given the title of Werewolf Liaison, Serena is determined to make things right for her people. When she ventures to The Dry, she meets Liam, the werewolf with hazel eyes, and her whole world gets turned upside down. As Serena discovers the real history between werewolves and mermaids, she is left wondering who her true enemies are.

Reviews for 'The Rising'

"It was a great ride. I devoured every page and loved the whole thing through." *by Ariel Avalon, Book Blogger*

"This is a wonderfully unique story." and "I recommend this if you enjoy mermaids or werewolves with some great action, mystery and a bit of romance." *by Darker Passions Book Blog*

"The book is fast paced filled with action that keeps you on the edge of your seat till the very end, add in a little romance and mystery for the perfect balance. The author has written a beautiful story that sparks the imagination. I loved everything about the story and can't wait for the next one to see what happens to both Serena and Liam as their stories unfold." *by The Reading Diaries Book Blog*